The Edge of a World

The Edge of a World

JD RIVERS

ISBN: 978-3-9826359-0-3 (ebook), 978-3-9826359-1-0 (paperback)

Book Cover by planetsandmagic

Type setting (cover & book) by Hermit

1st edition 2024

For David.

Without you this book would
have taken so much longer.

Chapter 1

Aaoran-peras,

How many turns has it now been since we last saw each other? I stopped counting them. I rise when the sun rises and sleep when it gets too dark to see. The turns are just drifting past. Since my last letters, many turns have walked the Seven Lands. I'm alive and as well as one can expect.

I have set out to map the ruins of the Ancients in the southern jungles, that grow along the mountain ridges. It's a tedious task, and yet one I enjoy, hopefully it gives us a clearer picture of these long-lost ancestors.

Since I left this morning, I have been followed by a flock of birds, which the locals named Lopi, because of their distinctive "lopi-lopi" call. I wonder if you have ever seen them on your travels.

The little birds, smaller than the palm of my hands, glint like jewels when they flutter around in the sun rays that find their way through the thick canopy. They are flighty birds, one could say, but very curious. I left them a few crumbs from my dinner last night, and now they probably hope for more.

Don't laugh at what I say next, but I find them comforting company. At least they are happier companions than my yardar. The bird beast is as full-tempered as always. The southern jungle is relentless and understandably hard on a creature used to the drier steppe climates.

There is not much I can report back to you; the last turns have been less exciting than I hoped they could be.

The same locals that told me about the bird also pointed me in the approximate direction of a hill structure that was too regular to be entirely natural. Together with the tidbits of a local legend, their claim that there was more hidden under the dirt rang true. And yet, upon further exploration, it was nothing more than a gigantic heap of dirt and stone. There are traces that could make it promising to dig deeper but would need an entire excavation troop, and I'm only one man. The jungle, thick and lush, has overgrown the hill, guarding what is hidden underneath—I won't be the person to pry its secrets away.

After that disappointment, I found myself at a crossroad. I could press on and find the forgotten tidbits that the jungle is keen on obscuring, but I'm tired of sweating through my clothing with no payoff. Also, I fear any longer and the yardar will just walk away. There is that glint in its eyes again.

The same locals who told me about the dirt hill and the birds told me about another legend. It's not a local one, but it's a ghost story that centers on the mountain range to the east. Similarities in their retelling with other legends lead me to believe that there is a yet undiscovered ruin hidden in those mountains.

I have set out to inspect it. There is also hope that I will come across a settlement with some traveling merchant who will transport my letters and notebooks to Rasanell and leave them at the university until you're able to retrieve them, just like we said when I set out for the first time.

I wish I had more answers to all our questions, but as always, the Ancients have left nothing behind besides stones and more stones and more questions.

I'm close to the southern island territory where you told me your community resides. Traveling alone differs from traveling with someone at your side, I have learned. It's different and seldom better, but you would know even better than me. You have traversed the Seven Lands more often and longer than I have been born. So I'll quit my maudlin thoughts here and close the letter with a few sketches of the hill in the jungle and what I found buried in the sand, because—

Otar squinted into the fading light. Unnoticed to him, the night had crept in, and he now had trouble making out the lines he was writing. He put the pen down and closed the inkwell. A slight breeze drifting in from the open window brought the leafy and damp smell of the early night.

He had arrived at this place, Piskus, five turns ago. Where he had hoped to find a small settlement, he had instead found a bustling village sitting on a salt-trade route from a mine that was just a few miles away. Merchants came through here often enough that it even warranted an inn, which unfortunately for him was fully booked. Yet the locals had been gracious to give him a modest hut that currently stood empty. They told him the previous tenant had died of old age in his sleep, and no one had claimed it yet. Despite the size, it was comfortable: it had a small fireplace, blackened from the many winters of use it must have seen; it had a rather lumpy bed, which was still better than the bare ground he had been sleeping on for most of his current travels; and it had a table, a chair, and a tiny trunk where he stored his things.

When Otar revealed he was a traveling scholar, the folks were very excited. Question after question they asked: about Rasanell, the Crown Jewel of the Wooden Lands; about the Southern Islands and their swimming cities; about the endless steppe and the Black Mountains; about the deep jungles and the monsters that lived in them; about how blue the Blue Mountains really were; and about many more peculiar places. Otar had tried to answer them as best as he could, and they listened to each of his words with such a rapt attention that it made him uncomfortable.

Being in the middle of things wasn't his preferred way to be. His mentor, Aaoran, was the opposite. They loved being the center of every gathering, but Otar escaped as fast as he could without appearing rude.

He rose from the chair, his stiffened muscles protesting, and went over to the tiny nightstand, nothing more than a wooden stool, and fetched the oil lamp. Once lit, he carried it over to the table before sitting down again and taking back up the pen.

He scribbled down a few more lines to complete the tales of his travels to Piskus, before throwing sand over the fresh ink and tapping it off after a few small-turns. It would have to do, he decided, and judging by the encroaching night, he had to hurry. The merchant willing to take on his letters and notebooks would leave early in the morning and, therefore, retire soon.

Otar folded and sealed the letter and added it to the others in the small package that also held his already filled notebooks and other reports he had made. It wasn't easy parting with them, but carrying them around and losing them in an accident would be even more devastating.

Carefully folding the wax cloth closed, he tightly bound it and checked to ensure it was secured as needed. The merchant he had bought the cloth from many turns ago had raised his eyebrow at the amount Otar had requested, but he was determined that every book was bound in its own sheet before wrapping it all together with a last layer. Better to be safe than lose any of it, as scholars have gone mad after finding their life's work destroyed. Otar checked the parcel one last time, and finding it sufficiently prepared, took it and slipped it into his thin overcoat and hurried out.

He walked down the small path that led to the local inn, which also functioned as the tavern. It was simply a glorified drinking hole, because, despite the trading route, there wasn't enough traffic in these regions to warrant a proper guest house. The three rooms were plenty for the traveling merchants and salt miners on the lookout for labor.

Laughter grew louder the closer he got. As the harvest was going well, the villagers were in good spirits as the summer had been generous this year. Otar slipped in through the door and waved at a few people, who raised their mugs in greeting. He ignored their requests to join them and made a beeline for a corner table at which the merchant Bedaran was currently eating.

Bedaran's hair was in one full braid down their back, and they wore the typical flowy garb of a shimmery midnight-colored fabric that the southern islands favored and the style his mentor Aaoran wore. For a southerner, their occupation was atypical. They'd explained it to Otar two nights ago as they lay together that they came from a family of weavers, but that they had no sense for the artistry needed. So, making themselves useful, they traded their family's tapestries and from there, their business grew. They had come here to check if investing in the salt trade was feasible.

Bedaran and Otar bonded over their shared stories from traveling through the Seven Lands, and how they both had differed from their families, seeking their fortunes elsewhere. The nights spent in mutual comfort had been a change of pace for Otar, and he was sad to see them go now that they had finished their business with the villagers.

Otar waited at the side of the table; even if they had found companionship in each other, he would never presume—being invited to eat was a privilege, not a right.

Bedaran paused eating and looked up, then smiled and inclined their head. Smiling back, Otar settled into the empty chair opposite them. He took out the small parcel and placed it on the table. Bedaran grabbed it without commenting and hid it in the many folds of their garment. Once Otar had asked Aaoran how many hidden pockets theirs had, but his mentor had winked at him and never answered.

The daughter of the tavern owner brought Otar's own meal and a mug of the local ale, a slightly too bitter brew. It was this or water, and Otar never much cared for the latter.

They ate in silence. The carousing of the locals ebbed and flowed around them like the waves of a sea. One merchant was playing a fiddle, and the rest were singing rowdy songs about their wild and amorous nights. The atmosphere reminded Otar of the steppe riders, who always laughed and sang when eating in front of the communal fire. Their songs had probably been as unruly as the locals' but Otar couldn't be sure because no one had ever explained them to him and had only laughed when he asked after them—maybe he had been too young. They had also traded stories and anything that had happened over the turn, calling to each other across the fire sparks dancing into the sky. There was a twinge in his chest at the memories, a mix of fondness and melancholy. Otar tried his best to ignore it.

After they finished, Bedaran walked them out and then around the building to a small pathway hidden in the darkness. They hadn't been overly open about their liaison, because Bedaran felt uncomfortable about it, so they kept to the shadows.

"I'll retire soon, so this will be our parting." Bedaran's eyes were dark fathomless pools, but they were smiling.

Once more Otar would miss the simple joy and the comfort they found in each other, although it had never been a grand love story. The monster inside him reared its head, unwilling to let the other go, but for once Otar had a tight grip on it.

"Safe travels." Otar raised his hands, drew Bedaran's face to him, and kissed them first on their eyelids and then on the lips—the traditional gesture of parting when leaving a loved one on the southern islands. Bedaran mirrored the gesture.

"Until we meet again. May you find whom you are searching for," Bedaran said with a teasing smile.

Otar rolled his eyes fondly. Then Bedaran was gone, the laughter spilling out into the air as they returned to the tavern and then became muffled as the door swung shut behind them.

Loneliness gripped him. For a moment he even considered going back inside as well, absorbing the energy of the surrounding people, letting himself drift in the crowd, but the more he thought about it, the more he found he didn't have the patience.

Instead, he turned away from the tavern, hoping to return to the small cabin and plan his next foray into the mountains. He wanted to find that ruin. Just as he was stepping onto his path, he bumped into someone and lost his balance. Strong hands grabbed him, saving Otar from an ungraceful tumble to the ground. Moonlight hit light hair and blue eyes—the village elder's youngest son, Marit.

"Master Otar," the youth stuttered, his hands still on Otar's waist. "I'm sorry," he said with a blush.

Otar sighed and took a step back so that Marit's hand dropped away. The boy, not yet a man, was infatuated with him, which was partly sweet and partly annoying. This was one of the reasons he hadn't thought long about Bedaran's subtle offer and all but jumped into the merchant's arms—to not give Marit the slightest hope.

"It's alright, but you're too close."

Marit stepped hastily back, his blush deepening.

Distantly, Otar wondered if he had behaved the same with his first infatuation. Perhaps he should ask the next time he saw him…or better not.

Marit shuffled his feet.

Otar resisted the urge to pinch his nose and show his annoyance and instead crossed his arms. "What can I do for you?" he asked. One thing was sure, Marit wasn't here by accident.

"I thought that…I mean," Marit scratched his neck, "now that your…lov—friend is gone, I could…"

Points for guts, deduction for not speaking plainly—Otar suppressed a sigh while Marit babbled on, and decided to put him out of his misery.

"Marit, it's poor form to want to go with someone moments after their lover left."

Dropping his shoulders, Marit's gaze shifted towards the ground.

Otar pressed on. "I've told you—I'm not interested in you at all."

Marit probably had latched onto him because he saw something grand in Otar that was different from everyone else in town—but that was just not there. Otar was a scholar, devoted to the Ancients and their ruins. No one could compete against that, and of the few lovers he had even considered being more, most had taken offense at being second to his studies.

With a clenched jaw, Marit hovered for a moment as if he had more to say, but he turned and ran away. Otar shook his head and strongly hoped this would be it.

His hopes were dashed the next morning when Marit arrived at his doorstep carrying the basket with Otar's breakfast and a letter addressed to him. Normally Marit's mother, who had taken a shine to Otar and wanted to fatten him up as if he were a plump chicken, would bring him his morning meal.

He scrutinized Marit for a moment and then sighed, hunger and his need for brew to wake him up won out. With reluctance, he moved to the side to let the intruder in.

As soon as Marit stepped over the threshold, he started talking. When he found the table occupied by papers, he put the basket on the trunk and pulled out the small portions of food they preferred for their morning meals in this region, each in a tiny bowl: three different cheese types, freshly grilled summer vegetables, a piece of a honeycomb, and warm fluffy bread. Sitting cross-legged on his bed, Otar ate in silence while Marit kept up his chatter. After finishing, Otar sipped the brew and closed his eyes in bliss for a few small-turns. Brew in these regions was a strong herby mixture, which was close to the ones the steppe riders made.

He sighed to himself.

"Shouldn't you be out helping with the harvest?" he asked when Marit paused for some air.

"I want to help you," Marit said instead, and he handed the letter over.

Otar raised an eyebrow at that, turning the letter over. It was from his mentor, Aaoran-peras; he put it to the side for the moment.

Marit's cheeks turned as red as they had yesterturn evening, but this time, he didn't run away.

"You have been searching for a way up the mountains these past turns. There are hidden passages, but finding and navigating them is difficult and often very danger-ous." Marit fiddled with the basket handle. "I know them, and I can show you the different ways. I have talked to Father," he plunged on as Otar opened his mouth with the intention of rejecting him. "He said it'll be fine. The harvest is nearly done anyway, and they're okay without me for the time being."

Considering the offer, Otar pressed his lips together and tapped his fingers on his thighs. Marit was right in one thing: the mountains were inaccessible to him. He had searched at the mountains' foundation for any sign of the ruin to no avail, and then he had tried to work his way up. They were steep, and he got blocked too often. But he knew they must be there. He felt it. He ignored the shifting feeling inside him, the monster was being restless.

And there was also the case of the ghost.

A guide would be helpful; finding nothing was tiring, and while he had the time, he didn't have the patience.

He exhaled, and after another small-turn of consideration, slowly nodded.

"As you wish."

Chapter 2

"They named the village after a fish called Piskus that grows plentiful in the close-by river. They eat the small fish to every meal, cooked in all forms imaginable. It was complicated explaining to them that I don't eat any type of meat, and I don't think they fully believe me yet, but as I have eaten all the other plant food they provided they seem somewhat mollified."

(Chapter: "Piskus", in: Scholar Otar's Notebooks, No. 26)

OTAR AND MARIT met up again in the late afternoon. Marit brought the provisions they would need, and they discussed the best route to take where Marit informed him about a small passage to the east they could use as a starting point. Otar had stayed up long into the night, studying the maps to find the best place where an ancient civilization may have once settled.

They set out early on the next turn. The sky was deep gray, but the village was already bustling with life. Marit was still half-asleep, unusually quiet and yawning every few steps.

The morning air was crisp; summer was turning into fall, taking the balmy nights with it.

They made good progress. From time to time, Otar would consult his folded-up map, but even with his state of exhaustion, Marit led him sure-footed, around the village, over the river, behind a waterfall, down a small cave, through a tight crevasse, and then back out into the open, before they descended another slope.

"We're going down again?" Otar observed with a frown. To him, that made no sense. They needed to go up.

Marit looked at him, puzzled.

"The walls can't be climbed. There are no paths that lead up."

Otar suddenly felt very dumb.

"Is that what you did?" Marit asked, mirth dancing in his eyes. His body shook. Otar was sure he was suppressing laughter.

He tried not to bristle, but it was futile, if the sudden broad smile on Marit's face was any sign. Best to change the topic.

"Where are you leading me, then?"

Marit accepted the change of topic with grace and pointed down the new chasm. It was tight, almost a cave. High above them, Otar made out a sliver of the blue sky.

"These holes lead to a cave system that stretches through the surrounding mountains. We'll start at the easiest entry point and see how far we've come, then we track back and choose a different one, until we have found what you have been searching for." He looked back at Otar. "No one has ever mapped these caves in their entirety, so we need to be careful." Marit turned to the crack and frowned.

Otar stepped up beside him and peered into the darkness, trying to find what Marit must have seen. "What is it?" he asked when he found nothing strange.

"There were once ways which led to too smooth walls that we always thought to be man-made. Maybe from settlers before us. It's a shame that those have caved in." Marit rolled his shoulders back in a half shrug. "The snow melts bring floods, and over time…" He trailed off, but it was clear what he meant.

Otar studied the path, his mind working. This was the tidbit of information he had been searching for, but no one had told him. He wondered what the reason could be. "Can we go parallel to the old way?"

First Marit shook his head, but then he paused, considering. "If we're lucky."

For most of the turn, they weren't. After they passed the crevasse and emerged into the cave system, the terrain became difficult to cross with uneven ground and stones loosening under their feet while the way led up. The air was cold and moist and often hard to breathe. Otar made notes when they came to an intersection, while Marit marked their way with colorful scraps of cloth.

When Otar asked for an explanation, Marit turned pink. "It's safer than chalk, water drips down here and may wash any symbol away, so fabric holds better." He took out a yellow scrap of fabric with colored blotches and embroidered symbols on it and tied it around a rock spire extruding from the wall. Marit's blush deepened when Otar pointed them out. "I made them last night," Marit mumbled and moved on.

When Marit was scouting out a path, Otar stepped closer to a scrap and examined it. It was a row of three signs Otar hadn't seen before. He sketched them with fast strokes and then hurried after Marit, who was calling for him.

After what must have been many small-turns, they found their way back out into the open. A grassy patch hidden between walls of rock opened before them. Otar tried to check the sun to gauge how late it was, but the high stones obscured most of the sky.

They settled down to take a short rest, and Marit handed him a flask with the local ale. Otar took it with a nod, and, after a swig, studied Marit.

"Why did you offer me help?" Otar paused and then added, "Besides the obvious reasons."

Marit's cheeks colored once more, and yet he didn't shy away from the embarrassment. "You have seen so much of the world. And I want to know about it so badly." Marit looked at a point over Otar's shoulder, his eyes flicking around. "The books and the tales the merchants bring—they're not the same. I wanted to go out by myself but Father says I have a duty to the people of the village, and he won't let me leave."

Otar thought back to his mother, who had said close to the same thing—the world outside was too dangerous, too unpredictable, too everything else. Otar knew where she was coming from. She feared she would be losing him as she had lost her husband. One turn, his father had gone out and had never returned.

And yet, she hadn't been able to stop him. He had packed his bag and had said goodbye.

At times, he sent her and his sisters letters, sometimes with money, often with stories.

Otar took another swig from the flask. "You know, you can just leave." As he had.

Marit turned his gaze to him, a flicker of hope dancing in it. "But where would I start?"

"At the first step."

Marit spluttered, but Otar said nothing else. Everyone needed their own beginning to decide for themselves if it was worth it.

Otar screwed the canteen tight and put his things together again. After a few moments, Marit mirrored him, but his mind seemed to be somewhere else.

While he waited for Marit to be ready, Otar hoped the other wouldn't insist on coming with him when he left the village. Taking him on would send mixed signals, and while Marit was attractive in a charming, boyish kind of way, Otar wasn't in the habit of having a bed warmer to stroke his own ego. He needed something different: a spark, a connection, something to hold on to. He needed…

He swallowed and shouldered his pack.

They crossed the grass field and slipped once more into the damp and cavernous darkness. Marit dutifully tied scrap after scrap around rock fixtures and anything they would be sure to find at every intersection they came to pass. After a particularly steep incline, the path leveled out, and they entered an enormous cavern filled with an underground lake. The water stretched dark and glossy before them. Nothing rippled on the surface; it was an endless mirror. Their small witch light barely illuminated the area beyond the shore.

Marit frowned at the lake. "This is new."

They walked down the waterfront then hit a dead end. Neither of them was inclined to find out how deep the lake was.

After a brief discussion about their next steps, they tracked back to the previous intersection and chose a different route, which this time ended after two twist and turns blocked by what looked like a cave in.

Otar tried hard to hide his impatience at the wasted time.

"Our luck seems to have run out," he remarked as he inspected the rubble and found no way through.

Marit sighed. "That wasn't the plan."

"And yet I've gone further than I have ever gone before," Otar said with a grin, and after a moment Marit grinned back.

Back at the intersection, they chose the third option that led them into a smaller cavern, this time with an exit at the other end. The ceiling hung low and at one point, they needed to crawl to pass through. Thankfully, it opened up into a round shaped underground chamber.

After brushing off the dirt from his clothing, Otar looked around. The place seemed too symmetric to have formed naturally. Neither stalagmites nor stalactites grew. The ground was even with a layer of fine dark dust, and the air dry. The opening they had come through appeared as if something had caved in or broken through.

Otar crouched down and wiped the dirt with his hands. The ground was stony, with no patterns or carvings or tiles.

"Found anything?" Marit kneeled beside him, the witch light throwing their shadows onto the wall.

"Not really. But it is odd."

Otar sat back on his feet and looked around. Confused, Marit did the same, unsure what Otar was getting at.

Otar pointed to the surrounding stone. "The cavern is too regular. There are no heaps of dislodged stones, and the walls don't have the same textures as the others. And the air is too dry." Otar scratched his chin in thought. "And yet, if this had been made by the Ancients, I expect the ground laid with tiles, or at least some markings. The other ruins never had bare floors like this here."

Otar put his pack down. He fished out his notebook and scribbled down a few lines of his observations before making some hasty sketches. Any anomaly was an additional step closer to uncovering the secrets the Ancients had left behind.

Marit rose and turned around himself. "So, another dead end?" There was no other way out.

It was, wasn't it? The hovering witch light was strong enough to illuminate the small cave. There were no shadows hiding anything.

"Master Otar?"

"When is your family expecting you back?"

Marit colored and scratched his neck. "They told me to enjoy myself."

Otar raised an eyebrow but didn't comment further. The less said about any of it, the better.

"We'll rest here and then decide what to do when we aren't so exhausted. This place is dry and not much can creep up on us."

They made a cold meal and then curled up in their bedrolls. Otar had gotten used to the bed in the hut, so sleeping once more on the hard ground was uncomfortable. At least it was not as freezing as Otar had feared. With the air being as dry as it was, no dampness settled into his bones. Still, he was restless through the night.

He woke early—or, he assumed it to be early. A glance at Marit showed him that the other was snoring away; turned to the side, the bedroll pulled up to his ears. The witch light hovered between them. It wouldn't take much to reach over and let himself forget everything for a few small-turns, let himself forget about the monster he was, the monster he carried with him…

Otar scrubbed a hand over his face to lose the dangerous thoughts, peeled himself out of his bed roll, and got up. After stretching his stiff muscles, he went to work. There should be another way out of the cavern. If this was part of an Ancients ruin, there must be a hidden mechanism. With Marit not hanging over his shoulders, he could try a less orthodox method that would generate too many questions if witnessed.

But first, he checked his notebook to find if there had been anything similar he had come across before. He cursed himself for sending the older notebooks away, the writing in this one didn't go back very far and as expected revealed nothing important.

Otar swallowed. He had one option left—but it came with a risk and always with a price.

There were legends surrounding magic.

In the south, the people held the belief that all had not just magic but that it was powerful enough to perform miracles, commune with the world around them, shape a mere thought born in their mind into existence—until they couldn't anymore.

In the north, the tribes described great monsters that consumed magic, and so our ancestors hid what they could until they had forgotten all about it.

In the west, they believed the gods took magic away as a punishment for an unspeakable crime.

And to the east, they assumed that everyone in the world never had much more magic than they had now, and that all that talk about past grandeur was only myth and nothing more.

There was a tiny spark of magic in everyone—not enough for creation magic—but they all felt a connection to the mysterious energy that lay beneath the ground, a steady hum that some called aether and others magic.

Those who have a stronger spark powered witch lights, knew that winter would come early, and could hear the trees whisper—but there was never enough to create something, as the old legends described.

Whatever happened in the past was unclear, but Otar was sure that at one point that kind of magic must have existed, maybe as a distinct form from what remained in these times, because only magic could activate the ruins.

He walked over to the stone wall and checked every inch. After a few small-turns, he heard his companion shuffle. At the sound he whirled around, overbalanced and caught himself on the stone wall. There was a tingle in his palm, and then the whole cave rumbled, the ground vibrating.

Marit sprung up, looking around with wide eyes. "What is going on?"

"I might have found the hidden switch," Otar said, forcing himself to grin while his heart was in his throat beating a fast staccato.

Marit blinked at him, almost owlishly, his mind still not there.

The room stilled; dirt trickled down from the ceiling for a bit longer. In fear of triggering anything else that might bury them under tons of rocks, they remained still as their eyes darted around the cave to assess the damage. Part of the wall had opened, right next to where Otar had pressed his hand against the stone.

Darkness awaited them.

Otar eyed it with trepidation.

"First breakfast and then we go onward."

Marit blinked at him and then laughed. If it sounded hysterical, neither of them commented.

Chapter 3

"I tried to dig deeper into their ancestry, but it's hard to determine where they have hailed from. Their skin is too light and their hair not the usual dark coloring you find in the southern regions. I guess they have wandered down from the north over many generations. Patterns in their weaving show similarities to the ones they have in the north-western settlements, close to the liveable line."

(Chapter: "Piskus", in: Scholar Otar's Notebooks, No. 26)

THEY DIDN'T HURRY through their cold meal, but they also didn't linger. Then they packed up, and slipped into the darkness, two witch lights now trailing between them dutifully.

The air was colder and crisper, fresher than in the small room, the space was narrow hardly wide enough for them to pass through stretching into two directions. When Otar turned left he saw the faint outline of massive boulders blocking the way. They turned right Marit pointing out a faint glimmer of light at that end.

The room they slept in had been barren. A testament to that once more, nothing besides the naked stone remained. Otar pinched the bridge of his nose. Devoid of anything besides pictures on the walls and symbols that might be words, the ruins were strangely empty places. Just as empty as this hallway. Otar looked for Marit, but the other was a hazy scheme further away.

Scholars often speculated on what materials the Ancients might have used that would decay so completely. A long-forgotten craft? Or did the Ancients take everything with them when they left?

Which was another point of contention: Had they actually left?

The hallway was not built as in other ruins, here it was tunneled into the mountain stone. Otar stepped closer and studied its walls. Yes, there were minerals laced through it, and the color hues were the same as in the caves they had just walked through. Usually, the ruins were made of a much lighter stone, a light gray or brown, but never this dark and built with almost invisible seams, a technique also lost.

In these hallways, deep lines ran at roughly the height of their shoulders down the entire length. In active ruins, they'd emit a pale light not unlike the witch light.

Otar followed behind Marit at a slower pace, probing the stone from time to time, hoping for a clue, a reaction, for anything, really, while his companion moved further away.

After a few small-turns he saw Marit disappear into another room. As Otar made his way to the end of the hallway, he emerged into a circular room with a domed ceiling and saw Marit at the opposite wall. Similar to the other ruins, every one of them had a dome entirely made of stone. The size differed depending on the overall scale of the ruin. Rarer to find was a ruin with more than one dome. The biggest dome was the main building, or what the scholars dubbed as the main. Around the outside of the building, spires would be evenly placed. Impossibly slender things curving inward, they seemed to be reaching for the middle of the dome.

At least, that was another assumption. Most tips had weathered away, and only the minuscule bend in their stoney bodies led to the theory.

Otar deeply inhaled the fresh air within the room and registered the massive windows on one side. They were open, no glass holding back the mountain wind that thundered through.

Instinctively, Otar took out his notebook and wrote down his observations. Ruins never had windows. Marit, who had been inspecting the walls on the other side, came up beside him, and they both stepped closer to them. Beyond their delicate frames, the cliff edge plunged down into a deep chasm.

Excusing himself, Marit took a few hasty steps back. "I've never been this high up. At least not immediately confronted with such a steep fall."

Otar nodded absentmindedly and made a few last notes. Looking around, he noticed the dome was on the smaller side, the mountains probably dictating the size. One half of the walls were still rough stonework. Otar walked closer and let his fingers drift over it. It didn't look like the masonry work Otar had seen in Rasanell, where thin lines, almost invisible, spoke of the tools that formed the stone. These were deep gouges, as if something impossibly big had taken a swipe out of it.

Otar turned back to survey the whole room. Marit was watching him. He felt his gaze prickling his neck, but he paid him no mind.

Something piqued his interest, something besides the anomalies. He looked back at the walls that were smoother and then it came to him—the murals were missing. He looked closer and noticed in one corner the rest of a faint star-like pattern, above a stylized ruin, the lines barely there.

Every ruin, no matter how big or small, had a mural painted onto the main dome walls. It illustrated strange plants and animals no one had ever seen before, with strange black symbols scribbled close to them. Scholars concluded that they either must be names or, at the very least, descriptions.

And yet, in this ruin, Otar saw nothing was painted on or had ever been painted on. No colored remains from the white undercoat or the flowers and the colorful animal skins could be seen.

Otar made more notes and sketches, sending the witch light this and that way, taking it all in.

Then he stepped into the middle of the room and crouched down, brushing aside the collected dust and stone to check what the floor was made of.

He found bare stone once more and the same flat underground they had seen in the small chamber. Even the typical gold and blue mosaic tiles were gone or had never been laid down.

There was no ghost waiting for him; that strange specter that seemed to haunt most of the ruins he explored.

Otar sat back on his haunches and considered all the things he had seen here. Was the ruin unfinished?

He racked his brain to remember if there had ever been an unfinished ruin, but in truth, they had barely scratched the surface in cataloging all the ruins scattered through the Seven Lands.

The Ancients built so much and left nothing behind, only stories and legends.

And ruins.

Who were the Ancients?

Otar recoiled when he felt a touch on his shoulders. Hurt flashing over his face, Marit stepped back.

"You startled me," Otar said, trying to get his bearings back.

Marit nodded after a moment but wariness remained in his eyes. "There is a way down." He pointed his thumb over his shoulder at another dark rectangle which Otar had previously assumed to be another window.

"There is usually more than one story," Otar said.

New excitement spread over Marit's face, whipping back and forth on his feet he asked, "Can we take a look?"

Otar couldn't help smiling to himself at the enthusiasm. It was refreshing to see someone as enthralled as himself at the prospect of discovering more. The other scholars always behaved as if they had seen it all even when they had not, and even Otar became weary of the same patterns over and over again in the ruins. Even if the ruins differed in size, they all followed the same plan, as if the Ancients had made one original design and had modeled every other ruin after it.

"This is why we have come. We need to take a look." He put his notebook away, and together, they walked to the opening. They saw stairs leading down.

If this ruin followed the normal pattern, then a set of rooms should be found on the next story, then below that a massive underground chamber with a slightly concave floor that would be the same size as the upper room.

That, together with the dome and the spires, was what every ruin had. At larger ruins, a cluster of smaller buildings outside of the dome could be found almost hugging its outer walls; connected by maze-like pathways and bridges. But everything stayed contained in a tight perimeter forming a rectangle.

The witch light hovered between them as they descended carefully, shining light on cracks in the walls and the stairs. At a few points, the ceiling had caved in, and stones and thick boulders made the passage difficult to navigate.

"Be careful," Otar murmured as he tested every step before bringing his full weight down on the stairs. Five summers ago, when he traveled the southern jungles close to the Green River, he had fallen through the stairway of a crumbling ruin, saved by sheer dumb luck—a save that wouldn't happen a second time because the person who had saved him was far away now.

They made the way down without an accident. Otar sent out the witch lights and exhaled.

The usage of the rooms on their current level was greatly theorized. Every ruin held an even number of rooms, the walls of each one painted in a different color.

These rooms were small, roughly double as wide as Otar's arm span, and were as barren as the other rooms in the ruins. Had they been used for storage? As living quarters? Priest chambers, places for rituals, treasure rooms? The questions went on and on, but there was never any clue as to what their purpose may have been.

The witch light illuminated the destruction. The walls between the rooms were knocked down, the rumble scattered haphazardly, as if someone big had taken a handful of dirt and rocks and flung it around.

Otar shivered at the thought of something powerful enough to leave this kind of mess. Still, he stepped closer and examined the crumbled edges of the walls. Some were blackened, but they didn't smell of fire and ash, at least not anymore.

He straightened up and realized how quiet it was down here. The level had no windows, so no wind thundered through, and no animal could be heard skittering around. There was only his breathing and Marit's steps. Otar looked back at the walls. They showed flecks of colors. At least this level seemed to have been finished, or as close to finished as it could have been, before disaster befell them.

He frowned and walked deeper. Only when he was already halfway through the room did he realize that Marit remained at the foot of the stairs.

"Marit?" he called.

Marit blinked slowly, his eyes owlishly large in the shadows thrown by the witch light. "Something sinister raged here," he rasped out, followed by a blush.

He really was young, wasn't he?

But his words rang true. Otar looked around. Something must have happened here, something big, something bad—so bad that the Ancients abandoned the ruin and never came back to finish it.

Otar returned to the broken walls, the black a stark contrast to the lighter stone. He touched them with his fingertips, and the stone crumbled away like sand.

The faint wispy sound was loud in the room. When the sand stopped, silence returned.

Otar couldn't even make out the faint humming of the ruin's core. This place had taken just enough energy from him to open up the door above. Besides that, it was dead.

Coldness crept into his body. Otar swallowed, cleared his throat—the sound danced between them—and said, "If you feel unsafe, you can wait here."

Marit's eyes widened, and Otar expected him to bolt. His whole body rigid, Marit placed one foot in front of the other and came closer, as if his feet did this of their own volition. Otar paused a moment longer to give him the time to change his mind, but when Marit didn't move away, he turned and picked up his exploration again, Marit close by.

The scholars who researched the Ancients had always hoped for the one clue, the one thing that would finally unravel all the secrets and bring the ongoing mystery to a satisfactory end. But even in this chaos, nothing remained of the Ancients or of those who might have caused their destruction.

Or had there been an accident? Similar to the one that cost Otar dearly? The reason why he had left the university, and why…

Had the Ancients unleashed something terrifying?

At the end of the room was another set of stairs leading further down. The darkness there seemed more absolute—even the witch light seemed dimmer. Marit paused once more, fear painted in the stiff line of his shoulders and the large eyes.

"Wait here," Otar said, taking pity on him. The dark shadows made Marit look even younger.

Marit looked relieved and nodded. He left the second witch light with him, and Otar walked down. Now alone, he trailed his fingertips against the walls, hoping to spark something again, but silence and stillness prevailed.

On the third level, the destruction was evident: broken-down walls, big boulders and stones littered the surface, ridges driven into the stone and floor. But there was something else.

Otar stopped on the last step and squinted into the pale light. The shadows watched him. They seemed to whisper strange sounds and emit high-pitched voices. Nothing lived here, but something was awake. His heartbeat loud in his ears, Otar waited, but after several small-turns, nothing moved, so he soldiered on.

Some rooms' entries were blocked by the fallen stones or entirely smashed, and only a faint outline pointed to where the walls once had been. Those he could access held nothing more besides more debris and colorful walls. He retraced his steps and considered his next move. Should he go back? Even if it was in a desolate state, the ruins had so far offered nothing new. They followed the same pattern as all the others.

Otar groaned as all the questions kept piling up.

There was another idea at the back of his mind, something he hadn't even dared to tell Aaoran-peras. A private theory that maybe would bring him a step further to uncovering who the Ancients had been. But he had yet to see the heart of the ruin. It was dead, that was true, but there was something he wanted to confirm.

"Otar?"

Marit's voice sounded muffled down here.

"Still alive," he called back. "I'll go down to the next level."

"You sure?"

No, he wasn't, but he was driven. The monster inside him was also drawn. There was something down here, something explicit.

"Yeah, I won't take long."

"Okay."

Otar moved down to the other side and, just as on the other level, he found an opening leading down once more. He descended.

So far, everything was as it should be. The stairs led down in an arch to accommodate the restrictions of the rocks—but this time the way down felt different.

The instant his foot touched the ground, Otar knew he wasn't alone. The monster also took note and reached beyond him. Whatever the monster sought, nothing answered its call. Ignoring it, Otar checked the surroundings.

The floor was marbled and decorated with long black and gold lines. Symbols were meticulously written along them, forming words that echoed in his mind. Everything glittered faintly when the witch light hit.

This is what he expected. This was what could be found in every ruin. Otar stepped closer and saw cracks on the floor, barely visible, but the witch light illuminated them. Otar noted that they widened the closer he came to the middle.

The monster stretched even further.

The center was supposed to hold a white basin with symbols along the edges and a big blue gem center piece its reflective surface almost like a mirror, but here these were obliterated, replaced by a deep crater opening where they would usually be, as if a giant fist had smashed through.

The surrounding air moved.

Dirt trickled down as if something moved overhead. Slowly, Otar raised his gaze to the ceiling and three red eyes stared back at him. For a moment, nothing moved.

The monster, the thing that lurked inside him, what he had once believed to be magic, pounced lighting-fast and reached for whatever lurked in the shadows, as if it were welcoming an old friend.

Familiarity began to suppress the terror in his bones, and the monster stretched and stretched, until—

There! It made contact, it knew it was—

The shadows roared and shook the entire ruins. Then they moved.

Otar fled.

He sprinted up the stairs, calling for Marit to run. But the idiot was still waiting for him at the top of the second-level stairs, watching him confused. He looked at Otar questioningly and then flicked his gaze behind him. He blanched and then screamed in terror.

Otar grabbed him by the shirt as he passed, but Marit was a boulder resisting the movement. Another roar thundered through the walls. Otar whirled around and saw shadows rolling closer, the three red eyes huge, like suns in the sky. Whatever it was, it had no discernible shape, but the menace rolled off it in waves. A void blotting out everything, coming to get him.

He managed to wrench his eyes away and clapped Marit hard on the cheek.

"Get a grip!" Then he pulled at the other again. This time, Marit came willingly. The witch lights dimmed with every inch the shadows crawled closer.

They crossed the second level, Marit almost tumbling twice, then ran up the stairs. Otar's lungs burned, his pulse thundered, and his legs threatened to give out under him at every moment.

On the first level, Marit finally came back to himself and ran on his own, a straight line down the dome and up the stairs.

They thundered down the hallways to the hidden door and into the small room. Marit was already going down the small passageway when Otar arrived at the threshold. Otar rushed into the room, his fingers scraping over the wall to find the switch, and hoped that closing the door was enough to fend off the raging shadow.

"Come on, come on," he mumbled while his fingers skittered over the cold wall. The shadow rushed closer, swallowing anything Otar could see through the open door. It was as if they knew that their prey was on the brink of escaping their wrath. They roared, and the hallway, the room, and everything shook. Otar pressed his teeth together and kept searching for the switch, the blood roaring in his ears, his heart thundering like the walls around him.

Finally finding the right spot and just as the shadows reached for him, the door slid shut. The walls thundered, and stones and pebbles dislodged from the ceiling and rained down on them as they made their escape.

He didn't wait to find out if the door was holding but crawled after Marit through the passage.

The shadows raged on behind him.

Chapter 4

"Yardar are strange creatures adapted to the steppe they come from. Since their domestication, they have populated the entire Seven Lands. Their massive, scaled two legs are perfect for work on most terrains, and they adapt to almost all climates reasonably well. Recently, scientists found adaptations in their feathers depending on the region they live in and how long their ancestors have been bred there. This is a rather remarkable discovery..."

(From: "The Yardar - Beast or Helper?")

OTAR FOUND MARIT huddled in a corner of the natural cave that led to the passageway. His whole body trembling, he hid his head under his arms and tried to make himself as small as possible. Otar crouched down before him, not touching.

"Can you walk?"

Marit uncurled slightly, just enough to look at him with an unfocused gaze, before his eyes sharpened and took Otar in.

"What was that?" His voice almost broke at the end.

"I wish I knew," Otar said honestly. He'd never encountered anything like it before. There wasn't even a hint of something this monstrous in any of the stories they collected about the ruins. Where did it come from? Did it destroy the ruins? And if so, why?

Otar rose and offered Marit his hand, but Marit chose to use the stone wall to get himself up again. Otar let his own hand drop and didn't comment.

Following the fabric strips Marit had tied, they walked back in silence. From time-to-time Otar would stop and listen into the darkness, but everything had reverted back to the state when they arrived. The red-glowing eyes and the shadows hadn't followed them down. Marit's back was rigid, his eyes remained front. Otar almost wanted to go back and study everything further. The monster inside welcomed the thought. And yet, he had feared for his life. Maybe one turn, when he finally knew more, he could tame that monster and analyze it. When they reached the small clearing between the walls, they settled down for the night. Darkness was upon them which made Otar wonder how long they had been gone.

Otar made a fire to chase away the lingering shadows. Marit gulped down a cold meal and then rolled up in his bedroll, his back to the flames and Otar, without having muttered a single word. It stung. Otar had forgotten how fast adoration could turn into fear and rejection. He had led Marit to a terrifying place.

When Marit started to cry out in his sleep, clearly in the throes of a nightmare, Otar sat next to him and rested a soothing hand on his head, carding his fingers softly through the short hair. Marit murmured something, then he sank deeper into slumber.

Otar returned to his seat and twirled a lock of his white hair between his fingers in thought. The band that usually held it together in a tight bun must have gotten lost in the flight. It now fell past his shoulders. After coming back from his last travels, he almost considered cutting it but found it easier to keep it out of the way in a bun.

Otar kept an eye on Marit the entire night, but the nightmares didn't return.

When twilight flooded the clearing Marit woke, and by unspoken agreement, they broke camp. They trekked the entire way back to the village in silence. Otar was on the verge of opening his mouth a few times, but the tight set of Marit's jaw and rigidness of his body told him it wouldn't end well.

When they reached the edge of the village, Marit didn't stop and made a straight line for his own house. Otar watched him for a moment, wondering if he should call out to him, before he shook his head and returned to his own hut.

Back at the table, he got out his notebook and wrote down as many details as he remembered. The absence of everything in the ruins, the destruction, the attempted eradication, the red eyes of the void monster—all of it was new, never documented before.

Did they wake a guardian? But how did the monster inside him reach for the creature as if it knew what it was? Was it something of the Ancients? Something built by another? Was there more than one ancestor?

Question after question spilled out from his fingertips onto the pages.

He scribbled down note after note in his small, neat handwriting, followed by sketches and everything else he pulled out of his memory. When darkness fell and he was about to contemplate turning on the oil lamp, someone knocked.

Otar sighed. Having a good idea who would be on the other side, he stood, stretched his cramped muscles, and then opened the door.

The elder was watching from under his bushy brows. He wasn't that old for having the title; he was a short man with a weathered face that came from working outside all his life. His hair was mostly gray, but there was still youth in his gait and energy in his eyes—eyes that watched him now intently.

"Elder, I was about to visit you," Otar said.

The elder raised an eyebrow. "Were you now? Well, this will spare you an errand."

Otar nodded and stepped to the side.

The elder swept his gaze through the room, but didn't move further than one foot behind the threshold. The door remained open, chilly dampness seeping in.

This wasn't a social call.

"How is Marit?" He genuinely wanted to know. Whatever happened had shaken Otar, and he had seen things. Marit must be beyond fear.

The elder nodded as if Otar just confirmed something for him. "He'll get better."

"I can leave instructions for a draught that should help to ease his sleep."

The elder hesitated and then let his shoulders drop. "That would be kind."

They stared at each other; the night cicadas took up their lone song, interspersed with the *ribbit ribbit* of the frogs from the river pools. Laughter drifted over. Someone sang a lullaby.

Otar finally gave in. "What did I wake?"

"We call it the Keeper."

"I've never heard of one." Otar inched to his table. He itched to write down the information the other provided.

The elder sighed, and Otar stared at him. The elder was avoiding his gaze and looking out through the open window. Then his eyes went to Otar, expression intense, and this time Otar wanted to run away from it.

"I never thought you'd actually make it inside. I never expected *you* could wake it." The elder paused. "There are legends passed from ancestor to ancestor. Legends that speak of an unprecedented evil. Once it resided in these mountains a very long time ago."

"The void monster."

But the elder shook his head.

"Something else. Our ancestors called them the white devils." His gaze flicked over Otar, surely noting his almost white hair, and Otar resisted hiding it under his hands. "We came once from the north, fleeing an evil that did unspeakable things. And yet when our ancestors arrived at this mountain the same devils had already been here, building the place you have now discovered.

"Our ancestors lost so much and had nothing more to give, so in their desperation they fought back, but they pushed too hard, not knowing what would happen. They woke the Keeper, the guardian the white devils had with them.

"Here, the legends are not clear what exactly happened, but the Keeper went mad and threw off its chains, chasing down friend and foe.

"The Keeper raged and raged, destroying everything in its wake, so our ancestors fled, hid in the mountains, and felt the tremble in the walls and the floors for turns and turns. The devils weren't able to contain the Keeper and so they fled as well.

"When the last of them was gone, the Keeper fell silent." The elder licked his lips. He shook his head and continued. "Our ancestors waited in fear, and they waited, and they waited, but the Keeper did not come for them, nor did the devils return. To be sure, they purged the stories and legends, and only the elder of the village will be told the truth. Hoping it would be enough to let the Keeper sleep, and for the devils to forget about us."

Otar tapped a finger against his chin. "This is the first time I've ever heard a story like this."

The elder didn't comment.

Otar let his hands drop and slumped. "You want me gone."

The elder inclined his head. "You woke the Keeper. You don't belong here."

The comment shouldn't sting as much as it did. But Otar was reminded that he belonged nowhere. Not in this village, not in Rasanell, not in his own home, and not with…no, every place he traveled to had rejected him.

"When Marit has recovered and is in the right mind to hear it, I'll tell him you said goodbye." The eyes of the elder weren't unkind, but hard. "Someone will bring you provisions and the letter that has arrived in the last turn."

Otar made a formal bow. "Thank you for your hospitality."

The elder only nodded and walked out, leaving Otar alone with the encroaching night and his thoughts.

Not long after, a woman brought the promised food and one message. Regardless of how they parted, the elder had been generous. The food was enough to last him a few turns.

The new letter was from Turas, the adviser to the Heir from Rasanell. He eyed it with trepidation, but then he noticed the letter from his mentor he had left on his desk before the disastrous trip. He opened that one instead.

Otar,

Whatever you are doing, leave it be and come to the steppe. We found something you must see. Ask for the Adabel ruin at the Patreshka University. They will arrange a guide to bring you to me.

Come.

Forever yours,

Aaoran

There was no date. He read the missive thrice, making sure he didn't miss a hidden meaning or any instructions, but those few sentences were all that was there. At least now he knew what to do next. He penned a short reply to send so that Aaoran had an idea of when he could expect Otar. He estimated it would take him roughly eight turns to make it to Patreshka, depending on his method of travel and the path he took. Then, if he remembered the map with the ruin locations well enough, it would be another few turns before he would reach Adabel.

He searched in his memories for what he read about the Adabel ruins. They were on the smaller side, close to a little mountain range cutting off the steppe to the ocean. Many summers ago, scholars had found small clusters of buildings hidden under sand and rock, but not much more. They suspected it might have been larger than it seemed, but other scholar factions hotly contested the idea. At the same time, the interest in the ruins and the Ancients waned, and the funding became tight. Shortly after, they abandoned the site.

Four summers ago, he almost did the treck to the ruins out there, but then he chose a different direction—now he was going, anyway.

It was hard to suppress the bitter laughter at the irony.

WHEN DAWN HERALDED the oncoming turn, Otar left the village without saying goodbye to anyone—the elder would spin his own tale on why he'd gone, and, despite their interest in him and his travels, he and the villagers hadn't been close.

It proved once more that he was nothing but a stranger passing through. Aaoran would call him dramatic at those thoughts, telling him he'd just not found his people yet, and that he should give it time.

It was slow going, the turns spent in the mountains still clung to his bones, making every step harder than it should be. He missed his yardar; it got injured right before he reached the village and needed to heal. He left a note for it to be given to someone in need because returning for it now would probably not be a good idea.

The ground was hard and cold, and the forest seemed to watch him more than usual.

On the third turn, he was lucky. He crossed paths with a traveling caravan of merchants that were going to Patreshka and were willing to take him on.

They didn't travel faster than he alone did, but it was welcome company. The run in at the ruin had sapped too much strength out of him. The monster inside him gnawed at Otar's bones. Here, with so many people, energy ran high and the monster could satisfy itself by taking bits and pieces here.

The group was a merry bunch who traveled on this route every season. There was a core group that had originally formed the caravan, and they had picked up and dropped off different people along their journeys.

The leader was a massive woman from the north with broad shoulders and hands that could rip Otar apart. She had a no-nonsense attitude and kept everything running smoothly. When he first asked to come aboard, she scrutinized him, eyeing his thin arms. Which was fair. He was tall but thin-limbed and gangly, and he looked like someone who spent all his time indoors bowed over books—which he did. However, his travels over the last summers had put a little more muscle on him and had added color to his skin.

The leader sighed when Otar said he could do anything, not quite believing him, but in the end she took pity and relented. "You can help Berat with smaller tasks, then."

And this was how Otar was tasked with doing chores when they settled down for the night. Getting water for the cooking, finding firewood, moving things in and out from the storage caravan for the cook of the communal meal. Berat, the other man on the job, was younger than him and nice enough—he reminded Otar a lot of Marit, but without the gleam of worship in his eyes. Instead, they held an edge that betrayed Berat's outward and easygoing nature. Otar had seen the same hardness in Aaoran's eyes when they talked about the past.

Then, everything had seemed larger and easier and newer. Now...

With a sigh, he brushed away the thoughts of the past and picked up another dry looking branch.

"That's a heavy sigh," Berat commented with amusement. He was close in height to Otar and heavier. His muscles had the same wiry structure Otar often saw on the steppe riders, even if Berat was missing the same hair color and complexion. Granted, he had only ever seen a certain faction of steppe riders, the ones Andres and his twin Onder had overseen to guard the Bakusaran ruins—under contract with Aaoran. The ruins were close to Otar's home village, and Aaoran had showed them to him when Otar was ten and six summers old.

It was hard to pin down where Berat was from since his accent was non-existent. This either meant he had an excellent education or he had moved very often.

"Otar?" Berat's smile shifted, showing an unfamiliar edge.

Otar shook his head. "I apologize. My mind was elsewhere."

Berat gave him a look that said it was evident, and Otar grinned ruefully. He threw the branch in his hands to Berat, and Berat caught it in one smooth movement. Otar whistled. Berat bowed and put the branch onto the stack.

"Boys!" the voice of the caravan leader echoed through the forest.

"You'd think being almost thirty summers would count for something," Otar grumbled, while Berat called back, "Coming!" Together, they hefted the bundle up and half-carried, half-dragged it out of the woods.

A blacksmith, traveling with the group for the second time, took care of the fire, while an old woman, on her last journey to settle down with a daughter in Patreshka, cooked. Berat and Otar cut the vegetables and meat and handed the cook everything when she needed it.

It was dark when they were all allowed to claim their own food portion. Berat and Otar kept close enough to the group in case of trouble, but they sat down sufficiently far away to have some privacy.

The meal was tasty and hearty, a mix between a vegetable stew and a porridge with a grain that Otar wasn't familiar with.

"What are you doing in Patreshka?" Otar asked after a moment of silence while they ate.

Berat rolled his shoulders back, his spoon scraping over the dish's bottom. When the food was gone, he put the bowl down and stared into the fire, his brows furrowed. "I did business on the southern islands, but I have been away too long. It is time to return to the steppe."

"Where is your tribe traveling?"

Otar possessed a rudimentary knowledge of tribe culture. In the past, he had pestered Andres and Onder with hundreds of questions about the way they lived and their customs, about the beads in their hair and the songs they sang every evening. They had indulged him, telling him all kinds of stories and tidbits, particularly about their own tribe that traveled the central part of the steppe. There were more tribes—along the eastern mountains, in the deep south, and the far north—all of them with their own unique customs and traditions, and none of them ever the same.

Berat licked his lips and after a moment, said, "They are dead."

"I'm sorry."

But Berat shook his head. "It doesn't matter."

Otar didn't press. Instead, he rose and extended a hand to Berat. He looked at it for a long time, and then he smiled, grabbed it, and let himself be hauled up.

They picked up their dishes, washed them at the basin, and then stored them dutifully. They informed the leader that they were done for the turn, and she sent them off with a lazy gesture.

Otar slept beside Berat in one of the storage caravans. It was a tight fit, and especially the first night had been awkward, but it also made certain affairs easier.

When they woke in the middle of that first night, almost on top of each other, neither of them looked away. Otar wondered if it really was a good idea, but the monster and him had been so hungry—a hunger that no people-food, no people-drink would ever satisfy, because it craved the energy, the life force, of living beings. When it went too long without feeding, it came for Otar.

Intimacy helped; in the throes of passion, energy flowed more freely, and the monster took its fill on what was given. And Otar himself sought physical contact with other people just as much. He wanted to get lost in them, explore every inch, let the monster loose to take it all and fill out Otar completely. It was a slippery slope, his control precarious, the chance of losing his hold on the monster always a constant undercurrent, as it had happened in the past—and yet, it was a drive for him, almost an addiction, one that was never curbed.

After they settled down together, Otar rolled over and kissed Berat, who came willingly, as he had since the first time, and Otar took what he could.

Much later, when Berat rested against him, already asleep, his breath hot and wet against his neck, Otar allowed himself for a moment to just be.

Chapter 5

"Sometimes I do wonder if I made the right decision in pursuing the Ancients and their secrets, as it has brought me much pain and loneliness, and seldom satisfaction. I understand now why some scholars leave their field after summers of fruitless search for answers or anything substantial. And yet, I push myself to go further..."

(From: Aaoran-peras' private collection of letters from the scholar Otar)

OTAR MISSED RASANELL, the Crown Jewel of the Wooden Lands. A sprawling city around a river. Encapsulated behind five city walls, he had surveyed the walls for turns to understand their construction, a knowledge he wanted to apply to the ruins.

Winds blew from the west through the alleys and streets at the height of summer taking most of the sweltering heat away, Otar had welcomed them together with his friends on one of the many terraces of the palace.

Rasanell had been the first place he felt as if he might belong, and even after he left, he loved the city with all his heart.

Patreshka differed, the Desert Rose of the Steppe Plains, had high walls and small gates to brace against the periodical sandstorms and bandit attacks, Andres had once explained to him. Clashes between the tribes and hit-and-run raids were other reasons settlements chose to wall up. Andres pointed out on a map that this happened more on the southern coastline, where fishing and more predictable rain for planting allowed for a permanent settlement to thrive. Otar still felt that tingly sensation as the turn he realized Andres had never ignored one of his many questions.

The steppe rider even told him about Patreshka's history. Sitting in a caldera, the natural high stone walls formed the first city wall. A long-ago monarch became so paranoid that he ordered an extra ring to be built for defense—he got his wish, and when the wall was finished, a revolt promptly disposed of him. The grievance? The increased taxes to finance the construction. Andres had closed that story with laughter, and all the steppe riders who had sat around the fire and understood Common joined in, murmuring about the idiosyncrasy of city folk. Otar had smiled and basked in the warmth of the fire and the camaraderie.

As it traveled closer to its destination, the caravan joined a stream of merchants and travelers. Otar was sitting next to the leader on the first wagon as she led the yardar with snarls and click sounds. She pointed out the different defense structures, while Otar wrote it all down and sketched what he could see. He tried to be as inconspicuous as possible so the guards overseeing the incoming road did not have any reason to accuse him of spying or, even worse, treason. Getting arrested on those grounds would probably amuse Aaoran, but Otar had no wish to embroil himself in that kind of headache, again.

The main gates were flung open, and a steady stream of people flowed in and out. The enormous doors were made of an unrecognizable wood and were reinforced with sheets of metal to withstand the intense battering of the storms. Otar had never experienced one, but the steppe riders spoke of dust towers so large they blotted out the sun and everything around oneself, with massive rolling waves of sand burying all. Otar wondered what it would feel like. The air was hot and dry and filled with dust clouds, making breathing hard. Fine sand grains clung to everything; Otar felt the gritty texture even on his teeth. The leader of the caravan cackled when he complained about it.

While trying to brush some of the sand off his clothing he watched the people around him. Left and right, they hauled around baskets and odd packages, drove loaded carts, or sold their wares on the way. The air was filled with the clucking of chickens, the brays of nervous yardar, and the clomps of the many feet on the stone bridge, underlaid by the creaking of wood and metal and leather.

For a moment, the walls loomed over them, and then they passed through the gate. The guards scanned the crowd, watching everyone like hawks. Tensing in fear of being discovered, Otar waited for one of the guards to point out his crimes, from the petty theft of cooling cookies as a little boy to the boiling monster inside him.

He forced himself to relax and instead concentrated on what lay inside.

Small houses made of stone and clay huddled close together, not an inch between them. The clay was found in the ground around Patreshka, and stones were aplenty outside, but wood needed to be imported and was expensive. Otar wanted to ask a local builder how they constructed the house without the support of beams.

The caravan followed the wider central road up to the main trade market, with the caravan leader telling him about where he could find which market. It was clear that both cities had a slew of separate markets, depending on the goods they offered. One for yardar and big livestock, one for wood and bigger metal works, one for fabrics, another for fruits and vegetables—there was also one for leather, but at least in Rasanell it was closer to the tanneries which lay outside the walls because of the smell.

The main trade market was the central place for smaller livestock and pets, teas and spices and food, and as well fine metalworks and general goods like bowls, cutlery, keepsakes, books, lamps, candles and everything else one might need in daily life.

Otar hoped they'd also sell brew cakes as his supply of brew had run out. He hadn't had a good brew since he and Andres… Otar stared ahead and wondered when it would stop hurting. Tomorrow? Sometime in the future? Never?

And why was he now thinking so often of the other man? They had parted ways amicably, both travelers and not to be tied down. Was it the steppe that made him nostalgic?

Maybe it was the grim-looking steppe riders who crossed their path as they rumbled up the road. Their colorful hair charms and beads in their braids glinted in the sun. Otar tried to determine the tribe region they hailed from, but the beads were only little dots too far away to make out, and he had never gotten the hang of reading the armor markings to identify their tribe and position. It didn't help that there was no unified system, but only a consensus depending on the region.

The caravan stopped in front of a guesthouse. Here it was time for Otar to part ways. The merchants would break off in smaller groups to sort out their business and wares, and Berat, who had ridden front on another caravan, said he would check in with an old acquaintance before heading out into the steppe. He was still close to a sister-tribe, in which relatives had married into and hoped that someone was willing to take him on. Otar kissed him goodbye and wished him good fortunes.

OTAR CHOSE A smaller inn and left his pack behind in his room. He was tired and in dire need of a wash, but he wanted to get the guide situation sorted out. The streets were a bustling mess of locals, travelers, and merchants. Locals wore a similar style of flowing garb that they also preferred in the hotter southern regions.

The first person he asked for directions to the university was a steppe warrior with scars covering half her face. She pointed him to an extensive building on top of a hill in the center of the city with hundreds of turrets barely visible through the dense buildings around them. Otar had assumed that it was the palace.

"One and the same," the rider said in a heavily accented Common when Otar commented on it. Otar raised an eyebrow at that, but the warrior was already hurrying away, joining a group of other steppe riders. Otar watched them for a moment, ignoring the longing unfurling inside him, before he walked in the direction she had shown him.

At first, the street was a gentle slope, then an almost steep climb. The higher he went, the more the tight cluster of houses opened up, giving way to greenery sprawled around him. In contrast to the rest of the city, he could glimpse extensive gardens and buildings that looked like palaces. Fewer people hurried around, clad in expensive fabrics and jewelry.

When Otar reached the top, he found himself in a lush garden, palm leaves and flowers waving lazily in a breeze. Small pathways led through the greenery, intersecting at different points. People strolled along them, alone and in clusters, speaking in loud voices and using energetic hand gestures. Otar grinned at that; academics wherever they were always discussed with a passion.

He followed a wider way down to an open gate and down into a big courtyard and then, when no one held him back, through a set of equally open doors into the building. The cold enveloped him, and Otar stopped and absorbed the change in temperature. The steppe could be freezing and sweltering hot. It was a warm turn, and the sun beat down unrestrictedly. Not even a passing cloud was in the sky to give temporary shade.

As he continued into the building he realized there were no guards. In Rasanall, they guarded the university to stop anyone from entering who didn't look like they belonged based on their appearance—like a windswept, sunburned, and dirty Otar.

A person rushed by, nearly pushing him to the side. Otar stepped out of the way and looked around. Where the city had been swarming with people, the university's main entrance was a beehive. Students hurried past, talking loudly, calling to each other, running to catch up with someone, or dragging towers of books. Hallways branched out in a star-like pattern, each flanked by open doors. Otar walked down one way at random and peered into a room. A lecturer talked advanced mathematics, pointing to complicated graphs painted onto the walls. Someone slipped in beside Otar and hurried up to a woman sitting three rows down making notes. The newcomer crouched down, and they both talked in hushed tones, while the lecturer and all the other students paid them no mind. In Rasanell, that wouldn't stand, depending on the professor, they either demanded that you talk after the lesson, or they threw the interrupters out.

Otar walked to another open door. Nearly the same as the first, the large room was filled with students taking notes and a lecturer who didn't care for who came and went.

A third one further down revealed a lively discussion happening with people crowding the entryway, throwing in suggestions and comments. Their voices, with all the others drifting from the open classrooms, were underpinned by the bittersweet melody of a flute someone played in the distance.

Otar scratched his arms and regretted not taking the time to wash up. Maybe, after he had secured the guide, they'd allow him to sit in on a few lectures. Some seemed to be in Common or Trade Common, and all the others were in the more widely used guttural Central Steppe language; the tribes additionally had their own dialects, usually some version of the central one.

Otar tapped the arm of a youth standing close by. "Where can I find the excavation department?" he asked in Trade Common, hoping it was easy enough to understand.

The youth blinked, his mind clearly not on the more mundane aspect of life like giving directions. His gaze cleared, and he raised a hand to point down the hallway Otar was already in and then made a gesture to the left, then dropped his arm again and turned away. Before Otar could ask for a clarification, the youth hollered something into the room and another shouted an answer back, and the entire room erupted with laughter.

Otar was clearly dismissed.

He sighed and took his chances. He walked down as the youth had indicated, and when he crossed the next path, turned left. Smaller rooms replaced the lecture halls, and what he glimpsed through the still open doors looked like offices. The first office was empty, with only a lazy breeze drifting through the open windows. In the third office, an old man was loudly snoring at his desk, books and documents stacked precariously next to him.

In the fourth, two women talked excitedly. Otar tried to get a word in to ask for further directions, but it proved to be futile, they were too engrossed in their conversation.

At the sixth, he finally got lucky. Again, it held two women. They had their heads together and were flipping through a book. They looked up when he knocked against the door frame.

"Yes?" the left asked in Central Steppe, her eyes big behind her glasses. It was one of the few words that Otar could discern.

"Peace upon you," he greeted back in Central. "I'm looking for the excavation department," he added in Common.

She studied him, while the woman to her right smiled. "You've found it."

Otar gazed around, taking in the multitude of maps pinned to the walls, the graphics of various Ancients ruins, and the many notes attached to them, a lot with underlined question marks. They even had some of the Ancient's word transcribed. Otar ignored those words calling to him—all in all it looked similar to the office Otar had frequented back at Rasanell.

"What can we do for you, stranger?" The left one asked, her tone not quite hostile but guarded. She even called him 'stranger' and not the more welcoming 'visitor'.

"I was told to inquire here about a guide to Adabel," Otar said in what he hoped was a friendly manner.

That earned him narrowed eyes, while the more amicable woman kept smiling at him.

"May we ask why?"

"I apologize, mistress. I'm Otar from Darell. I study under Aaoran-peras, and they sent for me." He took out his notebook and tugged out the letter Aaoran had sent him. It was flimsy proof but all he could provide. He slowly stepped closer, and the guarded woman took it, reading it three times before handing it over to the other.

"You're in bad luck. All the guides are currently in Adabel or otherwise occupied."

Otar cursed. "When will they be back?"

The smiling woman handed the letter back to Otar and then slid out a small ledger from under the book between them. She flipped through the pages and stopped. "We expect Jodan back in four turns, but his cycle has him then on a three-turn break, so you won't be able to set out for seven turns at the latest."

One or two turns wouldn't have been bad, but seven? That was too long. He was keen on pressing on, fueled by the burning curiosity of what Aaoran may have found.

"Are there any other options?"

The woman on the left tapped her finger on the wooden desk. "A handful of merchants supply the excavation and might take you on if you're in a hurry. But you will have to cover the cost on your own."

"Thank you." Otar secured the letter again and then bowed formally. At their nods, he turned to go but when he approached the door, he looked back at them. They both had their heads close together again, whispering to each other while turning the pages of the book.

The main entryway of the university was still busy, and Otar slipped out through the mess of constantly moving bodies. Stifling afternoon heat hit him like a hammer. The city was baking, the hot air above the stone roads flimmering. At the first street food merchant he found, Otar bought a skin of watered-down wine, some flat bread stuffed with roasted vegetables, and some white cheese. Then he chose a place off to the side in the shadows that held some upturned crates to sit down.

While he ate and washed his food down with the wine, he contemplated his next move. Hiring some random merchant could be risky. He knew no one here whose judgment and endorsement he could trust. If he wasn't careful, he'd find himself mugged and left alone in the middle of the steppe. He could wait out the seven turns, but the urgency in Aaoran's letter had more than piqued his curiosity. Since thinking about it, there had been a drive to get out here, as if something or someone was beckoning him. Which was absurd, and yet…

He thought back to the turn they handed him the letter and suddenly remembered the one from Turas, who was the advisor and closest friend to his Imperial Heir Jasner. Otar had folded it up and put it into the bottom of his pack, vowing to read it when he had a more peaceful moment, and then he had promptly forgot about it.

Once he found the letter, he turned it over and saw the wax of the royal seal was already cracked from mishandling it. Due to his position Turas was allowed to use that seal. A long time ago, Otar called him and Jasner friends.

Sometimes he saw them in his dreams, smiling and waving at him, before the monster took it all away.

With a sigh he unfolded the letter.

> Otar,
>
> We are still waiting for answers. Rumors have reached us that you'll be in Adabel. Await our arrival there. It is time we are done with this.
>
> Turas ad Temar,
> Advisor of His Imperial Heir Jasner

Otar let the letter sink and stared out into the streets. Another reason than to hurry to the ruin. Turas wasn't a patient man, and the little he had had been tried by Otar for the last summers now. Jasner wasn't getting better on his own. The mysterious illness that had befallen him seven summers ago had never lost its grip. But finding a cure…He drank the rest of the wine. It tasted like ash. He hopped down from the crate to move into the stream of passing people when a hand on his arm held him back.

Otar whirled around, ready to defend himself, or at the very least to throw the empty skin into his attacker's face, when he recognized who was standing before him.

It was Berat.

Chapter 6

"I'm sure it was your doing peras, but this time I will let your meddling slide. Because Andres saved me. I almost broke through a staircase but Andres, who arrived at the right moment, pulled me up again. I inquired as to why he was there, but he didn't really give me an answer. He simply insisted that he had been in the area, which he could only have been if you had told him where to find me. When I confessed to you in confidence, I didn't want you to take my complaints about loneliness literally. But, as I said, he saved me, and I'll let it go."

(From: Aaoran-peras' private collection of letters from the scholar Otar)

"You're still here?" Otar asked in surprise and, despite everything, delight, as with Bedaran in Piskus, he had been sad to see the other go and just slip from Otar's life.

Berat had been good company, and it was nice to know at least one face in the city. Maybe he could even help. Berat knew people here, so finding that trustworthy merchant had gotten easier.

"You are too," Berat said with a laugh.

Otar groaned. "I'm stuck here for now."

"Ah, that is a misfortune. What will you do?"

"I'll inquire with the merchants that travel in the direction I need to go in, and maybe one will be willing to take me on."

Berat furrowed his brows, then he looked down to the market at the end of the street. "You think that is a wise decision? You're not from here, and they'll try to rob you."

Otar shrugged. "With your help, if possible, it might just work. Seeing you, I'd hoped you or your friends can vouch for me, or at least steer me clear of the dishonest ones."

"Perhaps," Berat hummed more to himself. "Come, let's drink something, and we can sort this out."

There wasn't much more Otar could do, so he nodded. Berat took him by the hand and dragged him through a maze of alleys and wide hallways. He stopped in front of a small sign Otar would have overlooked and then stepped through a door into an open backyard. Low tables and colorful seating cushions were laid out haphazardly over thick rugs. Berat led them to a table in a corner, and right when they had sat down, a man came up to them and asked something in the Central Steppe language. Otar tried to make out the words, but Berat was already answering, a bit stilted but good enough, because the man nodded after some back and forth, left and returned shortly after with two drinks and some food. Otar's stomach started to grumble as he took in the smells of a thick vegetable stew with more of the fluffy flatbread, that was sold here at every corner, along with an array of dipping sauces in different colors.

They toasted each other. The drink was strong, sweet and spicy. It was a familiar taste and for a moment Otar's heart was heavy remembering nights in Bakusaran filled with the songs and laughter of the steppe riders, but Berat drew him in a conversation about his studies and soon everything else slipped from his mind. The afternoon soon gave way to the evening and then the night.

Berat explained the food they ate and their names and the customs surrounding them, and Otar told him of his travels and various embarrassing situations he'd gotten himself into.

Much later they swayed arm-in-arm to the inn in which Otar had taken his room. The host didn't bat an eye at the additional sleeper, and they stumbled up the stairway. Barely through the door, they were onto each other, shedding clothing and kissing every inch of newly exposed skin. Their coming together was freer than it had been in the caravan, with all the merchants sleeping close by. Otar curbed the hunger of the monster, careful and controlled to not overstep, the alcohol making it hard to concentrate, but for once it heeded his call.

Barely finished and snuggling into each other, Otar was sound asleep.

IN THE MORNING, they lay close, and Berat said, "I can take you there."

Otar stretched like a cat in the sun and considered it. He knew Berat, which was good. They had already traveled together, and Otar was sure the other wouldn't offer if he was unwilling.

The decision was simple. "Okay."

They decided to set out early on the next turn and use this turn to collect everything they'd need. Otar explored the general market, admiring the different craftsmanship that found their way seldom to the west and south. When he came across a bead seller, he stopped. The old woman manning it smiled at him. Her hair was done in tribe style, with long braids adorned with many trinkets and beads.

"Looking for something, visitor?"

"No, not really, but they are beautiful." His eyes kept straying back to a black bead inlaid with silver markings. It was a warrior bead, the kind awarded after a particular heroic act. Next to it was one cut from a blue stone Otar had never seen before. His fingers itched to take them into his hand.

The old woman had followed his gaze. "You have a good eye."

Otar looked up, startled, catching her smile. He nodded at her and walked away. He made it five steps in the other direction before he turned back and then bought them both.

The old woman didn't comment but handed him the beads in a small leather pouch.

Two streets down, he cursed at himself being an impulsive fool. But what's done was done, and bringing them back seemed to be a harder admission than he was willing to make. He could slip them to Aaoran in Adabel, and they could gift them to anyone without having any ties attached to it.

Gifting beads was a serious matter in a tribe. And Otar didn't want to be caught in a misunderstanding if he gave them away himself. But holding onto them would make him look like a bigger fool, clinging to a past that should be left buried.

He hurried to buy the rest of the things Berat and he had agreed upon, and then they spent another enjoyable evening together while Otar pressed all the other memories down.

They rode at dawn. Berat proved to be an excellent rider and, as already shown, a skilled companion. He blossomed under the open sky, and Otar finally saw the tribe-blood in him. He grinned to himself at that.

As soon as a steppe folk climbed on a yardar, they were all the same, a proud steppe rider on the plains. It was in the way they held their shoulders and their head, how they gazed in a straight line at the horizon, as if their eyes were caressing the line where the ground and the sky met; as if nothing could ever throw them off.

Five summers ago, when he traveled with Andres, the steppe rider had always grumbled about the thickness of the jungle obscuring the true horizon and making him uncomfortable, Otar had teased him mercilessly about it.

Berat and he didn't talk much while riding. He occasionally answered Otar's questions about the local flora and fauna or landscapes in the distance.

At night, when they made camp, they shared stories, with Berat always talking with a wistful expression.

"You know a lot about the steppe," Berat said on their first night, after their meal watching the fire glimmer down slowly.

"Not as much as you might think." Otar paused and searched for the right words. "Many summers ago I traveled with a few riders, and it always struck a chord with me on how they talked about the plains. Until now, I had never seen it with my own eyes to really understand it, but now…"

"Matresjka," Berat whispered.

Otar nodded. One of the few phrases Andres had taught him. It was more a concept than just a word. The rider was all alone under the open sky with the never-ending plains stretching before them, and yet they were free.

"There is nothing like it in the Seven Lands," Berat said with a reverence that made Otar shiver. "There's an endless ocean, endless mountains, and endless forests. But with none of them, you're surrounded by nothing but the sky."

"Stretch out your hand and grasp it, because you are made of nothing else but this sky and this earth." Otar closed the old tribe saying.

Berat smiled at Otar's words. "It's seldom that outsiders understand the concept."

Andres had taught him much more, when the two of them sat alone around their small fire at night, trading stories and tidbits of their lives—sometimes Andres would even sing.

Otar shrugged. "I was lucky that someone was willing to explain it all to me." He didn't quite meet Berat's gaze when he said it.

"Otar," Berat said and Otar looked over. His eyes danced in the sparks, and whatever he saw on Otar's face must have been enough, because he moved closer and kissed him.

And Otar, with the voice of another in his ears, let himself fall into him.

THE NEXT MORNING started early, they set out when the gray line on the horizon barely heralded the new turn.

At midturn, Otar took a swig from his water flask and noticed it was almost empty. Furrowing his brow, he tried to remember how much he had drunk over the last turn. He checked the remaining ones and, finding them in a similar state, cursed.

Berat navigated his yardar closer and they stopped. "Is there a problem?"

Otar turned the flasks over and found hairline fractures in them. How unlucky could one person be? That water merchant had been a swindler.

He let them sink and looked at Berat. "Looks like I'm running out of water."

Berat motioned for Otar to hand over the flasks. He eyed them critically. "All three of them?"

"Apparently. The fourth one is already empty."

Berat handed the flask back and turned the yardar to look out over the steppe. "I will give you one of mine and we'll share the other. They should still be full. But we'll have to make a detour to replenish the other one, so we do not run into any problems until we reach Adabel. We could make it. It would be a tight fit before we run out of water, but if we were delayed for any reason…" He tapered off and Otar's own mind filled in the rest.

"You know a place?"

Berat nodded with some hesitation. He slid down from his yardar and looked for a stick. He brought it back and then sketched a map into the ground.

"We are roughly here, and here are the ruins." He marked a point above them and then one to the right and slightly above it. "There is a mountain range." He drew a wiggly line over the first point and approximately on the same line as the ruins. "I know there is a river all-time-round. It runs mostly underground, but spills out into the open in the mountains." Berat looked up and pointed in the direction. "I estimate that we lose one, at worst two, turns to get there."

Otar considered it, squinting at the horizon. For the added security, it wasn't much of a detour. The decision once more was easy. "Lead the way."

OVER THE NEXT few turns, they traveled with new urgency. Berat distracted them with tales of his own tribe and his past life. It was all highly fascinating to Otar. Andres had been a grown man and a warrior and a leader of his people, while Berat had left when he had been ten and six winters—he had a vastly different experience and perspective.

With Andres, there had been a yearning in every word he had said and every story he had told. With

Berat, there was only sadness. It made sense, with all his people being dead—Otar ached for him.

THE PROMISED MOUNTAIN range was more of a hillside interlaced with deep trenches. As they traveled through, Otar spotted caves and more crevices. They heard the river before they saw it, a thundering sound echoing along the stone walls.

They stopped at the top of a cliff, while the water roared under them and whipped white foam against its stoney prison.

"You know a place where we can safely access it?" If they let the flasks down here, there was a guarantee they'd be snatched away.

Berat turned his head and then pointed to the side. "There should be a small beach close by, if you could even call it that." He added with a shrug.

Otar nodded, and they moved the yardar to follow the river.

Berat was right. After a few bends, the river broadened and small branches split off, becoming gentler streams that vanished again beneath the stone.

Calm wasn't quite the correct word, but it flowed slow enough to not rip the flasks out of his hands. Otar took the two from Berat along with his first one and then walked down to the water.

He took the first flask, popped it open, and bent down.

He heard steps behind him. He opened his mouth to say something to Berat, when suddenly…nothing—

Chapter 7

"And now tell me how Otar is doing? His mother asked me to include greetings to him and would like to hear some updates as Otar seldom writes to her. I do wonder myself about him, but I'm sure he is much happier taking in the wonders of Rasanell and learning about the world outside rather than being confined to the small village he was raised in. He took a shine to you and what you promised, and I can't fault him for that, but I wish…wishes are fruitless. Maybe you can bring him back with you when you come to visit, at least once."

(From: "Doctor Mare letters to Aaoran-peras", Vol.3)

OTAR BLINKED INTO sudden brightness, his gaze unfocused. Slowly, the world gained contrast. He groaned when he moved his head to get a better view of his surroundings. Everything throbbed. When he tried to move his hands to check if he was injured, he found he couldn't move them. They were twisted up, bound tight overhead with a cord to a pole his spine was pressed against. He hung awkwardly down, his bottom not quite making contact with the hard, stony ground. Carefully, he rose onto his knees and settled in a kneeling seat, hissing when any movement aggravated the head wound or jostled the overstretched arm muscles.

Then Otar took stock of what was around him, his aching skull making it troublesome to concentrate. Pale light filtered through what seemed to be a grayish fabric. Shadows moved outside, and the deep laughter of a group of men drifted over.

Had he been taken prisoner for a reason? He tried to remember the last bits, but it all came to him in pieces. Had they been attacked when he got the water? Had they been somewhere else after that? Had it been bandits?

Andres had told him of bandits that traversed the land, raiding what they could get their hands on. Dishonest men the tribes put bounties on.

Otar leaned his head back, careful not to knock it against the pole; it still hurt.

Could he talk his way out? But he had no connections to any tribe in this area. Yes, he had traveled with Andres for a time, and they may have been close at one point, but nothing to warrant a ransom.

And where was Berat? Otar looked around as much as possible, but his vision lost focus again. Nausea spread through him, and he concentrated on inhaling and exhaling for a moment, determined not to give up the contents of his stomach.

"Ah, he is awake," a deep voice spoke in Common.

In the tent opening stood a man who looked at him with a gruff and unwashed face, he had short hair and a scar running over his forehead.

"What's going on?" Otar slurred.

The man smiled and ignored Otar's question. "Yes, you'll bring us a nice, sizable sum." His smile broadened and Otar suppressed a shudder. The man turned and left again.

Money. The man wanted and expected to get money for him.

Otar swallowed as he realized this was worse than bandits. Slavers had captured them.

Andres had spoken about them briefly, only a throwaway line. In the past, many slaver bands had existed, but the tribes had hunted them down without mercy. There were some tribes who had cooperated with them, often those which were down on their luck or found themselves in an unfavorable position.

As the other slaver didn't immediately return, Otar pulled at his restraints, but it made the rope cut only deeper into his skin.

"You should stop that. It will only hurt you further."

Otar's eyes snapped to the front. Berat stood in the opening. Beyond it, Otar could make out a gray sky. How much time had passed?

Berat's gaze was steady on him, but harder than before, as if the darkness Otar had sensed in him on their travels had now taken over. For a second Otar felt relief flood him, because Berat was safe and free… and then the implication of it hit him.

"Why?" He sank down on his heels.

Swaying on the balls of his feet, Berat first shrugged and then said, "Money."

"I don't understand."

"When you are ten and six winters, and all alone, you need money. To survive, I made a deal. I help them, and they provide me with everything I need."

"You lure the victims in."

"Sometimes." His gaze focused on a point above Otar's head. "I also do the legwork in other lands. People tell me I have a trustworthy face." He grinned. It was all wrong.

"Does the steppe mean so little to you?"

"The steppe," Berat spat. "Did you know they threw me out, exiled me? Hunted me down because I dared to love someone different."

For a moment, understanding flickered between them.

He laughed. "Well, I made them pay for it. I led my new friends to them."

"You condemned them all."

Berat showed his teeth. "And why shouldn't I? You can't understand how it feels to not be accepted for who you are. Did you ever need to fight for your life? You, who has always been loved?"

Otar opened his mouth and clicked it shut again at Berat's words.

"Yes, my dear friend, you mutter in your sleep. And it's only one name: Andres. Andres. Andres."

Otar shook his head, wincing at the pain lacing through it. "You're wrong. He has never loved me." There. He said it. Otar had never mentioned love and Andres had never told him. They had come together for a short time and later had split again.

A crack formed in Berat's anger, a softening around his eyes, but before Otar could use it, another voice cut in.

"Don't be a fool, Berat." A large man slipped in, making the tent crowded. He laid a casual hand, littered with scars, on Berat's shoulder. His face was all harsh lines and deep shadows, dark eyes peering at him; he might even be called handsome in a rugged way. His hair was wild. At one time, there could have been braids. Otar glimpsed a few lone beads, now dull and chipped in the unkempt, tangled mess. Was he part of a tribe turned into slavers?

The man leaned forward, slipping an arm around Berat's waist. "He'll tell you anything to draw you in."

Otar tried to shrug, but it was awkward with the way his body was bound. "I don't lie." He omitted parts of the truth, but this wasn't the place to admit to that.

"It doesn't matter," Berat said. "I'm done here." He shrugged off the large man's hands and walked out, and with him, any hope Otar might have harbored of being set free again.

The remaining man, maybe the leader of this merry band, narrowed his eyes at Otar, while fiddling with a golden ring on his thumb. "Perhaps it would be more worth it to exchange you for a ransom."

Otar shifted his body weight to elevate his shoulders. It didn't help. At the leader's words, he sighed.

"I don't lie. I'm a scholar. There is no one who'd pay for me." Aaoran probably would, but they had no funds, or at least not sufficient enough that would satisfy these men—not when they could sell him. "I won't be missed enough." People may wonder what had happened and after time had passed, even mourn him.

The slaver watched him a moment longer and then nodded. He opened his mouth, then closed it again when someone called from the outside, "Chief, we need your help."

The leader growled and strode away.

Wonderful. Otar tried once more to tug at the rope, but as Berat predicted, it only tightened more. He shifted his weight around and finally found a spot that took some of the strain off his shoulders. It wasn't much, but for a small-turn, he could enjoy the sweet relief.

He leaned his head against the upraised arm and closed his eyes. The wound throbbed. The conversation had exhausted him, and his vision was still blurry. Hunger and thirst were an afterthought.

It didn't take long for darkness to claim him once more.

Hands on his skin woke him. Startled, Otar hissed at the pain in his arms and knees, and someone laughed in his face. Foul breath hit him fully—so repulsive, he almost puked.

The world was dark. Night had come.

"What—" A hand pressed over his mouth and nose, suffocating him.

"One word, pretty boy, and you'll regret it."

Otar's eyes adjusted to the pale moon light that illuminated the tent walls. It was the man with the scar who had commented that he was awake. And now his hands were on his skin, searching for…searching for…panic threatened to overwhelm him. Never did someone…never…

"Chief shouldn't have left you alone. You're mine now. Just a taste." More coarse laughter. Otar tried to roll away from the hands, but the slaver backhanded him, and for a small-turn, Otar was too stunned to react.

More amusement. "Better listen, little boy."

Never.

Take him.

Anger flared through Otar, burning through him, washing the world in hazy colors, narrowing down to what was in front of him.

And the monster rose inside him.

Hand contact was always easier. That way Otar might control the flow, even if the monster tried to slip his grip every time. But with only the hands on the skin of another, he could back away if needed when it became too much; overall skin-on-skin contact worked.

The monster was hungry, and Otar was so tired, unable and unwilling to fight it—so he let go. The monster pounced and took and took and took.

Outward, it looked as if nothing was off. The slaver still had that gleam in his eyes, and his hands never stopping roaming over Otar's body. Until they wouldn't budge anymore, sticking suddenly to Otar's skin. When the slaver registered that something was wrong, it was too late for him—he crashed to the side, eyes widening in surprise. He tried to pry his own hands away, but the monster wouldn't let him. Otar tried half-heartedly to reign it in again, but for once, he didn't care. The vile breath still lingered in his nose, and the feeling of the unwanted touch twisted his stomach, making him shudder. It all burned the last tendrils of compassion for another life away, and the monster ravaged the slaver until he was only an empty husk.

When the man stilled, Otar held his breath, listening for movements outside. Everything had happened so fast that the slaver hadn't had the chance to call for help or make any sound. No one moved.

Otar exhaled. Whenever the monster took, it stored the energy somewhere inside Otar, never giving it up. But some of it seeped into the cracks and nooks that made up his body, boosting his strength for a fraction of a moment.

He concentrated and grabbed for all the extra life force swirling through him. With all his might, he strained against the ropes, pressing his wrists in opposite directions. Sweat broke out, and he hissed through his teeth, praying to the lords and additionally any other deity that had once been worshiped.

With relief, he felt the ropes give, and his arms swung down, pins and needles shooting through them as the blood circulated through his limbs again.

Fatigue swept over him, but there was no time for a break. With deft hands and bile at the back of his tongue, he searched the body and took the slaver's dagger. Carefully, Otar furtively poked his head out of the tent. There were five to six more tents, but most of the slavers laid as lumps around a dead fire. A loud snore sounded to his left, and Otar flinched and slipped back into the tent. Someone shouted from the other side. There was a grunt followed by silence.

Otar waited for another heartbeat and then tiptoed out. The pale moonlight was barely enough to make out a path. Pebbles shifted under his feet, and he stubbed his toes more than once against a big rock. He pressed his teeth together to avoid cursing out loud. Rounding to the back of the tent he was held prisoner in, he stopped every few paces and checked to ensure that no one had woken up. After what felt like forever, he crept past two more tents and was finally at the outskirts of the camp, the sleeping bodies of the slavers in his back. There was a big boulder that would obscure his figure, so he crouched behind it and considered his options.

On foot, they'd catch up to him easily.

He peered around the stone and looked back, suppressing a curse. He had chosen the wrong way. On the other side of the camp were the yardar, their moving silhouettes barely distinguishable from the night. Creeping over and mounting one would mean waking the entire camp. The birds hated to be disturbed.

He could circle the camp back the way he had come and take the risk, but it would add to the chance of someone getting up and spotting him. Maybe they even had guards up, and so far, he had been lucky.

Exhaustion crept through his bones. Another hunger, the bodily one, swept through him. When had he eaten last?

The monster was unwilling to help—besides what slipped through the cracks into his body, the monster guarded its price jealously. Nothing more would be coming. He barely had enough energy left to stay on his feet and keep his mind sharp. It was a terrible state to be in.

Only one choice remained: he needed to risk stealing a yardar.

Otar stepped around the boulder, and someone moved in the shadows. Berat's hair was mussed, his naked chest littered with dark spots.

"Leaving us so soon?" he drawled.

"Your hospitality was a bit lacking."

Berat snorted and opened his mouth, and Otar reacted on instinct. He lunged forward, tackling Berat to the ground pressing a hand at the same time over his mouth.

"Don't," Otar said imploringly. "You'll regret it."

Hatred flared in Berat's eyes. Whatever connection they might have shared, it was all gone now.

"Please," Otar tried, "I can take you with me." But Berat bit him and in surprise, Otar moved his palm a fraction, allowing enough space for Berat to take a deep inhale to shout, but before he could do so, Otar pressed down again and let go.

The monster, still simmering under his skin because of all the agitation, came readily, sucking the life force with glee.

Berat reacted fast, drew a small dagger, and plunged it into Otar's side. Otar almost let go, but the monster was in control and held onto its prey.

It was over in a few heartbeats. Berat's eyes turned dull, and Otar let the body sink down. Wild energy coursed through him; being sated like this was exhilarating and wrong in equal measures.

He moved fast; the new overspill of energy would soon dissipate. He winced when he turned. The dagger felt uncomfortable in his side, and running with it would be impossible. Onder, Andres' brother, had warned him once to never draw out something pointy stuck in him; well, it was a risk he now needed to take. He slipped out of his shirt—the dagger had only grazed the edge of it—rolled it up, and dragged the dagger out, hissing out between his teeth at the pain. Then he knotted the shirt tight around his waist, putting as much pressure as possible on the wound, just as the doctor in his home village had taught him a long time ago.

He glanced down at the dagger and back at Berat. With a sigh, he put the weapon down on the other's chest and curled a hand around it.

Once finished, he checked his surroundings, eyeing the yardar on the other side of the camp once more. Pale light on the horizon warned him that his chance was now gone.

He grimaced, turned, and ran.

After a few steps, a hound howled.

How did he miss the dogs? He cursed when he heard shouting near him, followed by the sound of scrambling of feet, and more hollering. Otar hurried down the nearest path into a narrower path, hoping that the more massive bodies of the slavers wouldn't be able to fit through.

He rushed down, thinking fast. They had his pack. Was that enough to pick up his scent?

When he left the narrow pass, he found himself at the shore of a small river, its murky depths drifting past lazily. Otar checked on the bandage and winced at the blood seeping through. Going into the river would be a bad idea, but that was his only option. He exhaled and waded in. The water was freezing, and the riverbed fell away under him fast. Swimming sapped the strength right out of him, and he was not sure how he made it to the other side. He heaved himself out onto the opposite shore and lay still to catch his breath, then he staggered to his feet and hurried on.

At intersections, he chose a path at random until he reached a cave mouth. Otar stumbled in and dropped to the ground. He rose again, and slipped deeper into the cavern, retreating as far back as he dared, all the while hoping that nothing larger had already claimed it.

With the cave wall behind him, he drew his knees up and let his head rest on them. Everything had happened so fast, and the details were now fuzzy. What stood out in his mind was the death of two men—two men *he* had killed. He had done the one thing he swore to himself would never happen again: let the monster take blindly. But how much control did he have over it in the end?

He wanted to feel remorseful for the lives he had taken, but he had protected himself from a crueler fate. And yet hadn't it been the monster itself that had protected, and he, unwilling to stop it, had given in to what lived inside him and tormented him since he could remember—always waiting for a slip-up, for a chance to take?

Had there been another choice?

Later, he told himself, later he would find justice somehow, find a priest if possible and donate something to the lords, begging for their mercy.

Before that, he needed to get out of the hillside alive and escape somewhere. The map Berat had drawn appeared in his mind's eyes. The ruin lay to the east. Pale light filtered through the cave opening, barely penetrating the gloom. With all the stone walls and crevices that obscured the sky and the path of the sun, it would be difficult to make out in which direction he needed to go.

Getting out unseen was at the top of his to do list. Afterwards, he should head east or find a friendly merchant or even a traveling tribe to take him.

In Adabel, he would be safe, and then he could alert someone about the slavers roaming around close by.

While the light would make it easier to see, he'd be clearer to spot as well. Under the cover of darkness, it was less risky, but harder.

There was no choice.

He sighed and closed his eyes.

Chapter 8

"The Southern Islands are situated right off the south-western coast of the Altek Kingdom. Past kings have made many futile attempts to invade, until under Barek II, a long-lasting treaty was signed, promising the five major islands and their surrounding archipelagos sovereignty."

(From: The Southern Islands, in: "The Seven Lands in its Entirety", Vol. 25)

OTAR PAUSED AND listened to the sounds of the night. What was that skittering sound? A foot crunching on the track overhead? He exhaled. It was probably a restless animal.

He crept forward again. Thick clouds obscured the moonlight. As predicted, the path was hard to see. Otar trailed a hand along the stone wall to not get lost. He snorted at the irony. In the ruins, he had done it to wait for something to happen. Here, he hoped nothing would.

When he slipped out of the cave as soon as night had descended, he chose a direction on a whim, praying to the lords that this one would at least lead him out.

Stones clattered somewhere. Otar stopped again waiting to hear the more rhythmic clicking of a person walking down a path. But just as before, it must be a skittering animal hurrying away into the darkness—no one seemed to follow him. After waiting for some time, he no longer heard any noise, so he moved on.

Wincing when he took a wrong step and aggravated the wound, Otar checked his side, blood was still seeping out and the bandage was damp. He was sick. Flashes of hot and cold shivered down his spine. His vision held dark spots, and his forehead was too warm.

Maybe he should hope to die out here, because when the slavers caught up with him, he would pay dearly. Two dead by his hands wasn't an offense easily forgotten, regardless of what money he might bring them. They would take their revenge.

Another round of pebbles clattered down onto the path and Otar froze.

Too many, too often.

And then he heard the clicking of nails.

They had found him.

Otar squinted into the shadows, imagining them moving and twisting, reaching for him. He reconsidered his plan to escape into the steppe. The hounds had the ability to trail him, and out in the open, they were capable of racing. Could he outrun them?

A shot of pain raced down his side, reminding him why it would be a stupid idea. He gnawed on his thumbnail; once more he was running out of options. Exhaustion had slipped into all the places the energy had been before.

Endurance. It all came down to that.

A shout nearer than he would have liked, and he clamped his mouth shut, fearing his breathing would betray him. He turned his head up, making out moving shadows. Terrified, he pressed his back against the stone wall. His heart was hammering so loud they must surely be hearing it. It was a miracle the earth wasn't thundering with it.

Words in their own tribal language drifted down to Otar, they didn't speak in Common anymore, so he couldn't make out their plans. There was more shouting further down the path, and the shadowy men turned in the direction they had been coming from. They must have discovered his tracks. Now it was only a matter of time.

The ravine he was using as a path was sloping downward, and another river arm waited at the end. He moved and clenched his teeth, pressing his jaw together to not cry out in pain. He fingered the bandage and found the surrounding flesh hot to his touch.

Could he make it through the river? Well, there was only one way to find out.

He hurried and didn't stop when the freezing water hit him. As he swam, the current was stronger than he'd expected.

Otar paddled as close as he dared to the high walls towering over him on the other side. Searching for an opening, he let himself drift until he caught sight of a small outcropping reaching down into the river. He tried to grasp it but slipped, his fingernails scraping painfully over the wet stone. Taking a moment to breathe through the pain, he grabbed once more and heaved himself up.

He exhaled and climbed. It was slow going; fumbling more than once, he slipped down the rough stone, catching himself at the last moment with his fingertips. Their skin broke open, and he flinched at every grip he needed to make, until he finally scaled over the cliff. On the other side he stumbled through more stone walls, following a twisting path until he found himself on a gently sloped hillside. Pale light appeared, washing the horizon gray.

Otar swallowed and moved. He ran through the hills, always listening out for thundering yardar feet or the howl of the hounds. But nothing came.

Hopefully, that last bath had thrown them off for good. Still, when the sun flooded the steppe, he chose a small bower and rolled himself into it, waiting once more for the night to cover him.

In the twilight, he crawled out, shaking and stiff. The voice of a lone wolf rose; Otar flinched but didn't stop and ran. His gaze flicked around, hoping to find the light of a settlement or a fire, a beacon to safety. But there was nothing but blackness; the moon had ended its cycle and was nowhere to be found, so darkness pressed in on him from all sides. He stumbled, caught himself, and kept on moving. The moment he stopped, he knew he'd fall down and never get up again.

Twilight shifted around him. The sun rose anew, its light harsh and hot.

Otar kept running. One foot in front of the other.

Wetness seeped down his side. His hand came back red and yellow. He cursed, but there was nothing to be done about it now.

He ran.

At roughly what should be midturn, his steps slowed. Not because he wanted to, but his body wouldn't obey anymore. He willed his legs to go further and further, just one more step, just one more mile. But his muscles didn't listen. His vision was blurry.

In the distance a dog barked, another answered.

Otar stumbled forward. Then his knees gave out, and he crashed to the ground, his arms useless appendages at his sides. It hurt. He was surprised he still felt anything. He groaned and then struggled to get back up again, trying to move his arms, his legs, but it was as if he was stuck to the hard soil, a force holding him down, pressing him deeper. Otar tried for a trickle of the life force the monster had taken, willing it to return some of it, to help, to keep them alive, but it didn't budge.

Another bark, closer now, feet that thundered over the earth.

A snout in his hair, the hot stinky breath on his neck.

There was nothing left to give, as everything went dark.

BLACKNESS STRETCHED AROUND him, with no end in sight. He was just a speck, without thought, without agenda, floating through something too vast to comprehend.

A heartbeat flickered, the darkness shifting from gray to white, flooding his senses. Otar tried to squeeze his eyes shut, but he couldn't because he was nothing. He was…

You have come…

The light hurt him. He wanted to run away from it, hide his head and his eyes between his arms and escape the brightness.

With you, we finally can go. Bring the last piece.

No, he hadn't, this wasn't…

His eyes sprang open into blissful darkness. He shifted and found that he wasn't able to move. His body refused to obey him—his hands, his arms, and his legs, no muscle twitched.

The slavers must have captured and sedated him, waiting for him to wake up so they could take revenge.

No, no, no, no, no…panic thundered through him, his pulse a staccato beat, his breathing…he wasn't getting enough air…he opened his mouth to scream, but nothing came, no sound, the world swam around him.

He was—

He—

"Shhh," a voice close to his ear cooed. One breath, another. He flicked his gaze to the side—a shadow crouched beside him.

Had they—

The specter shifted, holding up a witch light. Blink by blink the face next to him sharpened. He could see dark eyes, a wicked scar down one cheek—the result of a fight with a thunderbeast—and a tangle of braids encrusted with beads and ornaments tied back and slung over one shoulder.

"Andres?" Otar croaked. Was he a figment of his imagination? And even if so, it was a lovely one. The panic rescinded, and his breathing eased.

"You are safe now," the Andres-mirage said.

Otar smacked his lips. His throat was parched.

"Water?"

Otar nodded and winced when pain laced through his skull. He remembered the unchecked tumble to the ground, and before that, whatever Berat used to knock him out. The Andres-mirage curled his lips in a teasing smile and bend to the side to grab something out of Otar's line of sight.

There was the trickle of water.

Andres turned back, carefully wriggled a hand under Otar's head and neck, and lifted him up, as if he was nothing more than a puppet. Then he pressed a shallow bowl to his lips.

"Slowly," Andres said gently. He only allowed Otar a few tiny sips.

It was heaven. The cool water was soothing. How many turns had he been out there? After Otar emptied the dish, Andres laid him down again, still achingly gentle.

"What happened?" He asked when Otar found a comfortable position.

Memories danced through his mind. Sand and water. Stone and darkness. Panic. Shadows that flowed in the night. The empty eyes of Berat. He was sure he wasn't able to explain anything right, so one word needed to be enough.

"Slavers."

Andres' eyes narrowed. "Where?"

In what direction had he run? His thoughts were sluggish, sleep tugging at the edges of his awareness. The sun had risen to his side, and then moved in front of him. Golden and deadly. That meant…

"North." And then, "River underground. Many caves." He coughed, his throat hurt, he was thirsty, he wanted more water, but also sleep. Sweet slumber.

Andres touched his face, caressing Otar's cheek with his thumb. His eyes were half-hidden in the night shadows, but they felt like burning coals. "Sleep now. No more harm will come."

Otar wanted to say more, wanted to ask—

Sleep claimed him once more.

GRAY SUNLIGHT HAD crept in. Otar blinked into it, his eyes slow in adjusting. He traced the outline of wooden furniture and canvas walls. It was a big tent, the type the steppe tribes used on the plains.

Sun rays filtered through the air duct at the top, Otar raised a hand to catch them, and this time his arm moved. He nearly wept.

It was painful. Every tiny movement of his body brought pain. He had overtaxed himself, running for turns through the steppe would do any person in. Otar might even have snorted at the ironic thought, if he had the energy.

His memories were still a scrambled mess. Had he really envisioned Andres? Whoever had helped him had at least been kind. Otar wouldn't ask for more.

Shouting rose outside, drawing him out of his contemplations. Otar rolled onto his side, winced at the pain from the stab wound, and then fought himself up on one elbow. His body protested, making it clear that this was a bad idea, but he failed to tame the panic that gripped him.

He tried to sit up further as more shouting rose. It swelled like a wave through what must be the entire camp, followed by the heavy steps of warriors on a mission.

Had the slavers come? Were they attacking the tribe that had been gracious enough to save him?

Otar planted his feet on the ground, his toes sinking into a plush and colorful rug. While he was wondering if it was a good idea to get up, the tent flap moved, and an old man hurried in. When his gaze fell on Otar, he raised an eyebrow. With surprisingly fast steps, he was at Otar's side and pressed him back into the bed.

"None of this now, visitor."

"But…" Otar protested, his body already following the command, melting down.

When Otar finally lay still, the old man checked the dressing at his side, probing it a few times before humming, satisfied. "It's healing." He laid a hand on Otar's forehead. "The fever has broken as well."

The noise outside swelled to a crescendo, then yardar thundered past, the ground vibrating under their powerful feet, as if an army were taking off to war.

"What is going on?" Otar croaked out, his voice failing at the last word.

"The warriors have gone hunting."

Andres had explained to him once that the tribes supplemented their food with smaller game they'd hunt in the plains. But why so many of them?

Otar nodded as if he understood.

The old man's eyes twinkled. "Don't make it your concern. Whatever may happen, we'll take care of you, visitor."

Visitor. A stranger who came, who was taken care of, and who left again. Maybe he should inquire which tribe this was, maybe he should also—he blinked into the light. Otar was tired, exhausted. He had never known that someone could be this fatigued.

He was—

"Sleep, visitor."

HE DRIFTED IN and out of slumber. The old man left the flap open to let the sun and the wind spill in. It allowed Otar the pleasure of catching glimpses of the outside world. Other tents made up the backdrop, while people flitted in and out of his field of view. Women carried laundry baskets; children chased each other, their laughter soothing the darkness inside Otar away; a warrior patrolled on a path outside, wandering repeatedly through Otar's view, his hand on the pommel of his sword, the other in his sash—the same way Andres and Onder always walked around.

For a few precious moments, it allowed Otar to just be. At midturn, when the shadows grew longer, the ground vibrated anew. For a moment, everyone in Otar's periphery froze, then the warriors ran in one direction, and the women and children in another.

Otar fought himself upright, tried to stand up. The old man appeared in the tent opening and all but ran to Otar, hooking one arm around his chest, and together they wobbled out into the open.

In the distance, beyond the camp, Otar made out a dust cloud, advancing fast. Warriors, he could glimpse through the opening in the tent wall, took up a defensive position on the outer edge of the camp, while the old man kept them both moving along until they reached a circle of women armed with daggers and swords. Inside huddled the children. The ring opened for them, and when they passed through, closed.

Small-turns trickled by. The blistering sun was unforgiving. Sweat ran down Otar's temples and back, his heart drummed in his chest, and his vision turned blurry. The old man held firm. No one spoke as they watched the approaching cloud reach the settlement, the pounding feet of heavy animals reaching a crescendo.

After another tense moment, a call came from the other side of the camp. There was a pause, then another call came again. The women eased their stance, they sheathed their weapons, and shooed the children into another direction.

The dust cloud swept over them, spitting out yardar after yardar, each carrying a grim-looking warrior.

The hunters had returned.

In the middle, on the most magnificent beast Otar had ever seen, rode Andres. Otar was unable to take his eyes away.

The other warriors sat down, but Andres kept going. Otar's gaze met with Andres', and Andres swung the massive black yardar into Otar's direction, the birds' extended wings almost touching the walls of the tents on both sides. Andres stopped right in front of Otar and the old man, who was still holding him upright.

With a thud, something landed at his feet. It was a bloody scarred hand wearing a gold ring on its thumb.

The hand of the slave leader.

Otar gulped. He looked back at Andres, who watched him with solemn eyes. He swallowed once more, then he bowed as deep as he dared without toppling over. The old man helped him upright again. The world swam. He kept his gaze focused on Andres. Gone was the forbidding and cold man; his shoulders were relaxed, and he had the beginnings of a smile on his lips.

He slid from his yardar, handing the reins to another warrior, who led the beast away.

Otar wobbled. The old man grabbed for him, but all strength had left Otar, and he stumbled to the ground. He squeezed his eyes shut, bracing against the impact, but it never came. Strong arms enveloped him, a body smelling of steel and leather and spice pressing him close.

"Enough running around for you," Andres said and hefted him up, carrying him back to the tent and into the bed. Otar, too tired to care, let his head rest against Andres' chest and closed his eyes.

Sleep was upon him before Andres had settled them both into bed.

Chapter 9

"I don't know what my brother is thinking, or if he is thinking at all. I want to take him and shake him until he finally tells me what is going on, but no, the stoic leader is taking on all the responsibilities and fights the battles within himself and doesn't rely on or even trust me to help him. I'm a leader as well! Why have I earned his scorn in this matter? Please explain to me Aaoran. Does he fear I won't support his decisions? Does he think so little of me?"

(Letters from Onder to Aaoran-peras)

THIS TIME WHEN Otar woke, he wasn't alone. Distantly, he wondered when he would be able to just stay awake. At least he didn't dream of darkness and voices again. Had that been the ghost? But then it usually only came to haunt him in the ruins.

"You with us, visitor?" The old man asked. He was sitting at Otar's side on what seemed to be a small stool, leafing through a book.

"I hope so," Otar whispered.

The old man smiled and helped him to sit up to sip some more water. He settled back with a sigh, then remembered the bloody hand. Otar hesitatingly asked, "Should I have done more?"

The old man watched him with clear eyes.

"The hand," Otar added, "should I have said some grand words or a specific vow?" His throat was scratchy and painful, and his voice was almost drowned out by the calls outside.

The other shook his head. "You didn't reject the gift. We burned it as an offering to the lords." Then he checked Otar's wound.

The silence felt oppressive.

"I'm sorry they had to take lives." Life was sacred for the tribes.

The old man straightened up and threw him an unreadable gaze before answering. It was clear in his stilted voice that he was choosing his words carefully. "Slavers aren't tolerated in these lands, and they know if they are caught that death is their punishment. The tribes settled the matter a long time ago. And yet, they come."

So in the end, it hadn't been about him at all. Yes, the slavers had wronged him, and Andres had offered him the hand of the leader as proof that justice for him had been served, but in the end, they would have died either way. Which was fair. Slavers were a menace, and Otar was sure nightmares would haunt him for many turns to come. And yet, for one moment, he had wanted it to be about him, because apparently Andres wasn't a fever dream, and parts of him were slowly catching up with that revelation.

"Leader Andres was furious though," the old man added after a small-turn, as if he was reading Otar's thoughts.

"Old man, you talk too much," Andres' voice slipped between them. They looked over and found him standing in the tent opening.

"Do I really?" The old man smiled serenely. "Isn't talk all we old people have left?"

Andres rolled his eyes. Cackling at Andres' expression, the old man pointed at Otar's wound. "He is healing nicely. But it will be a few turns before he can be on his way." There was a clear emphasis on the last three words. Otar tried to not let it get to him.

Andres nodded. "I'll talk to the council."

"See that you do, leader." The old man winked amused at Otar, and then he was gone.

Andres pinched the bridge of his nose, then shook his head as if he was dispelling whatever had taken hold of his thoughts. He looked at Otar, and for a moment, all the summers and winters that stood between them melted away, as if they had said goodbye merely a few turns ago, and they grinned at each other in old understanding.

Andres crept closer. Here, on the ground, he differed from sitting astride his yardar, fury and anger vibrating through his posture. The imposing leader.

Here, he was a mere man with soft eyes and an almost impish gait.

Here, he was Andres.

He stopped at the side of the bed, and Otar scooted to the left to make enough room for him to sit down if he wished to.

Andres perched on the edge.

"I thought I had imagined you," Otar said after the silence between them stretched on too long.

"Believe me, it was quite the surprise to discover you, half-dead at our very doorstep." Andres interlaced his fingers on his lap.

"How did you find me?" He remembered howling dogs and the impact of hard, sunbaked ground.

"The hunting dogs took an interest in you. We let them out to hunt on their own, and we heeded them no mind at first, but they wouldn't shut up. So, one patrol checked on them."

Another lull in the conversation, broken by the sounds from outside of grinding metal, the ever-present laughter of the children, and singing.

Otar took in Andres' harsh profile—the furrowed brows, the stiff posture.

"You killed them all?"

"Yes," Andres said without hesitation. His discomfort at the admission was clear; Otar could still read that much on his face, even after all this time.

He touched Andres' arm. "Good."

Some of the stiffness drained away, and a smile flickered on Andres' lips.

"What happens now?"

Andres raised a hand and laid it on Otar's cheek, who couldn't resist turning into it. Andres' eyes glittered in the oncoming shadows. "For now, you sleep."

Fighting against the command, Otar yawned involuntarily. He'd just woken up. Sleeping was the furthest thing from his mind. And yet, the sweet call of darkness crept upon him and then claimed him once more.

SLEEPING WAS THE only thing he did over the next three turns—as the old man smugly informed him when Otar could stay awake for more than a few small-turns.

Once more, the old man was sitting in the chair beside the bed, leafing through a book. He raised his head when Otar moved around, watched him for a moment, then closed the book with a nod.

"Leader will be pleased." And with that cryptic message, he walked to the tent flap and tied it back onto a small wooden hook. Fresh morning air crawled in, bringing a slight chill. The old man stuck his head out and called out a few words; it took only a small-turn before someone shouted back. Then he shuffled in again.

"Water, visitor?"

Otar found himself too parched to speak. "Please," he croaked out after a few attempts. But before the old man could follow through with his offer, Andres stood in the tent opening, his chest heaving as if he'd been running.

"I'll take care of him, elder."

The old man crooked his head to the side. "See that you do, leader." And after a clap on Andres' shoulder, he was gone.

Andres stepped further into the tent and took the water jug, filling up the shallow bowl they had used before. Otar fought himself into an upright position, breathing through various spells of dizziness. For a moment, Andres hovered haltingly, then he held the dish out.

Otar smiled and wanted to take it with his trembling fingers, but Andres shook his head, put the bowl into Otar's hands while holding it steady with his own.

Otar tried to not dwell on the feelings that the gesture evoked. Instead, he concentrated on the sweet tasting water—it was tepid, but he savored it like the finest wine from the Palace of Rasanell.

"Don't make yourself sick," Andres chided, and Otar did his best to control himself.

After the water was gone, he let Andres take the bowl and waited. His stomach twinged, but the water stayed down.

Avoiding Otar's eyes, Andres looked down at the dish in his hands, turning it around.

"How long do I have?"

Andres sighed and returned the bowl to the jug. "The tribe will ride in seven regular turns."

Otar exhaled. It was to be expected. He nodded. "Please carry my thanks to the council to grant me that much time."

"You can thank them yourself. The old man has been watching over you."

That meant…Old Man: it wasn't an endearment for a beloved older figure or even a father or grandfather; it was a title. His nursemaid was the leader of the elder council. Tribes had two councils: the actual leaders, whose numbers depended on the size of the tribe—Andres was one of five leaders; and the elder council, who functioned as advisers and voices of reason. Both often attended the overarching council sessions, the All-Council, when the different tribes came together.

Otar stared at Andres, willing him to tell him he was joking. But Andres shrugged his shoulders. "Men in power gravitate toward you."

There was a truth to Andres' words he couldn't deny. He buried his face in his hands.

Andres, Jasner, Turas, Aaoran, they had all exuded that powerful charm. Perhaps the attachment from Marit made more sense now as he was the son of a leader. But what about Berat? Otar racked his brain about what Berat had told him. Remembering he had been the son of a rich merchant.

Andres nudged his leg, and Otar made space for him as he had done before. For a moment, they breathed together. Finding the other so close was nerve-wracking and unbelievable. He just needed to reach out and touch Andres. At moments, he still believed he would wake up and everything would just be a dream.

"How did the slavers get the jump on you?" Andres' gaze filled with curiosity.

Otar tapped his fingers on the blanket, smoothing over the fine material and exquisite ornamental stitches. For the first time since waking up in the tent, he mourned his notebook.

"Someone who I trusted sold me out. I think he manipulated my flasks, and then he led me to the mountains promising fresh water so that we could make it all the way to Adabel."

"Trusted…" Andres repeated slowly with a grin. "How pretty was his face?"

Otar swatted at him, making Andres laugh.

When he quieted down, Otar slung his arms around his knees and rested his head on them, looking sideways at Andres.

"Why have you been so close to those mountains?" If Otar remembered Andres' stories correctly, the tribe should have been farther to the east, closer to the Black Mountains that bordered the lands by the big ocean.

"Rumors about new slavers have been circulating for a while. The All-Council decreed the more battle-experienced tribes investigate various sightings and previous known hiding places." Andres interlaced his fingers. "Witness reports told us they must have taken camp in the mountain range you pointed us to, but we hadn't yet decided on how best to approach them." He grinned. "You kind of made it clear where they would be."

"How funny."

Andres' smile deepened, turning into the one that dimpled his cheeks and always made Otar's heart beat faster.

When they had traveled together five summers ago and parted on friendly terms, he had thought there had never been more between them than easy friendship and sexual compatibility—he had been very wrong.

At midturn, after Andres had excused himself murmuring something about tribe business, the Old

Man brought him a stew, or a less rich version of what the tribes usually cooked. Andres had cooked a few times in their time traveling together, and the broth had always been thicker and spicier. Here it was thin, almost devoid of bits and pieces, and blander. At least the bread was fresh and fluffy.

Otar had watched Andres go with mixed feelings. He wanted to say so much more, wanted to reach out—but he'd clawed his hands into the blanket around his knees instead.

Their parting had been amicable. Andres wasn't a nobody; he and his twin Onder, as well as three other steppe riders, governed this tribe. The Kruson tribe was one of the biggest tribes in the eastern and central steppe. It was split into smaller segments, each led by one of the five leaders, and was supported by the elder council.

Andres took up the mantle of leadership when he had been very young, barely twenty summers. The Kruson tribe didn't follow hereditary leadership but elected those they wanted to follow and Andres proved by his very nature that he was a fair and level-headed leader who was also a fierce warrior. He was a proud man who loved the steppe.

When Otar had accepted Andres into his bed, he acknowledged that there would never be more between them as Andres would never leave the tribe. Not that Otar wanted there to be more, as he shied away from emotional connections—always living in fear of the monster inside him. He was also unwilling to follow a travel pattern dictated by others, not until he fully discovered the Ancients' secrets, a task that seemed even more impossible with every passing turn.

Why was he even thinking about this now? Andres was probably married by now. Otar hadn't taken a closer look at the mess of beads in his hair. Maybe there was already a kid running around, a little adorable fierce looking menace.

And yet, Otar missed him fiercely. Upon seeing him again, everything rushed back, the longing he ignored, the pain after parting, the loneliness he pushed away, the—

"Not hungry?" The Old Man's voice startled him. Otar almost dropped the bowl in his hands. The other was watching him with furrowed brows.

"I was lost in thought." As if to prove his point, he took a spoonful of the stew and ate. It had smelled heavenly when the Old Man had handed it over, but it tasted even better, his body not caring for the missing spices. Despite its appearance, it was more of a porridge. Thin, but earthy and sharp without being spicy. Otar had eaten nothing like it in any of the Seven Lands. He almost choked at their thoughtfulness; his stomach still tender.

The Old Man hummed. He settled down on the small stool and drank tea. With the bowl, he had brought an additional jug and two cups made of fine silver with intricate ornaments driven into them, covering the entire outer surface. It itched inside him to draw them.

The aroma from the second jug was rancid and spicy at the same time. Otar found it a better idea to concentrate on the stew first, forcing himself to chew before taking the next spoonful. He was famished, and yet he waited after every few bites and listened to his stomach before eating more. Soon he was dabbing up the dregs with the fluffy bread.

His hunger was soothed, even if the famished feeling never went away. One moment the monster was sated and therefore was Otar, and a small-turn later, the craving gnawed at his bones again.

"How long have you known leader?"

Otar looked at the Old Man, but his face only showed curiosity. He wasn't sure why the other wanted to know, but saw no harm in telling him. "Since I have been ten and six summers."

The Old Man nodded in thought. "And you're what now? Twenty and five?"

Otar grimaced. "Twenty and nine." It might be even thirty now. He'd lost all sense of time, not bothering with the calendar since he had begun exploring the jungle.

"Ah," the Old Man said, and then he said nothing at all.

While the silence stretched between them, Otar handed his empty bowl over. The Old Man took it, put it to the ground next to his feet, and then picked up the second cup and filled it with the contents of the other jug, handing it over. Otar wrinkled his nose at the acrid odor. The Old Man chuckled.

"Elder, I hope I'm not too presumptuous, but what am I to call you?"

The Old Man studied him for a long moment and then nodded to himself. "You may call me Borroi."

Otar inclined his head in acknowledgment, then sipped the beverage. And while it wasn't pleasant, it wasn't as horrid as he had feared. Borroi chuckled at the expression of disdain Otar couldn't suppress.

"Fermented yardar milk, leaves from the southern regions, rock sugar, and spices. It'll make you strong and healthy."

Otar took another sip. It was better than the first, and while it would never become his favorite drink, he could get used to it at moderate intervals. And it was warming.

"Leader is a fair and, what is the word in Common…" Borroi spoke as if the previous conversation never stopped between them. "Ah, stoic. He is a fair and stoic man."

Otar knew that, and he was about to say as much, when Borroi threw him a look that said he had more to impress on Otar.

"Leader always thinks his actions through. He never rushes without considering his options or consequences." Borroi took a sip from his cup, his gaze steady on Otar, a degree cooler than before. "At least, that is what I thought. We tracked the slavers for turns and turns, waiting for the right moment, finding the best approach, making sure we had them cornered, that none of them could escape justice." Another sip, a gaze over the rim of the cup. "And then you arrived."

Otar swallowed, unable to bear his eyes any longer, and looked down into his own cup.

"At first, after we found you, we thought you were dead, or soon to be gone. But you clung to life with ferociousness. Leader, when he saw you dangling like a doll in the arms of the patrol, was ready to march to war right then and there. He was beyond anger, a beast barely tamed on the insistence that we needed to care for you first, that we still didn't know where they were, and that you could have crucial information." Borroi topped up his own cup. "But when you were stable and had uttered the location, he called for the warriors and rode to war."

War was probably an exaggeration, but Otar didn't dare voice that opinion under Borroi's penetrating stare.

"Tell me, visitor, are you more a stranger or a friend to the tribe? Will you bring fortune or ruin?"

The words shook Otar to the core, feeding right into the deepest fears he held locked away. If he examined them too closely, he was sure he would never find the strength to move forward again.

Andres' return saved him from answering. The moment the tent flap moved, his entire attention latched onto it.

"Old Man," Andres greeted Borroi, who smiled serenely back. The elder rose with a nod, took the empty bowl and his own cup as if he was a mere servant, and with a last unreadable gaze directed at Otar, he was gone.

"Nosy elders," Andres murmured after Borroi was out of earshot. He unclipped the silver cup that always dangled from his belt and poured himself yardar-tea from the tea jug. He offered to top Otar's up, but Otar shook his head, murmuring something about spices and his delicate stomach. Andres, looking right through him, chuckled. Then he sipped the tea and closed his eyes in bliss.

"Rough turn?"

Andres winked at him and perched on the bed. "Every small-turn, there are additional problems." He took another sip, savoring it. "Problems the tribe members could solve themselves, and yet they rely on the leaders and stop thinking for themselves." He sighed, looking tired. Otar ached to take Andres into his arms. "Sometimes I want to leave it all to Onder, and settle down somewhere quiet."

Otar grinned. "You'd miss the steppe."

Andres shrugged, his gaze far away. He focused back on Otar. "How are you? And be honest."

The 'I'm fine' was ready on his lips, but he backtracked. "Getting better. The wound is still tender, moving around aggravates it. I'll have to live with some discomfort for a while. It was a good stab," he tried to joke, but Andres didn't laugh.

"Killing them was too merciful."

This time Otar gave into the impulse and reached out, laying his hand on Andres' arm, ignoring the sudden quickening of his heartbeat at the skin contact. The monster stayed away, surprisingly. "I'm alive, and they can't hurt me or anyone else ever again. You and your warriors made sure of it."

Andres nodded, but the muscles under Otar's fingers didn't relax.

"Andres?" He had never seen the other man like this, closed off and guarded, bowing under an invisible weight.

But Andres turned the empty cup in his hand over and over. His mind was heavy. "For a tribe leader, there is a path. A path that is entwined with traditions, with beliefs, with rules. Handed down from leader to leader to keep order in the tribe and between the tribes. Stepping off the path brings war."

"Okay," Otar said carefully after Andres stopped, the silence stretching between them. He moved his hand away, but Andres grabbed it, keeping it trapped between the arm and his own warm hand. The monster twitched before settling down again.

"When we first met—you, me and Onder," he chuckled mirthlessly, "you were nothing more than a boy made of skin and bones, with big curious eyes and too many questions." He shook his head, shifting on the bed, turning more to Otar. His gaze was still lost in whatever memories must play in his mind. "At the Bakusaran ruins you were always underfoot, sometimes you were even funny, but you were also something to protect."

"Ouch." But Andres had a point. He had been very young, very naive, and very annoying, pestering everyone with question after question.

A smile flitted over Andres' lips. "When we met again many winters later, you were different and yet the same. Still curious, with a hundred more questions. Not a boy anymore, a man, but still something to protect." He paused and shook his head. "No, someone I wanted to protect. Someone I wanted to hold onto—but you didn't want me to. And there was also duty."

Otar licked his lips, the words confusing him. Had Andres always wanted more? He never assumed, had even mentioned to the other, that they had a nice and easy friendship. Had told him to go when the letter from Onder arrived calling him to the tribe.

And now it was too late.

"I understand," Otar said in a whisper.

"You don't," Andres shot back and waited as if he expected Otar to argue, but he had no words inside him.

Andres exhaled and picked up his tale again. "I chose duty, but I didn't comply with it. I angered the elders with decisions I made, born out of the chasm between us. But I didn't care because I made a promise. When we parted, I promised to find you again."

He had, in a way. That morning when they parted ways, Andres had held Otar's hand, kissed him one last time, and told him he would find Otar again, wherever he was. Otar had assumed Andres meant as a general term, like when Otar was in trouble, not as the specific intention that Andres would return to him. His heart beat painfully in his chest.

Clearly, from the way Andres was looking at him now, it had been a wrong assumption. All the memories of them pressing in, all the little gestures and touches they had shared, the quiet moments Otar had always dismissed as easy companionship. He searched for words, a treacherous hope spreading through his body. Was it possible he wasn't too late?

Andres kept talking, oblivious to Otar's turmoil. "But the matters with the tribes took too long to settle, and you had said nothing encouraging for what was between us, so I convinced myself that it was better to move on, to not return, to break my promise, and for the moment put it on hold. And I thought I was free again."

"Andres…"

But Andres shook his head. "When I realized it was you, bloody and broken in the arms of the scout, never in my life have I felt such rage." He looked down at his hands now. He loosened his grip on Otar and clenched his hands into fists. Otar laid his own onto them, spreading his fingers.

"I took pleasure in killing them." Andres' voice pitched so low, Otar needed to lean forward to understand him. "I made sure their leader understood why we had come. I relished the terror in his eyes."

Otar closed the gap between them, winding his arms around Andres' stiff shoulders, hugging him close.

The *path* Andres had spoken of was one of life. Steppe people cherished life. The lords they answered to had strict rules about killing. Steppe riders hunted down bandits and slavers with a solemn mindset, executing them without joy, but with sadness and reverence. Those who found excitement in bloodshed were exiled, often banished from the steppe.

Will you bring fortune or ruin?

Otar closed his eyes and hugged Andres closer.

Chapter 10

"Brew is a very delicate drink, and a brew cake should be carefully prepared so that the full flavor is developed. Never chop off too many of a chunk from the entire cake, and do not mangle the edges badly. Loose leaves will lose flavor quickly, so take less than you think you will need. When you add the leaves, the water should have boiled but not be boiling hot anymore. Let it sit for the desired strength, but not more than one turn, otherwise the bitterness will be overwhelming."

(From: „How to make the perfect brew")

"Aaoran is worried about you."

Otar looked up from the book he was leafing through, a distraction while he sorted his thoughts. After Andres' confession, he'd slept through most of the turn, drained by the emotions inside him.

"Onder!" He exclaimed surprised after he registered who was standing in the tent opening.

Onder grinned and stepped in. Andres' twin had always been fun to talk to. Of a similar temperament as his brother Onder had answered all of Otar's questions about the tribes and the steppe riders with a smile and a twinkle in his eyes. In the few letters that reached Otar from Aaoran, his mentor consistently included news about them both.

Noting the two jugs, one with fresh tea, Onder unclipped his own cup from his belt and poured himself. He offered to fill up Otar's as well, but Otar pointed to the water.

When Onder took the first sip, he closed his eyes in bliss, as all the other tribe members did. Otar shuddered and made a face as he remembered the taste.

"Not fancy enough for your western tastebuds?" Onder commented on his expression.

"It surely is an acquired taste."

Onder waggled his eyebrows and settled on the stool beside the bed.

"Aaoran is alright?" Otar feared his mentor himself might have been ambushed.

"They are waiting for you at the ruins." Onder took another sip, savoring the taste in the same manner Andres did. "They were surprised when you didn't arrive in the time frame you gave in your letter. And when I brought news of what had happened, I could barely calm them down. They were ready to go after the bandits themselves."

"Slavers," Otar corrected.

Onder winked at him. "As far as they are concerned, they were bandits, otherwise…" He let the words taper off.

"Doctor Mare would have killed us all."

They both chuckled. Aaoran's chosen partner was a fierce and protective man, well trained in the art of healing and all matters of death.

Onder raised his cup and watched Otar over the rim. "Andres killed them all."

"He told me." Otar returned the steady gaze, but his fingers danced restlessly over the intricate pattern of the blanket, feeling the different stitches and ornaments painted onto it with the twine. "I'm sorry."

"Otar." Onder's hand settled on his, but Otar snatched them away. The monster crawled under his skin. This morning, it had risen from its slumber and was a constant undercurrent, ready to pounce.

Would the monster ever have enough?

"Please go." Otar clicked his mouth shut to stop more words from tumbling out. He didn't say that it might be better to send him away, to get rid of him, to never look at him again. This was why he didn't get close. Whatever had possessed Andres, it was clearly Otar's fault, as Borroi implied.

Onder watched him a moment longer and sighed, disappointed. Guilt settled in Otar's stomach, along with the other regrets and the many fears about being wrong and causing people he cared about pain. Onder had been good and nice to him, and yet…

Onder rose without another word, gone before Otar could call him back. Numbness spread through his limbs. He had done it, had successfully driven the other away. Now he needed to do it with Andres, cut the ties that seemed to keep them and then…He drew his knees up and let the camp sounds settle around him. The monster's presence meant that he was getting better and was becoming restless. Borroi had advised him to stay one more turn in bed to make sure the stitches would hold. He closed his eyes, not sleeping. He had slept enough for several lifetimes, but he was unwilling to face reality. When someone entered the tent, he didn't react, or the next time, or the next, until the aroma of food reached him.

He turned his head, and there was a bowl filled with what seemed to be a similar porridge he had the turn before on the makeshift nightstand, accompanied by two thick slabs of bread. At the sight, his stomach growled, and he realized he was famished. The porridge was thicker this time, with a bit more spice. His belly accepted the food without complaining.

He was dabbing up the last dregs with the bread when Borroi stepped through the tent opening and closed the flap behind him. He didn't come closer, but hovered in the semi-darkness.

"How is your stomach?"

Otar's smile was genuine. "Better, and whatever this was," he held the cleaned out bowl up, "it was delicious."

"You should move around soon, to build up your strength again."

Time was running out. They wanted to move on, yet Otar's state was preventing them to do so. But what should he do out there? Wander aimlessly through the camp? That didn't sound appealing.

On top of it all, he was bored. Once more, he felt the painful loss of his notebook. With it he could at least sort through his notes, he could…he perked up at the sudden idea.

"Borroi, could I be allowed to observe and record your customs?"

The elder crossed his arms, studying him. "The council will decide."

Otar inclined his head. "I'd be grateful." He put the empty bowl on the nightstand. Borroi stepped closer to help him to the chamber pot and then back to the bed. Otar endured it with flaming cheeks.

After Otar'd settled again, Borroi sat down.

"I think I should apologize, visitor."

"Why ever?"

"I judged something that wasn't mine to judge."

Otar considered the words while sun beams streamed through the air vent, shifting slowly with every small-turn wandering by. "You spoke the truth. I was the reason he turned mad with anger and diverged from the path your lords have shown you. It's in your right as protector of the tribe to question my intentions." He paused. "To be honest, I never would have guessed Andres would react like this. I thought he would be angry, yes, as we were…friends, companions for a while. I hold him dear, but we were never close. At least, I thought…"

"You love him."

Otar flinched at the words. He always shied away from them, but over the last turns he did nothing but think about how he felt, and what role Andres had played in his life. Was it love? Was it friendship? He didn't recognize where one ended and the other began. Or did it even matter?

Was it really as easy and as complicated that he loved Andres?

"I don't know."

Borroi hummed. Laughter echoed outside, and a gaggle of children ran past, their shadows like a puppet theater dancing over the tent canvas.

"Are you ashamed?"

"No." At least he could say that with conviction. He never experienced embarrassment about the people he took into his bed.

"You turned away at the words," Borroi pointed out.

"I dread them. I fear losing him." Even if he never had him. A door he closed himself, he realized. Andres took revenge on the slavers for hurting him, but that didn't mean there was still more, or that Andres had forgiven him for driving him off the path.

Borroi didn't roll his eyes, but it was a close thing. "Do you know whose tent you occupy?"

Otar crooked his head. His fingers never stopped stroking the beautiful patterns on the blanket—a gesture that brought him much comfort over the last turn.

His gaze went from the blanket to the rest of the tent they'd put him in. For the first time, he was able to take a closer look, registering the finely carved furniture, the draped carpets with bold colors that felt soft under his feet, the expensive and well-cared knick-knacks scattered throughout, even the embroidery under his fingers. Everything was lavish and beautiful.

"Oh."

"Not everything is lost, it seems. The young finally opens his eyes."

"This doesn't mean—," Otar protested.

"Onder!" Borroi called in a sharp tone. The tent flap shifted, and Onder poked his head in. Had he been listening in the whole time?

"Bring leader," Borroi commanded. This was the man that led an entire council, making decisions others obeyed.

"As you wish," Onder said with amusement in his gaze.

Otar narrowed his eyes. He felt as if he were missing a few pages in a book, as if they all assumed… but there was nothing to it. Even after his breakdown, Andres had left without a word, without a backward glance. Andres wasn't his, and now, never would be.

As if summoned by Otar's own thoughts, Andres appeared in the tent opening and held the flap to the side with one arm, his eyes roaming over Otar.

"You look alright." Andres furrowed his brows in confusion.

"Leader."

"Old Man."

"Come and sit and prove that not everyone is so stupid."

Andres eyed Borroi warily but did as he was commanded—he shuffled in and sat down on the stool Borroi had vacated. The elder pointed a finger at Otar. "Talk, or you'll need to find another tribe to take care of you."

"Old Man!" Andres jumped up with clenched fists, his eyes flashing, anger bristling through his posture.

"Shush." Borroi laid his hands on Andres' shoulders and pressed him back down. And then he left.

Andres pinched the bridge of his nose. "I must apologize. I think his age is catching up with him."

Otar smiled faintly. He settled into a cross-legged seat and considered how to do this.

"What happened to my pants?"

Andres eyed him, probably deciding that all of them had gone mad, but he walked over to a trunk that was at the foot of the bed and pulled them out. Otar could see that they had been washed and even mended. He took them from Andres when he handed them over and searched for the secret pocket hidden at the seam of the waist. His shoulders slumped when he found the small bag with the beads he got in Patreshka still there.

He fumbled it out, and reached for Andres' right hand, who met him in the middle. For a moment Otar let his fingers dance over the skin, taking in the new and old scars and calluses that spoke of a life lived.

He opened the small bag with his other hand and teeth and took the black bead out. With a sudden sense of clarity, he knew what he needed to do. Clearing his throat, he met Andres' curious gaze from under his lashes. Then he laid the bead into Andres' palm and closed his fingers around it.

"Akamar daro." You reside in my heart.

Otar was sure he had gotten the pronunciation wrong, but it would have to do. In Andres' tribal language, this was a declaration of deep love—at least Onder had told him many summers ago, in the night's depth, when they both couldn't sleep. When Andres didn't react for a moment, he felt embarrassed and wondered if Onder had jested.

Then Andres' eyes widened, and Otar couldn't decide whether he looked elated or wretched. Well, here went nothing. Before the courage could leave him, he plunged on. "This is given freely from me to you. I won't have anything returned, nothing you are unwilling to give. There have been many things done and said wrong between us because of me. I'm not expecting anything from you, but only that you understand, whatever may be I'll always be your friend."

Andres looked at him and then at the bead, the one given when an important battle was won. It was fitting for the extermination of the slavers but also for the fight that waged within Otar himself. And if Andres wished so, he could see it as finally winning Otar over. He almost snorted at the ludicrous thought.

A range of complicated emotions played over Andres' face, when a sudden commotion from outside broke the moment.

"Leader Andres," someone called urgently.

Andres sprang up with a curse and strode out barking orders before the tent flap had even swung shut behind him.

Everything happened so fast. Otar sat frozen for a moment, before he chuckled embarrassed, ignoring the wetness that stole into it, while clutching the leather bag and the remaining bead in it tight.

By the lords, why did he say those words? What possessed him to offer his heart to a man who had moved on from him? There was nothing but pain, and yet the world was still moving. On the heels of hurt came relief. Maybe one turn he could even look Andres in the eyes again.

This time, a giggling woman, who also collected the empty jugs and cups, brought him food and water. Otar thanked her in stilted tribe, which was answered with more giggles, and then he was left to his own devices for the rest of the turn. Neither Borroi, nor Onder, nor Andres visited.

Was this a sign that he had said the wrong thing? Borroi had seemed eager for him to say something. Had he put Andres now into an even more difficult position?

Or was he just being dramatic? The world did not revolve around him, and all three held important positions and had things they needed to attend to.

Otar scrubbed his hands over his face. There was nothing to be gained by dwelling on it. He turned his gaze inward. But besides the ever-constant tendrils of hunger, the monster was silent.

He wobbled out of bed, to relieve himself, and almost wept when he was able to do so without help. Exhausted, he crawled back under the blanket and closed his eyes.

A NOISE WOKE him. He opened his eyes a sliver. Around him, the world was pitch black.

There it was again: a noise, a movement in the darkness.

Otar held his breath, while letting his gaze drift to the side. He squinted and found a different shadow hiding between the other shadows. As silent as possible, he shifted, his hand searching for anything he could use as a weapon. Had one slaver survived and was now seeking revenge? Had something more sinister come to him? A tribe member angry about the slave raid? Turas—

A witch light flared, and Otar relaxed his movements. How often had he seen that silhouette in the shine of a fire, broad and safe?

Andres unclipped his sword and stripped layer for layer out of his armor.

He turned and stopped when he found Otar watching him.

"Don't stop now," he drawled sleepily, falling easily into the old banter they had once shared. That Andres had returned did something to Otar's insides that he was unwilling to name.

Andres chuckled and crept closer, stripped down to a thin shirt and close-fitting pants. He perched on the edge of the bed and Otar wanted nothing more than to curl around him. Maybe this was how a moth felt near a flame.

A hand settled in Otar's hair; fingers carded through the long curls. As it always did with Andres, the monster uncurled lazily and took a small delicate bite. Every contact with Andres sparked a brief exchange of life force, not only when they slept together. With Andres, the monster was docile, never going out of control.

"Allow me to sleep next to you." Andres' voice was low, hesitant of his welcome. Otar reacted without thinking. He scooted so far back that he almost fell out on the other side. Then he held the blanket up in case Andres had missed the point.

With that soft, dimpling smile, he slipped in.

The witch light threw harsh shadows over Andres, deepening tattoo lines and scars. They faced each other, eyes darting back and forth between them.

"Hey," Andres whispered, while the light flickered out, the charge empty.

"Hey," Otar whispered. He wanted to add more, but Andres ghosted his hand over Otar's cheek, settling it at the base of his skull, scratching soft lazy circles. A gesture they both knew would put Otar to sleep.

He glowered at Andres, but the other just watched him, a soft soothing expression in his eyes, barely perceptible in the darkness. Otar fought against the sleep, but to no avail.

"Sleep, ana."

And Otar slept.

Chapter 11

"Jasner may have saved you from a worse fate, Otar, but I won't ever forgive nor forget."

(From: Letters to Otar from Turas ad Temar)

OTAR WASN'T SURPRISED to wake alone. He rolled onto his back, wondering if last night had just been a dream. Well, there was nothing to it now. He pressed his fists into his eyes for a moment and then sat up. Hopefully, they'd allow him finally to move around. His gaze wandered through the tent and caught on the sword leaning against the table. Otar blinked, but the weapon didn't vanish. There had never been an instance, besides Andres sleeping, where the sword belt wasn't slung around his hips. It was always the first thing he did in the morning: roll out of his bedroll or the bed of the inn they'd stayed in, grab the sword and fasten it.

And now it leaned abandoned against the table. It didn't make sense. His head was too sluggish to deal with it. He eyed the water jug and was about to reach for it when the tent flap moved. Andres stepped in, still only wearing his shirt and pants, both ruffled from sleep.

Warmth flushed over Otar's cheek at the thought of Andres walking out like this with all of his tribe knowing where he'd spent the night. By the lords, he wasn't a blushing virgin anymore, but the heat only deepened.

When he found Otar awake, Andres smiled. He held up a tray and walked over, setting it down on the bed next to Otar before settling opposite him in a cross-legged seat. The tray held two bowls of porridge, which looked more yellow this time, and a cup that smelled like brew. Otar stared at it for a long moment before Andres nudged it closer to him with a smug look.

Otar took the cup, sniffed it, and after taking a sip, closed his eyes in bliss.

"Why, by all the lords taught, has no one ever brought me brew until now?" He demanded.

"Because this is from my secret stash. Only Onder knows about it, but my brother usually knows everything—well, almost." Andres winked at him.

Otar groaned and put the cup down. He picked up the porridge and savored it. It was a mild grain, fluffy and buttery—delicious.

Interpreting his expression correctly, Andres explained, "We trade it from the south. They grow it near the ocean. The farmers claim the sea winds give it its unique taste."

"It's heavenly." He already found the stew one of the best things he had ever eaten, but this topped it all. It was melting in his mouth and slightly spicy, as if a blanket was draped over his shoulders, welcoming and warming.

It became clear now how much they must have tamed down the spices when they cooked for him while he'd been ill, which also meant that they had specially made the meals for him, which again meant…

Otar let his spoon sink as the realization hit him. "To them, even if they call me that, I'm not a mere visitor, am I?" He groaned. "An elder looked after me," Otar hissed. "They think I'm viewing for being your wife, or at least a mistress." The puzzle pieces were finally falling all into place. Why Borroi called him out like that being the ruin for Andres, why the woman giggled when he talked to her.

Andres coughed. "Your injuries were too severe. There was no other choice but to put you in my tent, as it was the one with the least disturbances, and the others just assumed."

"I think it has more to do with you going to war." It slipped out more sharply than Otar intended.

Andres winced, and for a moment, shadows settled in his gaze. He blinked, and they shifted away. "Are you angry about it?"

Otar, who had retrieved his spoon to scrape the last bits out of the bowl, let the spoon sink again and shook his head.

"What is it then?" Andres' eyes were gentle.

"You came to me last night—I'm not sure I understand."

"Ah," Andres said and looked to the side.

Disappointment crawled up Otar's throat, choking him. He hoped with Andres coming to him that he wasn't too late, that there might be a chance for…what exactly? They were living in completely different worlds, which seldom crossed each other. Even meeting here was only a coincidence.

"I see."

Andres exhaled—it sounded almost rueful. "No, you don't, but that is my fault."

Otar shrugged, chewing over the last part. He wasn't sure what the other could have done differently. "We decided to split. We never spoke about this between us." A half-truth, Andres, as per his word, did promise he would return to Otar, but nothing beyond it.

They never spoke about how they felt about each other.

"We both knew that something was there, and I broke my promise to come back."

In the distance, the yardar brayed, quarreling with each other, a shout nearby, laughter passing by the tent, a song, slightly off-key, the sounds of the tribe twirling around them but the silence between them stretched. What more was there to say?

Andres sighed, his bowl untouched. "For the moment, allow me to sleep beside you."

It was an innocent request, but Otar should say no, firmly, cut his losses, use the last remaining turns to get over the man, and then bury himself in the ruins and be done with this drama. But those eyes, dark and bottomless, drew him in.

No.

This was the line, no further than this: Nurse the broken heart, return to being friends at some point in the future, and nothing more.

No.

One word.

Otar opened his mouth and said, "Yes."

THE GROUP OF women sewed with deft fingers. Otar could barely follow their movements. Under their hands, the garment grew with every stitch—as if it was puzzling itself together. It was large, elaborate and decadent. Thick and lavishly embroidered with colorful twine, sparkling beads and golden trimmings. It almost looked like the blanket Andres and he had slept under in each other's arms—Otar wrenched his thoughts away. Since confessing to himself and to Andres that he loved him, everything returned to that moment. And Andres had remined silent about it. His love life had become a total mess.

Mistress. Wife. He scoffed at the words and swallowed down the yearning.

Finally allowed to get up, Otar slipped out of the tent after breakfast—Andres had long gone to do whatever leaders did the whole turn. Outside, no one paid him any mind. They flowed around him as if he was nothing but a temporary obstacle, a passerby, a *visitor*. Even if some thought of him as something more, Otar knew he was just a traveler.

As he wandered through the tribe, he found a big open tent where the women were working on the garment. At his arrival, they looked up for a moment and then returned to their work.

Fascinated at the craftsmanship and their speed, he stopped to observe them. He wanted to keep watching, so he'd tried to explain his intention to them in Common. But all the women shook their heads, not grasping his intention. Onder, who wandered over from a neighboring tent, came to the rescue, after winking at him. Then he did the translation for him.

Not many scholars or even travelers had written about the steppe, or at least none of those texts had made it to the library of Rasanell—one of the biggest libraries in the Seven Lands. Aaoran groused some time ago that not even Patreshka held many works about the culture and traditions of the different tribes. So, now with idle time on his hands, Otar wanted to use the opportunity to take some notes to rectify that oversight. Borroi had given him some paper and a pencil after he brought back the news that the council was allowing him to study their customs, only if he kept out of the way and didn't pester those who were unwilling.

After all the explanations were done, the women shrugged and returned to their work. Otar took that as a hint and settled cross-legged in the shade. After a few small-turns, one woman began to sing, with the others joining in one after the other, every stitch marking the rhythm. When the song ended, they all laughed, babbled over each other, until another one started a new song.

As that one ended, an elderly woman with many golden earrings, bracelets, stacked almost to her elbow, clicking at every movement she made, and long braids, said something in a low tone, and the one sitting next to her giggled. Another woman with shorter hair, hundreds of tiny braids full of baubles, and a nose ring, rolled her eyes. Her gaze met Otar's, and she winked at him before she returned to watching her stitches.

He had already made a handful of sketches when a younger woman with particularly elaborate braids stood up, stretched, and walked over. She eyed the picture that lay next to him and then started talking loudly to him. The others looked at each other, stopped working, and came over. After studying his sketches a few moments, they all spoke at once.

Otar gulped, pressing his current sketch to his chest. Did he do something wrong?

Drawn by the sudden commotion, one of the guards stepped over. He eyed Otar and then turned to the women, listening to two of them talk while the others almost seemed to vibrate. The guard nodded and then shouted for Onder.

The women fell silent at once, their eyes flicking from Otar to the illustrations and back. Otar couldn't quite place their energy or what they were so excited about. He had drawn parts of the pattern, making close sketches of the needles and how they were held, and had made a series of the different movements and how they added the beads. From there he sketched their different attires, braids, faces of concentration, and laughter. Did he overstep?

It took a short moment for Onder to come, closely followed by Andres.

Andres stopped by Otar and crouched down while Onder walked up to the women, who instantly bombarded him with words and rapid hand gestures, pointing between the garment and Otar. Was the problem the pattern?

"What happened?" Andres' voice was close and low.

"I don't know. I sketched what they were doing, and the pattern." He blinked. "Should I not have done that?"

"What do you mean?"

"Is it sacred?"

Andres chuckled. "Not really. It is a tribe pattern, but it never has been holy. Patterns are based on our history. They are telling our story, wishing for happiness and luck, a bountiful hunt, strength in the face of enemies; but they have never been associated with the lords." He smiled. "And believe me, Borroi would have told you if there was a restriction on what you could observe when you asked for permission from the council. We even gave you the pen and paper to do it."

Otar exhaled, relieved. They both turned to Onder, who was still debating with the women. Then he shook his head in exaggeration and walked back over to them. Otar rose with Andres' help, his muscles stiff. The women fell silent, hanging behind Onder like an ominous cloud.

"Did I insult them?"

Onder's eyes twinkled. That didn't bode well. "You did! In not telling them what an amazing artist you are."

"What?" Otar asked at the same time as Andres laughed. He patted Otar on the shoulder and with a wave walked away.

"Don't leave me alone here!" Otar shouted after him.

Andres turned around again, walking backward for a few steps. "You have this well in hand." He called for his hunters and was gone.

Otar turned with a sigh and found that all the women had moved closer, forming a half-circle around him and Onder. Their bodies were strung tight with anticipation, but there was also hesitation on their faces.

"But I only have this black pencil, no colors."

Onder translated, easily slipping between the Trade Common and the guttural tribe language. "It doesn't matter, we know the colors," Onder translated their answer.

Otar licked his lips nervously. "I hope I'll be able to do them justice."

Onder relayed that, and a few of them laughed, while the younger ones wore rosy cheeks.

"I'm sure you will try your best." Onder chuckled.

"Okay," Otar said, but his eyes went to the half-finished garment.

"Don't worry, it's not needed yet."

Otar knew he shouldn't ask, but he did. "What is it?"

There was one possibility. Usually, only one type of garment got that much attention in every culture he visited.

"A wedding mantle."

"Ah." His mind whirled with all the unasked questions, but he shook himself out of it and looked around. The light was good enough for embroidering, so it would be alright for drawing them. "If they want to change into something special, they should do so now."

Onder told them. The tribe tongue flowed in an almost sing-song melody, hypnotic and strange. Memories rose in his mind of flickering fires and a voice singing him to sleep.

The women shook their heads. They carefully folded the mantle up and made space to sit down on the cushions, facing Otar and Onder eagerly.

Otar smiled. He'd never drawn another person while they sat for the drawing. He was only an observer—always looking in, catching workers in their grueling labor, craftsmen in concentration, priests mid-sermon; but the process was still the same. He settled down and sketched.

He got lost in his work as he always did, be it his research in dusty libraries, exploring unknown ruins, or tracking down long forgotten legends. His mind sharpened, time flying past. Every time he finished a page, he handed it over to the waiting woman, and another one would take the place directly in front of him. They smiled and glowed, their eyes sparkling with satisfied pleasure. They kept talking and joking in the background, and once more Otar was gripped by their energy, so different from the people he had encountered before.

From time to time men and women would pass and call out to them, probably something teasing, and they shouted back and giggled, until an older woman, the one with the nose ring, would call them to a semblance of order.

It never held long.

After Otar handed over the last sketch, the women bowed and then scattered to attend to their duties. When he looked at his hands, flexing his fingers to loosen the tight muscles, he found dark smudges, blackened from the coal. These fingers brought joy, with just a few strokes on paper, and yet it felt so strange—these hands had also killed. Even if it was the monster, it was a part of him, and he did not try to stop it. Would he kill again? He wanted to deny it, but couldn't. Slowly, he was losing who he really was. Was he Otar the scholar? Otar the orphan? Otar the lover? Otar the traveler? Otar the murderer? Otar the—

"You good?" Andres crouched before him, watching him with worried eyes.

Was he? He searched inside him, poked the monster, which only grumbled back. Since arriving at the tribe, it had behaved more like an overgrown cat than the terrifying thing it had been for most of Otar's life—a fearsome force that acted on its own. The monster settled, leaving him for once with a strange, content feeling.

Some of it must have shown on Otar's face, because Andres' shoulders relaxed. "You must be hungry."

Right before Otar could deny it, his stomach growled.

Andres snorted and then helped Otar up again. He dragged him through the middle of the camp to the communal fire.

Dusk had risen, and Otar made out the first stars sprinkling across the dark blue sky. He always wondered if those small dots meant there were more worlds like this with people like him. When he was young, he had often stretched his hand out to the firmament, not sure if he had wanted to grab the stars or be grabbed by them.

Five women tended to the fire and the food, the aroma of fresh bread and stew heavy in the air making his mouth water. Andres pressed him down into a cushion next to Onder.

Onder smiled at him, while three other steppe riders who were in a conversation with Onder when Andres approached with Otar eyed him curiously. One was a big woman with curly hair; another was a broader man with laugh lines around his eyes; and the last one was a haggard man with a constant frown. They all wore the same cluster of golden beads Andres and Onder wore— the markings of the leaders.

Otar resisted the urge to hunch his shoulders making himself smaller under their scrutinizing gazes and forced himself to settle in a comfortable seat.

"You ready for tomorrow, visitor?" The woman asked in slightly broken Common, her dark eyes burrowing into his soul.

"Tomorrow?" Apprehension rose in him.

"The travel north, to the ruins, no?" She flicked her gaze to Onder, who rolled his eyes and smiled ruefully at Otar.

"We wanted to tell you after the meal," he said pointedly, while the female leader shrugged her shoulders.

The broad man leaned forward, his gaze apologetic. "It is time for us to move. The ground has tired of the tribe, and the family is getting restless."

"Leader Andres is needed elsewhere," the haggard man added, as if they were trying to convince Otar to let

Andres go. As if he were holding him back. The haggard man took a sip from his cup. "His betrothed is waiting."

Otar interlaced his fingers in his lap to hide the sudden tremble in them. "Who will accompany me?" Surely after what had happened, they wouldn't send him out alone.

Onder mock saluted. "I drew the short straw," he said with a laugh—it was all a joke to them, and Otar was the punchline.

His appetite was gone, and everything inside him was falling apart. Why was he still doing this to himself? He rose slowly, measuring every movement, and bowed to the leaders.

"Please excuse me. I will turn in early." He pivoted and left.

No one called him back.

Even with the flap dropping close behind him, Otar could hear them laughing and singing. He stopped in the middle of the tent, closed his eyes, and breathed. He tried to make sense of himself and the world around him. The ground was grabbing for him, taking, taking— the hunger roared to life, gnawing at his insides, poised to devour his blood and skin and meat and bones— until there was nothing left to give.

He was a lost boy, left on the outside, always the intruder looking in. On trembling legs, he crossed to the bed and sank down, burying his head in his hands.

He would never belong.

At the sound of the flap moving, he looked up. Andres stepped through, carrying two bowls of stew in one hand and bread in the other. His face was unreadable.

He settled down on the carpet and put one bowl down while taking the other. Otar didn't move.

"Come, you need to regain your health," Andres chided and began to eat.

"So that I can be finally shipped off."

But Andres didn't rise to the bait and kept eating.

Otar sighed. Even with his stomach in knots and his appetite gone, he was hungry, and he conceded he needed to build up his strength again.

With great reluctance did he rise again and settle down opposite Andres, taking up the second bowl. The stew was tangy and spicy and Otar knew he would miss it, the same as he would miss the tribe—or more the sense of community, family, home…not that they had ever wanted him to stay.

A home… His family loved him, but he had been brought in. His father had found him wandering around in a forest in the north, alone and dirty and confused. No one from the nearby settlement had claimed him as theirs, so his father took him home to his wife and daughters. The village made room for him, and yet with his pale skin, his golden, almost white, hair and his lanky build, he stood out. Perhaps if that had been all, he could have settled, but he was curious, always wondering what lay beyond the next bend in the road, the forest, the horizon.

When he came across an injured Aaoran in the forest close to his village, he didn't think twice about bringing them in while pestering them with all the questions, about their dark skin, the strange clothing, the rings in his ears. Aaoran, blessed by the lords, showed more patience than anyone had ever had before, answering every single question. Then they took him with them to the nearby ruin, Bakusaran—there everything began.

Soon after, Otar had stepped out of his home village for good and never looked back.

Maybe he could have found a home in Rasanell, but that tie broke as well and he drifted untethered—until Andres.

In him, Otar found something he didn't know he had craved, a connection that took and gave in equal measures. On their travels, he'd never been hungry, neither inside nor in his mind. He had been sated, content.

But he had seen his own feelings too late. His fear obscured everything.

Otar scraped the last bits of vegetables out of his bowl and chased down the sauce dregs with the remaining bread.

"Talk to me," Andres said in a rough voice, his gaze heavy.

"I knew that this turn would come soon."

"We wanted to tell you in a more gentle way. Leader Amadea stepped out of line."

"She only spoke the truth." Otar avoided Andres' gaze. "It doesn't matter."

"Otar." How could his name be spoken with so many emotions at once?

"Is it true then?" His eyes flicked to Andres' furrowed brows.

"What is true?" There was genuine confusion.

"That you are to be wed." All the questions he had shunned when Onder told him that it was a wedding mantle the women had been working on. Elaborate enough for someone high in the tribe hierarchy. His mind had suspected instantly, but having it laid out like this hurt.

"Otar."

"For once answer me!" Otar hissed, anger boiling through his veins. Everything he feared was being confirmed. He was too late, and any dream he may have held was now shattered—all he wanted was the truth.

Andres closed his eyes and nodded. Otar wondered why the admission could still shake him to his very core.

It did make sense. Not that he had expected to fall right back into Andres' arms, not like this. Maybe, he'd thought, he could persuade the other man over time, through letters and visits, but Andres was more distant than five summers ago. Less easy going, less amicable.

This was the end, wasn't it?

"I see."

Andres fiddled with his spoon. "Do you want me to go?"

There would be nothing more to gain here, nothing would come out of it—Otar would leave in the morning, and Andres would travel far and wide and get married, start a family, lead the tribe, fight its wars, and surely he'd rise above them all. And Otar? He would just be a distant, maybe even bittersweet, memory.

And yet, tonight, no promises were made that couldn't be broken. No one had fully claimed Andres—no one but Otar.

Otar swallowed and said, "Stay."

Chapter 12

"I left, Otar. I packed my bag and I left, setting out as you have done. The only regret I have is that I could never apologize to you. My father told me what you have done for me, the potion that would ease my nightmares and help with the lingering fear. But no one could or wanted to tell me where you had gone to, so I can just write this down and hope one turn this letter will find you."

(From: Marit's unsent letters to the scholar Otar)

WHEN OTAR WOKE alone, he knew it was time to say goodbye to an impossible dream. He climbed out of bed, washed up, put on his clothes, and gathered his things.

Andres and Onder had given him a new pack and a few more replacement items for the ones that the slavers had destroyed. He fingered the small leather pouch with the remaining blue bead—he debated with himself, but this was the last opportunity, and why hold on to something he would otherwise never pass along? So before he could decide against it, he put it on the table and left.

When he stepped out, half of the camp was already dismantled and stored in pull wagons.

"You should have woken me," he told Onder, who was standing beside the flap.

"You're still recovering, and it's early enough."

"Andres is out?"

Onder nodded.

Otar considered that for a long moment. "Let us ride then."

Onder watched him, Otar could feel his gaze burning into him, but the other said nothing and instead led them to two waiting yardar already saddled, provisions secured. Otar resisted the urge to check the water flasks. It would be a grave insult to the people who had saved him, but it agitated him.

"You can look at the flasks," Onder drawled from the side and Otar blushed, his stare must have been obvious.

"It's not you or the tribe," Otar said slowly, looking over at Onder.

Onder shrugged. "I understand."

Still, Otar resisted, the indecision paralyzing him.

Onder stepped closer and laid a gentle hand on Otar's shoulder. Then he moved to the pack and took out the flasks, inspecting them himself before he stored them back with care.

"Thank you," Otar forced out through his clenched jaw, his fingers twitching at the side. Onder only patted him on the back and then moved to his own yardar, checking the flasks as well.

Otar seized the reins of his beast and mounted the animal with one smooth movement, turned it, and looked down at Onder, who had his eyebrows raised.

"What?"

"I'm impressed." He grinned. "You've come a long way since you were that gangly kid that tagged along with Aaoran and who had never ridden a yardar before."

Otar blushed again and turned his head away, shrugging. "I picked up a few things while traveling."

Onder grinned, then he called a few words to the people loading up a wagon. They shouted back and waved. Then he mounted his own yardar, and together they set out into the rising sun.

THE TERRAIN WAS made of smooth rolling hills, filled with sand, rocks, and pebbles, overgrown with yellow grass and low scrubs. Lizards scurried away at their approach, forming rippling patterns in sandy patches. In the distance, the slender silhouette of a steppe wolf weaved through the shadows of large desert palm trunks.

After a few miles, Onder pointed out a stone marker. "We are now on the main road."

Otar squinted, but there was nothing discernible that could be called a road. There were only more hills, more grass, and even more sand.

Onder laughed when he remarked on that.

"We call them main roads. They're paths that have proven to be safe enough. We mark them down on maps, and pass them around."

Otar nodded in understanding.

"And don't fear, I have traveled back and forth to the ruins in the last big-turns. I know the way."

They settled into an easy but steady pace. Otar suspected Onder wanted to spare him as best as possible. While coddling peeved him, it also allowed him more observations. His previous journey through the steppe had been fueled by the concern about the water and filled with trading stories about their travels as a distraction, but nothing more about the steppe itself, and when he had fled, taking in the sights had been the last thing on his mind.

When the sun slipped low and the darkness was crawling in, they stopped at a spring a few paces from the main road. There was a stone outcropping, a small stream leading away, and a shallow natural pool. The stone overhang created an almost cave like environment, which would protect them from an attack from behind.

After Onder pointed out that any smoke would be visible for miles, they did not light a fire. They feasted on cheese, baked bread, apples, and, in Onder's case, dried yardar meat.

Exhausted, Otar rolled himself into his bedding and then turned onto his back, his eyes seeking the blinking stars.

Many had tried to explain what they were. Some said the lords put them there, and others claimed the Ancients had painted them to give the people something to look at. Others like Otar wondered if they were worlds, just like their own.

When he looked at them for too long, a falling sensation started in his navel. It was as if the sky was pulling him in, and he wasn't lying on the ground anymore but turned up-side down. Beckoning him closer and closer, singing a sweet song about adventures and mysteries, whispering words of comfort, speaking of…home.

"Otar," Onder's soft voice broke the spell.

Otar blinked, and he let the thoughts go. He turned his head, but in the darkness, it was difficult to make out Onder's dark eyes.

Onder was sitting upright, his back against the stones, using their sun-baked warmth and his bedroll around his shoulders to keep him comfortable enough through the freezing night. Taking the watch hadn't been a question for him—he would take all the watches, he had told Otar when he protested. Onder assured him he was trained to be awake for long periods of time, a few turns would be nothing.

Their eyes met.

"Please forgive him."

Otar exhaled. "What is there to forgive?" Andres had chosen, and it wasn't him. It hurt, it hurt so much, and yet Otar didn't regret it. He had told Andres what he felt, and now he could move forward. The time for "What if's" and "What could have been's" over.

He closed his eyes.

Onder never answered him back.

OVER THE NEXT two turns, nothing changed. They traveled the steppe at a steady pace on an invisible road, settling down for the night in a semi-protected spot, forgoing a fire every time as the nights were cloud free.

Onder tried to engage Otar more than once in a discussion about Andres and him, but Otar changed the subject to cultural insights or threw in a question about an animal or plant he had seen out of the corner of his eyes and didn't yet know about.

The third night they settled down, Onder handed Otar his food and said, "Andres has his reasons."

"Good for him," Otar muttered, filling his mouth with oat cake to stop himself from blurting out more.

"Otar."

Otar swallowed, fed up. "Stop it. He has chosen and made that choice clear." He took a swig from the water flask to wash down the oat cake. "I don't know what you think you know, but we didn't part as lovers. There was never a promise. I discovered my own feelings too late, and Andres has now moved on. So it's all good and I'll survive. And one turn, all this will be in the past. So by the lords, let me be, and let it rest."

Silence settled between them. Otar almost regretted his outburst, but he was done.

Onder didn't move, his gaze frozen on Otar. Then, he put his food down and opened a leather pouch clipped to his belt. He fished out a smaller bag and held it out to Otar, who eyed it warily as he took it. Half expecting to find a bead inside, he shook out its contents. Instead, it was a small round stone on a leather band. The stone glinted blueish in the fading sunlight, the hue close to the bead he had left behind. He stroked his fingers over it and caught ridges. When he held it closer to his eyes, he could make out symbol-like characters etched into it all over.

"What is it?" He looked up at Onder, his fingers running over the lines.

"A gift from Andres," Onder said with great reluctance. He looked like a man who had not only lost a battle but an entire war.

Otar looked at the stone, then back at Onder, puzzled by Onder's reaction.

"You look unhappy. Should I not accept it?"

That earned him a raised eyebrow and a faint twinkle in Onder's eyes. "Would serve him right," he muttered under his breath, but he didn't elaborate. He sighed and looked up into the sky. "It shows that my brother is a bigger fool than I had thought possible."

Otar kept staring at him, but Onder returned to his meal, eating in silence. After it was clear the other wouldn't say more, Otar studied the stone, wondering what the characters meant. There wasn't much in terms of a recorded tribe language; agreements between the tribes were written either in General Common or more often in Trade Common. Internally in tribes, stories, legends, and rules were communicated verbally, often in tales and sometimes in woven patterns.

What should he do with Andres' gift? He sneaked back a look at the other, but even after he had finished his meal, Onder resolutely avoided his gaze and stared out over the steppe.

Following an impulse, Otar slipped the leather cord over his neck and put the stone under his shirt. It settled over his heart, warming to the temperature of his skin—soon it felt as if it had always been there.

AT AROUND MIDTURN of the fourth turn, Onder pointed out a mountain range in the distance behind which the ruins lay. Together they estimated they would make it by nightfall.

Otar was thankful because he was exhausted. Everything in his body hurt—his butt, his thighs, his back was one big throbbing mess. How a few middle-turns of not being able to move had reduced him to this bundle of pain grated.

"Are you sure about nightfall?" he asked, more to distract himself from the pain than for Onder to confirm, even if it seemed impossible far.

"Only if we don't take a break."

That would hurt, but then they would also be safe. Otar didn't want to admit it, but being caught by slavers had shaken him in a way nothing had ever before, and with the tribe he had felt protected. Enough warriors and people around him to step in if someone came. But out here? It took everything in him not to jump at shadows that moved, and he knew his nights had not been as restful as he would have liked, even if Onder never said a thing. But there was an understanding glint in his eyes every morning.

Thunder rolled.

They both looked at each other and then turned in their saddles to look back. Dark clouds gathered, piling higher and higher into an ominous anvil-like shape. Lightning flashed, and more thunder traveled over the steppe, loud and booming. The yardar shook themselves at the sudden sound, but remained calm.

Onder cursed and checked the landscape beyond the side of the road. "We could seek higher ground and wait out the storm, or we go for it."

Otar looked back once more and tried to make out their distance from the storm. He had experienced thunderstorms in jungles and mountains, but Andres had told him that out here they moved differently and could literally drown you.

"You think we could make it to Adabel?"

The clouds came rapidly closer; at the next deafening thunder, the yardar danced anxiously on their feet.

"We'll get drenched to the bone, but we should be able to outpace its center."

"Let's go."

Onder snarled, and the yardar picked up the pace. Yardar were sturdy mounts but bred for long-term running and not sprinting. Stubborn creatures who would rather bury their feet in the sand than follow commands that exhausted them. But out here they didn't disobey and ran faster and faster, never slowing down.

The hard ride aggravated every muscle in Otar's body, but the quickening thunder and blinding, almost staccato-like lightning, spoke of the urgency that they needed to make it to shelter. It felt like turns before they finally raced into the mountain landscape. The rain reached them before they made it to the opening that would lead them deeper into the mountains to the excavation camp. Cold hard drops pelted down on them, drenching them to the bone, as Onder had predicted. Otar was sure he looked like a drowned rat.

Two guards who had sought shelter behind a stone wall, shielded halfway in, still checked them over, before ushering them through. More sentries eyed them from different hideaways along the path and above them. But then one of them recognized Onder, calling something down in Tribe, and Onder laughed before answering back. The remaining guards, relaying the news from one to the other, had friendlier faces, but they never took their eyes off the newcomers.

As soon as they were through and out in the open again, people came running. After Otar dismounted, dark fabric and the smell of sun and spices engulfed him.

Otar hugged his mentor back. "I have arrived, Aaoran-peras."

Chapter 13

"Don't think I didn't see the new earring in your right ear. There was just no time to mention it or to even congratulate you. I wonder if you ever thought that life for you would turn out like this when I found you injured in the forest and brought you to Doctor Mare. And now you are wearing the token of his affection as your tradition demands. I congratulate you two. I know with you traveling all the time it hasn't been easy, but I'm very happy that the Doctor takes you on your own terms."

(From: Aaoran-peras' private collection of letters from the scholar Otar)

AFTER AAORAN COULD be convinced to let Otar go, the rain coming down hard still, Aaoran led him into the heart of the camp. Dozens of tents in all shapes and colors were clustered there under a massive stone overhang, barely supported by thin, rocky columns carved out by wind and rain. Onder detached himself from the group and pointed to a setup that looked more tribal, mentioning that he would ride back with first light. Aaoran nodded at that, and with a wave, Onder was gone.

It took a dizzying number of lefts and rights before Aaoran deposited Otar in a small tent, almost all the way at the back of the encampment, and promised to send someone with something to warm him up and that they would talk later.

Despite its size, the tent was comfortable, and more important, dry. It had a low bed, a table with a chair, and a trunk. Otar put his pack down and pulled out all his meager belongings, kept dry by oilcloth, and stared at them. He was grateful to be alive and yet, losing all the tools ached; they had been the first thing he had bought when he arrived at Rasanell, it had made his new path in life so more real. Perhaps Aaoran could spare some before he was able to buy some from a merchant.

He slipped out of his wet clothing, hung them up over the chair, and then put on the ones given to him by the tribe. They were sturdy enough but Otar was hesitant to use them for crawling around in a ruin, as they were of finer quality then his other clothes, and a gift. Another thing he needed to inquire about with Aaoran: new clothes.

He slipped into the shirt, undergarments and the slightly loose pants, leaving out the heavy coat with an expensive-looking waxed outer layer—Otar had resisted taking it, but Andres had insisted. Now Otar was even more grateful for it—should the rain persist; he would at least stay somewhat dry.

The tent flap opened, and Aaoran stuck their head in, eyes closed. "Are you decent?"

Otar snorted. "I am."

Aaoran stepped in, water pooling at his feet, and closed the opening behind them. Sweeping a critical eye over him, Aaoran said, "You look ill."

Otar shrugged and busied himself with moving his things around. He pulled out a new notebook Andres had found somewhere and paper and pencil and set them out on the table, then shoved a few more pieces of clothing into the trunk, and finally set his pack beside the bed. "It has been rough. My strength is still not quite there, but it's getting better. We also crossed over in four turns."

Aaoran smiled grimly. "I won't insult you by asking if you're up to it, but are you sure you're up to the task?"

Otar raised an eyebrow, which seemed to convey the correct answer, as Aaoran nodded, satisfied.

"Let me know if you need a break. Onder told me it looked very bleak when they found you."

Otar sat down on his bed. "I remember little of it." There was darkness, and a voice, and something else, something intangible.

"Maybe it's for the better." Booming thunder almost obscured their words, followed by shouting and the noisy chatter of the yardar. Aaoran sighed, when they didn't shut up again. "I need to check this. Stay inside and get warm again. No sense in getting a coughing cold on top of that still healing injury."

After a stern gaze to drive their point home, Aaoran swept out.

Amused, Otar shook his head. Aaoran was still the same after all the summers they hadn't seen each other—a comforting thought that some things remained the same.

He checked his damp clothing, then skimmed through the notebook and the papers he had used for the wedding mantle sketches. He made a few notes.

Every time he glimpsed the elaborate piece of work, his stomach lurched, and after one too many times, he put the drawings to the side. Instead, he added a few observations from the journey through the steppe and sketched in rough strokes a few more of the animals he had spotted. A steppe wolf cub peeking out from a depression in the ground, a mouse scurrying past, a bird of prey soaring high in the sky.

Otar let his thoughts drift back to his stay with the tribe and found himself drawing some of Andres' newer tattoos, intricate patterns full of stories, shivering slightly as he remembered tracing them on skin, Andres' wild gaze, and the softness of his touch. The monster had feasted, and Otar had felt alive.

"Anyone in?" A thin voice called over the still booming thunder.

"Yes," Otar said, distracted.

A slender man bustled in with sparkling blue eyes and a ready smile. He was wrapped in what looked like a heavy tunic and a thick woolen mantle, water dripping down from his soft-looking hair.

"The head sent me to bring you food," he held up a tray.

Otar nodded and pointed next to him on the table. There was a bit of space left between the spread papers.

The man put the tray down and hovered at Otar's side.

"Anything else?" Otar asked after a few moments when the other didn't move.

"My name is Deron."

Otar stared at the other. He was exhausted, cold and hungry—he was in no mood for games.

The young man hovered a heartbeat longer, then his smile slipped when Otar said nothing else. He slumped his shoulders and slouched away.

Otar waited until the flap closed behind him, then he walked over and secured it.

The food he had brought was a porridge made from some unknown grain topped with a dark sauce and preserved vegetables; the tangy acidic taste strong on his tongue. It was a blander meal than the tribe had given him, but it was warm and filling and everything he needed at the moment, but it left him disappointed.

With a sigh, he pushed the empty bowl away and settled into the bed, burrowing down under layers of blankets and furs. He closed his eyes and listened to the pelting rain and moving thunder.

Now that he had finally arrived, excitement spread through his body. He was curious about what Aaoran wanted to show him. He was looking forward to exploring the ruin, ever hopeful he could pry some secrets out of the Ancients' long dead hands.

At the same time, he was lost, untethered, as if he was missing a part of himself, as if—

He forced his thoughts away from that slippery road and rolled onto his side, drawing up his knees. The thunder passed over them, the rain picked up, voices called outside—Otar concentrated on the noise and let it lull him to sleep.

THE VIBRATING SOUND of a gong woke Otar. He opened his blurry eyes and wondered where he was. The tent he had stayed in ten and six summers ago at the Bakusaran ruins? The different inns and caves he stayed in his travels? The tribe's tent? They all blurred together. In the last turns, his thoughts had become increasingly sluggish to keep up, the memories all overlapping each other, running into one big mess. Bit by bit, he was losing the grip of what was present and what was past. As if he had somehow reached the capacity of what his mind could hold.

Seeing things where nothing should be didn't help his state of mind. Things like the ghost in the ruins. The one in the mountains didn't had one. But would the ghost be waiting here? And if so, would it for once reveal some of its mysteries?

At the thought of it, the monster perked up, its tendrils reaching for something that wasn't there yet. Otar tried to suppress it again, but it only settled down a fraction and kept shimmering under the surface.

With a sigh, he peeled himself out of the bedding, feeling more rested than he had in a while. The air was cold and damp, but the thunderstorm seemed to have passed.

He washed his face and pulled a thick woolen shirt over the one he had slept in. When he slipped into his boots, he made a face at the lingering dampness in them and then stepped out.

Having inspected ruins on his own for the last summers, he had forgotten how overwhelming a whole dig site could be. People were already bright awake, hurrying in various directions, calling for each other in Common or more regional languages. A group of Peral scholars, somber in their black robes, stood around a table with notes thrown over it, locked into a heated discussion; workers armed with buckets and shovels marched into the direction where the ruins must lay, shoving each other and laughing; a merchant, just arriving through the passage he and Onder had ridden through the night before, was being led to a big tent, his yardar braying in agitation.

The gong sounded a second time, the last call for the morning meals, and Otar followed a stream of people hopefully in the direction of the kitchen tent. His stomach growled, and he was sure he would find Aaoran there, sweet-talking the kitchen matron into giving them a second or third portion—Aaoran was always hungry. They were seldom sitting still, constantly on the move, looking for something, inspecting, wondering— the same as Otar. It was probably why they got along so well.

Otar nodded at a few vaguely familiar faces. Scholars he might have encountered at the university in Rasanell, or at one of the ruins he had traveled to that had an excavation running. They greeted him back in the same superficial manner. Otar had never entrenched himself into the research circles, always staying apart to keep his own secrets from being discovered.

Because the ghost, which called itself Maugi, talked.

Otar hurried into the food line. A woman pushed a bowl with a grain porridge topped with nuts, dried fruits, and a small dollop of honey into his hands. He smiled his thanks before turning around and after a few more steps, claimed the first free seat he saw.

They'd put up rows of long tables, as well as areas with seat cushions for those that preferred sitting that way. For Otar it was a table, a bit off to the side, slightly obscured by the massive kitchen tent. He ate. Once more, he was missing the spices he had gotten used to in the last few turns with the tribe. And he should really stop comparing the food—he needed to let go and clinging to these thoughts wasn't helping.

A few moments later, a cup of brew was put before him, and another person sat down on the opposite side.

Otar eyed Onder. "I thought you'd already left." The sun had been up for a while now.

"Eager to get rid of me?" His tone was flippant, but harshness lingered on his face.

Yes. No. It was complicated. Otar settled on, "Maybe."

Onder, in the middle of taking a sip from his own cup, paused and let it sink. "That was the most honest word I have ever heard out of your mouth."

Otar rolled his eyes. His feelings for Andres and where they stood with each other were out in the open by his own doing. It was time to move on, and Onder was a literal reminder of what he couldn't have. Symbolical and physical—they were twins. Even if Onder didn't have the same scar, was thinner, and had different braids and tattoos.

Either way, his presence wasn't helping his peace of mind at all.

"Otar."

Otar swallowed and met his gaze. Onder smiled, but it held a painful edge. "It's alright, I understand more than you think."

Something heavy was pressing Onder down. It was unusual seeing the confident warrior so insecure.

"You know I was born as a sister to Andres, but I always wanted to be a brother. When I was very young, I fell in love with a boy from another tribe. We would meet at the trade markets and make plans, encouraged by our families, waiting until the winters would catch up, until we were old enough to be able to wed.

"When I decided not to be a sister anymore and became Andres' brother, my love wasn't able to accept it. Called me all the awful names people had thought up for those who were born different. It hurt, it still does, but I got over it and him." He smiled more genuinely. "So yes, I do understand the devastation of a broken heart."

Before Otar could say anything else, a voice cut in.

"Why are you looking so somber this early?"

They both looked over. Aaoran had arrived carrying a bowl that held twice as much porridge as had been in Otar's.

Otar grinned. "Morning greetings, peras."

Aaoran rolled their eyes and sat down beside Otar in one fluid motion.

"You haven't been my student in a long time. No need to greet me like that anymore, Otar."

"You took a chance on me, and I wish to honor that."

Aaoran shook their head and turned to Onder instead. "When will you set out?"

"As soon as I'm finished."

"Stop by the staff tent." Aaoran flicked a finger to the left, pointing out a bigger tent with a line in front. "They'll give you provisions as always, and a few letters for leader Andres and a few for other tribes. I'd be grateful if you could distribute them further."

Onder inclined his head in assent. "As you wish."

With that Aaoran rose, his bowl and cup of brew already empty. "Otar, a word?"

Otar scraped the last bits of his own food out, chugged down the brew, and stood. He looked at Onder, who winked at him.

"Stay safe," Otar said with a formal bow while holding the empty dishes.

"As you shall," Onder answered with smiling eyes.

OTAR BROUGHT HIS used utensils to the designated collection area and joined Aaoran, who talked to a passing group of scholars. When Otar drew close, they excused themselves and waved Otar closer.

"Tell me, how are you really feeling?"

Otar started walking with Aaoran falling into step beside him. "It has been a couple of eventful big-turns."

"Found anything special on your last trip before getting knocked out?"

Otar eyed them from the side, but there was nothing on Aaoran's face that indicated that he knew what had transpired in the mountains. Not trusting his voice (Aaoran had always read the lies in his tone), he shook his head.

Aaoran clapped their hands together and smiled gleefully. "Well, but I have, and I dare to say it'll be a treat for you."

They stopped by Otar's tent so he could collect his notebook and pencil, then Aaoran led him out back to the passage. Otar commented on his lost tools, and Aaoran assured him the staff would see to his needs.

They stepped onto the main path, which started at the crevasse and went in a straight line past the camp, further into the distance. Otar could make out another, much narrower crevasse. There, the road passed through a second rock formation.

Stone blocks as tall as Otar, driven into the ground, paved the way. They fit neatly together, the seam lines hair thin, as if it was one big slab of stone. He crouched down and brushed the dirt and sand to the side, letting his fingers graze the stone under it. It was smooth.

"The Ancients built it?" he said half to himself and half to Aaoran.

His mentor hunched down beside him and nodded. "So far, we haven't been able to determine why. As you saw, they didn't build any roads to or from the ruins, only a few pathways between the outer buildings. This one leads all the way to the main dome. There is nothing in the canyon and beyond, in either direction."

Otar looked up and down the road. Then he fished out his notebook, scribbled down a few words, and made quick sketches with more notes, which he would fill out later with more details.

"This is remarkable," he muttered. Everything that deviated from the norm was noteworthy. Even if they were left with more puzzle pieces and no clue as to how they all fit together.

"Ah, don't use up all your excitement! There is more to come."

Otar studied them. Aaoran was almost giddy with anticipation. He narrowed his eyes at them while he rose. Aaoran pointed down the road to the other crevasse and, with their other hand, patted him on the shoulder.

"My dear friend, my most beloved student, this, I promise you by the lords, will be the best turn of your life."

Chapter 14

"Onder told me you are currently in the southern jungles at the Blue Mountain ridges, and if this letter finds you in time, may I ask a favor? You might remember my student Otar. He is on an extended excursion through the southern jungles, close to the Green River, and I worry about him being alone while researching crumbling stone and unknown regions. If you could check up on him, I would be most grateful. The last known location…"

(From: "Letters to Andres", Vol. 2)

THE SUN SIGNIFICANTLY changed its place in the sky when they finally arrived at the stone gate. Otar was hot and sweaty. At least the way through the hill had brought a moment of sweet relief. Walking downhill in the blistering heat had taxed him, but he had enough energy left to gape at the sudden stone gate.

"A gate?" That was also unprecedented. The Ancients ruins followed a rather formulaic pattern, depending on their magnitude. A cluster of low buildings in a dense rectangle form, cut through with five main roads that originated in a star-like arrangement from a middle spot—the main dome. Those were the big ruins. Of them, they only ever found a handful. More common were the smaller ones. They exhibited the same type of central dome, often in the same size, but fewer constructions clustered around it. Roughly half of the ruins, they found somewhat intact, were just the dome alone. The assumption was that this central building was the point of origin from which the ruins grew in a strict pattern depending on how big the population would be.

Otar stepped closer to the archway. It had no doors and was made of the same smooth rock as the road. Beige stones, not showing even the slightest tool usage from the masons. With no visible seam lines, the blocks fit together like puzzle pieces. The gate straddling the road didn't show that there had ever been something inside the arch to close the way. And yet it must have a meaning.

"Why put a gate here?" Otar asked while he made more sketches. There wasn't a sign of a wall or a fence. One could circle it completely with no obstacle. Scholars and workers flowed around them; some nodded at Aaoran, who smiled back.

"You'll find that many things are different here." Their voice held a peculiar note.

Otar squinted at them, taking in the barely contained tremors running through their body and the sparkle in their eyes.

"Oh." He said and turned around, taking it all in. "You think this is Eitin, the first settlement." He blinked. "But—"

Aaoran shook their head. "We don't know if Eitin was the first. And therefore I sent for you. Regardless, you should have been here right from the beginning."

The legends about the Ancients were as clear as they could be. The texts and stories called them travelers, arriving from the east, from beyond the Great Ocean. They settled on these shores and then spread out through the Seven Lands, until they disappeared one turn, leaving nothing behind beside slowly crumbling stones. Some myths and old scrolls referenced one city, the biggest and most amazing a person could ever lay eyes on, filled with wondrous and impossible things. The text fragments called it Eitin, the only surviving city name. Scholars contested if it really was an Ancients name, or a name that the people later had given it.

Either way, it had never been found, and nothing they discovered did the descriptions justice. Some thought it might be up in the northern mountains, buried under snow and ice, in one of the thousands of hidden valleys and crevasses; others searched for it in the southern jungles hidden under the thick green canopies; some suspected it to be in the waters on the coast, believing it must have sunk into the sea. Finding nothing put a damper on that research. Money dried up, and the scholars turned to other fields of interests.

When his Imperial Heir Jasner and his right-hand man and adviser Turas sparked a new interest, fresh funds came in and scholars spread through the Seven Lands again.

Otar's eyes roamed as they walked through the gate and down the rest of the road. They encountered the same narrow buildings as in the other ruins, not higher than three stories, interconnected by a dizzying number of stairs and small bridges—everything in pristine condition.

The main road led down to the dome-structure. The central one was the biggest, its sides each nestled a smaller one. They were connected by a small bridge on both sides. The main dome counted eight spires curving over the top, with the smaller domes having four. On top sat a smaller spire pointing into the sky. So far, all domes they'd discovered sprouted such spires, but always fewer than eight.

The sun was hitting the stone from behind, invoking the faint glimmer many ruins showed. A handful were built from a grayer stone, usually the ones in the mountains, but a number of those had darkened with time with plants growing over them or encrusted with moss and dirt.

They never found the building material in a natural environment, and analyses had given no answers about its composition.

Another mystery atop so many. It was as if everything else would unravel should they ever be able to answer just one of the thousands of questions.

Aaoran led him down the pathway to the main dome. Along it, workers shoveled sand and scientists crawled like ants over every inch, shouting measurements to each other. Artists made sketches from all angles. From time to time, Aaoran would point something out, and Otar wrote a quick note or did a hasty sketch of his own.

At first glance, Adabel was in perfect condition. One more mystery scholars didn't understand. Some ruins appeared as if the Ancients had built them yesterturn, while others had crumbled to dust heaps. A popular thesis was that they had been protected by some kind of magic that must have run out or failed for those that were now destroyed. But there was no evidence.

Otar kept silent about his own theories, as voicing them would open a box of fishing worms he could never close again.

They both sighed with relief when they stepped out of the sun's heat into the cooler and darker interior of the central dome. It was almost gloomy. A multitude of witch lights swaying around gave it an eerie atmosphere. Still, Otar's eyes needed a moment to adjust to the difference, before he could take the structure in.

A dome was the primary building of an Ancients ruin. Every domed building was perfectly round, not even a speck off. The floor was always tiled in a dark blue mosaic, with the tiles not being larger than Otar's hand. The main wall on which the dome rested circled the entire floor. Painted onto it, running the whole circumference, covering the complete wall, was a mural depicting flowers, plants and animals, and strange things, no one had ever seen or recorded in the Seven Lands.

Otar could name them all.

A popular theory was that this flora and fauna were long extinct; others hypothesized that they'd be found in the lands beyond the ocean, where the Ancients hailed from. A few in the minority waved it all away, scoffing that they were entirely made up.

Aaoran led him over to the pictures and Otar's eyes sought out the strange symbols that accompanied each of the different drawings automatically, forming words that echoed in his mind.

Attraquer. Ziarav. Beltrider.

Words he wasn't able to match to Common or any other language whispered in his mind. For him, they were just empty names.

In every dome, though, they were the same. At least they usually were.

Otar frowned at the thought and stepped closer. The words were the same, he was sure, and yet…he crooked his head and squinted.

He sidestepped a scholar who was crouching down to copy a tree-like plant called *Edes*. Otar was now almost touching the wall with his nose and turned his face this way and that.

"What do you see?" Aaoran had followed him.

Wasn't that a strange question? Otar put it to the side and concentrated.

"They are the same," he said slowly, "but there is something…" He fished out his notebook and, after scanning through it, cursed. The relevant notes were stored at the university. "I think they're different. Tiny changes." He pointed to the plant that was called *Ziarav*. A blueish-purple flower with five buds and dark green leaves with thin yellow stripes. He remembered counting those buds in all the ruins he'd gotten access to, writing the amount repeatedly: Five buds, three leaves, with each leaf having three stripes.

This flower was painted with four buds and three stripes, and while that number matched, the stripes ended halfway up the leaves.

Aaoran put their head right next to Otar's, squinting their eyes. "I can't be sure myself. I'll tell the other scholars to make a comparison. We have some sketches with us which were taken from other ruins. We should have a result pretty soon."

Otar hummed in confirmation, his mind already working on coming up with a conclusion—were these painted first and then copied over? And if so, why? And how?

Aaoran waved someone over and instructed them to compare the pictures. Then they tapped Otar on the shoulder.

"There is more to see."

Otar raised an eyebrow. More? How could there be more? And why did they only discover this now, when Adabel had been known for a while?

Aaoran guided him with a light touch to his lower back, around the bustling scholars and then to the small opening that would lead them down a staircase to the deeper levels. They stopped short at the level with monochromatic chambers—they didn't seem to differ from those in the other ruins. Otar made a mental note to take a closer look, to be sure.

They walked the rest of the stairs down and found themselves in front of two massive stone doors propped open. A slew of witch lights swarmed around.

"The lights aren't working?"

Aaoran looked at him and then back into the chamber. "No, we haven't been able to revive any of the energy systems."

Sometimes ruins burst to life when anyone entered them, yet more often they remained dormant or dead—like the one in the mountains. He always shuddered when he went into one.

They stepped onto the even ground and further into what Otar thought of as the heart of the ruins. It was a circular room located under the main dome and was about the same size. It varied, but was never off by too much. The middle points always matched.

Just off the threshold, Aaoran turned them around and pointed to the opposite, there half-hidden behind the stairs, was a closed second stone door.

"I'm assuming this is the gate to the sibling dome?"

"Yes, there is another one beyond this chamber."

"And the bridges outside?"

Aaoran spread their fingers. "There is nothing in the ceiling that indicates there is a way out, and we couldn't check the smaller domes. These doors seem to be the only point of entry, but they're shut tight."

Otar furrowed his brows, looking back to the center. "The main chamber was just open?"

Aaoran nodded.

Then they walked inside. Scholars and workers surveyed every inch here. As soon as they stepped closer to the well, Otar held his breath, waiting with trepidation for the ghost to come—and found himself equally disappointed and relieved when nothing happened.

The monster rattled around agitated once more, grasping for something that wasn't there, just as it did in the mountain ruin. Otar pushed that firmly to the side, and after another burst of reaching, the monster settled down.

Otar looked up, fearing red eyes peeking once more down at him, but all he'd see was the rough stone of the ceiling.

The chamber was as overwhelming as the dome above. Tiny white tiles gave the ground a scaled look. From the middle, thick black lines fanned out in a star pattern to the walls—a star with too many beams. Otar never counted so many. A lot of the other ruins had a handful, but this seemed to be, at first glance, more than two dozen.

Along those lines, the Ancients had scribbled more of those tiny symbols that they had also painted onto the mural walls.

More words and names, Otar knew.

Pahrasha. Escrin. Zydarra. Leontar.

The symbols, or maybe letters, were strange and foreign in his thoughts, forming impressions of cities and landscapes. His eyes stopped at a thicker line with a small border around it, which was almost imperceivable in the dim light. His gaze stopped at a name for several small-turns before his mind accepted what he was reading.

Eitin.

Otar swallowed. He searched for Aaoran, but his mentor had moved further to the middle. Otar hurried after them. They stopped at what the scholars had named the well. A round translucent area that glowed in a soft blue when the ruin was alive. Here it was dark, indicating it either was dead or had run out of energy. Otar looked down at the empty pool and then studied once more the lines that originated here.

After comparing maps and layouts, a scholar had discovered the markings corresponded with actual existing ruins. Following a line and walking straight, eventually the traveler would arrive at one.

At the end of the Zykara line laid Zyvkan, another ruin in the mountains in the west; Escrin was the line to Bakusaran, the excavation close to his own home village, and the first ruin he had ever entered; Pahrasha pointed to Patreshka. Which was ironic because scholars had written many theses about the question: Was the principal city of the steppe built upon a ruin? They never found a ruin on the line, just rocks and caves and at the end, Patreshka. But they could never satisfactorily prove that a ruin lay under the city.

Otar could lay all those speculations to rest, but that would reveal his ability to vocalize the symbols, and he was still grappling with the implication of that after all these summers.

All the time Aaoran was silent, but let Otar see and feel and experience. After a nod from him, Aaoran led him to the other side through the open door there and into the other staircase hall. As they'd said, there was another set of stone doors firmly closed.

Ruins were symmetric, everything had an opposite in the same shape and form.

They climbed up the stairs and through the main dome and walked back out into the sun. Otar soaked up the warmth. There was something peculiar in staying an extended period of time in the dim light or even in the darkness of a ruin. It latched onto them, claiming pieces of those that walked in them, chilling them down to the very bones. Otar thought back to what he had encountered with Marit in the mountains, the black shadows coming for him. Had that really happened? At least Marit had seen it as well, so…

"This is all for the moment."

Otar blinked, his thoughts returning to the conversation. "I think this is quite enough."

Aaoran chuckled.

"Aaoran, I grant you that this is one of the greatest finds we have ever made, but why did you call for me?" He wasn't a scholar of the university anymore, but more of a rogue researcher not outwardly bound to the enforced rules to be allowed into the dig sites. No one denied him access when he asked about taking a closer look. He suspected Turas' and maybe Aaoran's influence there, but the higher ups must have vetoed the decision to invite him here.

"Besides being one of the most knowledgeable experts on the topic?"

"My opinion does not carry much weight."

Aaoran shrugged in a lazy way that showed that nothing of this mattered to them. "You have already proved that calling for you was the right thing. You've seen a difference no one else has remarked on so far.

And you have never laughed at my more silly theories. I want you to find out if this is the first—if this is Eitin."

"That's a tall order, and a futile one," Otar said. Eitin, as the line showed, must lie somewhere else. But he couldn't tell Aaoran that, it would reveal his secrets.

But even if this wasn't Eitin, it was something different, something worthy to take a closer look at.

Aaoran looked around and then back at Otar. "This time I'm sure we will uncover some of those tightly guarded secrets."

Otar thought back to the underground chamber, and the line to Eitin, thought once more about the shadows haunting him, and further back when he'd first encountered the ghost that spoke to him in riddles and unknown words.

He shook his head. "Be careful what you wish for, peras."

Aaoran's eyes twinkled.

Chapter 15

"Words. They form words in my mind. I can read them, I can read whatever the Ancients have written on the walls of the murals. I'm baffled. It is all gibberish to me, I can't translate them, but I know them deep inside me. I asked Maugi about it. But it just repeated the names—which gave me confirmation that I'm not imagining the words. How should I process this? How is this even possible? I haven't slept for turns trying to solve the puzzle, but I'm too much of a coward to allow myself the obvious conclusion."

(Notebook burned)

After that, Aaoran left Otar alone to explore. Otar wandered around, peered over the shoulders of workers and scholars, inspected corners, and took a deeper look at the colored chambers.

A kind soul gave him a preliminary map copy so he could mark down his findings, and those others told him about. He made a note of the different murals, the strange bridges on the outside dome, and the line to Eitin. He didn't write Eitin on his plan directly but marked the lines' differences and the direction it was going with question marks.

When he passed a group of scholars in front of the right-handed smaller dome, chatter about restoring the energy drifted over. They wanted to get the lights on, and, even more importantly, the closed doors to open. A scholar told Otar that the gates were made of stone blocks, beautifully carved but impregnable. Getting through them the old-fashioned way with a pick and a hammer would take time.

But how did one restore energy that was believed to be run on magic without enough magic to actually do something? Fueling the witch lights was easy, but funneling the necessary amount into the ruins to make them light up was impossible—at least for them.

Otar turned away from the group and his knees wobbled. A nearby worker grabbed his arm and steadied him before Otar could crash to the ground. At Otar's impressive stomach growl the worker pointed him with laughter in the direction of the kitchen tent.

The sun was already setting, and Otar must have missed the gong for lunch and dinner. His throat was parched, his vision doubled, but the kind worker guided him down to sit when it became clear that this wasn't just a passing spell. He got out a water flask and thrust it into Otar's hand.

Otar guzzled the sweet water in two large gulps and then blushed, embarrassed.

"I apologize for taking your ration."

The elder laughed. "We all have been there when we were young—getting lost in the work is nothing new."

He winked. He had long gray hair that flowed freely down his back. His attire was the same flowing robes of the Southern Island Aaoran also preferred, but where his mentor wore them in dark colors, his were of a much lighter tone.

"Still, please accept my thanks. I will inform the quarter master to hand you an extra ration."

The elder inclined his head. Otar handed the flask back and then carefully stood up. When it was clear his legs would obey, the worker trailed away, and Otar made his way to the kitchen to beg for leftovers.

THE NEXT TURNS followed the same pattern. Otar got up, explored the ruins, looked over scholars' shoulders, exchanged notes with anyone who wanted to—and they all did, because the more they could find out, the more they stood the chance to understand the secrets of the Ancients—and then, in the evening, he strolled back when the dinner gong traveled like an echo through the excavation site.

Sometimes he talked to Aaoran about what he had found so far, but more often, he sat at the small table in his tent refining his notes, making references and annotations. When darkness had long fallen, he crawled exhausted into his bed, and slept through the night with no dreams until the morning gong woke him. It was a rhythm he happily could live on for the rest of his life, but he knew, remembering Turas' letter, that this was only a temporary reprieve.

He had loved studying at the university—a world filled with knowledge right at his fingertips. In the library, he'd first met Turas and then in his wake, Jasner. They had traded stories and theories. Otar had presented his thoughts about the Ancients, and the other two had showed him a world beyond dusty books and long-forgotten legends; allowing the monster to feed regularly at their close, sometimes more intimate, contact. It had been perfect, the closest to being happy Otar had ever been. Until one day it came all crashing down, leaving Jasner's health in tatters and Otar on the run to find a cure.

ON THE THIRD turn, Otar studied the well closer. It was smooth and round, sitting right in the middle of the underground chamber. The black lines fanned out from there, as if something could travel along it. A few times, he wondered if he found the right switch, the correct spell—if they could let energy travel down, they could…

What then? Otar pinched his nose, dispelling the thought. Pure speculation. It was frustrating how much belief it all was and how small the things were Otar could contribute.

If he told Aaoran about any of it, the words, the magic, the monster, would they laugh at him? Or worse, cut him off from all the future work?

No, it wasn't an option, it was too risky. He sighed and looked down at the smooth surface.

It was grayish blue, and there was nothing to see beyond it. His fingers brushed the black lines running into it, but nothing happened.

Otar sat back on his toes, his eyes wandering around the room. Many scholars had left for lunch and to get a bit of sun time. The ones remaining were occupied by the walls, marking down the endpoints of the lines that ended in circles that were as tall as an average person. No one was paying him any mind. This was his chance to test a theory.

He crouched forward and then laid his hand flat on the smooth well. It was cold and warmed slowly to the temperature of his skin. A zip went through his fingertips, but nothing happened beyond that. Otar sighed, disappointed, and was about to move his palm away, when the voice came.

It was a garbled mess, unknown words mixed with some Otar recognized, underpinned with strange sounds. It broke off with a crack and silence reigned.

Otar waited with bated breath.

The voice returned to his head.

I have adjusted my speech. Please confirm if you can understand me.

Otar nodded and then rolled his eyes at himself.

"I do."

A long pause followed.

You have woken me from a long slumber. It needs to wake up. There are enough resources remaining to allow for the procedures. Give it time. It's faster when asleep.

"Okay." The words didn't make sense to him. The ghost, or was it even the ruin, had never spoken to him like that.

It's faster when asleep.

He blinked and wanted to move his hand away, but it wouldn't budge; it was as if the well was holding onto him.

It's faster when asleep.

Was he meant to do something here? Should he say something? He looked around, but still no one was paying him any attention. He licked his lips and then whispered, "Go to sleep."

Going back to sleep.

And then his hand was free again. The smooth surface was still dark. Otar crooked his head, looking closer. Was there now a faint blue glow? He squinted, but it was hard to tell in the light. The words buzzed through his mind. The voice had reminded him of Maugi, the ghost of the ruins, but it had never been without a visual manifestation, even if it sometimes had been very distorted.

Otar stood and, as inconspicuous as possible, walked away.

THE NEXT MORNING, he woke to excited chatter. The sun was barely up, and the interior of the tent was still a murky dark gray. Otar blinked into the shifting shadows, concentrating on the commotion to understand what was going on. But more and more people chimed in, creating a cacophony of Common dialects and other languages. Otar sighed and rolled out of his bed. He pulled on his robe, and driven by curiosity, forwent the belt and slipped out, right into a gaggle of scholars who seemed to have chosen his flap entry as their gathering point. They spoke in that shout-whisper tone that could be heard for miles. The entire camp had probably woken up by now.

Otar looked up into the sky and watched the rising sun for a small-turn to gauge how early it was, and then to the left where Aaoran was already striding over, put together perfectly, even this early. Once more, Otar wondered if they ever slept. He remembered in Bakusaran, the midnight oil had always burned at the doctor's place in Otar's village, when Aaoran had come back with him to visit.

As soon as Aaoran arrived, the scholars fell silent.

"So, people, what has gotten us all so agitated before the sun is even up?"

A pot-bellied man moved forward, his hair almost gone, with lines around his kind eyes and mouth.

"The door to the right dome has opened!"

The information was accompanied by the thrilled whispering of the scholars that had arrived with Aaoran.

Aaoran clapped their hands together, their eyes dancing with glee.

"And?"

"It's full of black stones. Big black stone blocks." The pot-bellied scholar stretched his arms out and made a motion to indicate that they were bigger than himself. "Some are noting down their dimensions and placements. But we have never seen anything like that."

More excited chattering. Aaoran hummed and all the eyes moved to them. The tide of anticipation turned into their direction—the energy rose, tickling Otar's senses. The monster was waiting, for what exactly Otar couldn't quite fathom, but the last few turns it had been a constant presence in his mind.

Aaoran's amused voice cut through his thoughts, addressing the still growing circle around them. "So, get to work. Remember to take precautions and rotate through, so everyone can take a look."

They nodded, some murmuring words of affirmation, and the crowd dissolved, breaking down into smaller clusters. Aaoran talked to a few remaining scholars, older men and women, before they turned and their eyes met Otar's. They crooked their head. "Breakfast?"

Otar squinted into the sky—the gray had barely lessened—and Aaoran chuckled. "The kitchen has already opened. There always seems to be someone awake enough to put on the brew."

Otar shook his head. Maniacs, the lot of them. He made a hand gesture to indicate he would follow after them, then dived into his tent to change into more appropriate clothing. Aaoran waited for him.

They walked over together, running scholars crossing their path. Otar was sure half of them forwent the breakfast just to check out what had happened. Before the sun was up, the ruin would be crawling with them. The kitchen staff was up, their big pots going with breakfast and brew. With the drink just boiled, they took their cups and settled at one of the long tables.

Aaoran sipped with their eyes closed in bliss. Then they exhaled and their gaze went to Otar. "Excited?"

Otar raised an eyebrow—images flickered through his mind and panic gripped him even if they were barely there. As if the image was broken into tiny pieces, never quite coming together. It lasted only a fraction of a brief-turn, then it vanished. He hadn't gotten a vision in so long that he assumed he had finally overcome them. The last ruins he had visited had all been dead, the core either gone, or splintered as the one in the mountains, or buried under sand and rock like in the jungle or over-all black. Was that the reason? Now that he was here, the ghost had returned?

Maugi. When he first met the ghost in Bakusaran, he had asked for its name, and it told him "Maugi." For a long time, Otar believed it to be a figment of his imagination, that something had broken in his mind due to his overexcitement. It had appeared right at the moment he had set his first step into the main dome over there, babbling strange words interspersed with static.

Otar took another sip from his brew, welcoming the bitter and acidic taste. The tribes softened it with milk and honey when they had it, sprinkling spices over it, that gave it a somewhat peppery note. It would also turn the brew into a pretty amber color and soothe anything that needed to be soothed.

"Otar."

"Yes?"

Aaoran opened their mouth then closed it again, scrutinizing Otar, who hid his discomfort behind his cup. After another intense gaze, Aaoran shook their head and took a sip of their own drink.

"Ready?"

Was he ever really ready? But Otar drained the brew and handed the cup to Aaoran, who had extended their hand. They brought it back and exchanged a few words with the kitchen matron before joining Otar. They walked through the sea of tents in silence, before shifting onto the stone road.

So far, no ghost.

At every ruin, it was the same, with some changes. The ghost itself always had the same stature and face, the same clothing and the same demeanor, but how it presented changed. At some ruins, it was only a murky blotch, bobbing up and down, eerily silent, and at others it was a full-fledged person with long, white, flowing hair and golden eyes that were eerily familiar. What would it be here?

They crossed through the crevasse and under the stone gate. With every step he took, Otar braced for the ghost to pop up, and yet it didn't come.

When they came closer to the main entrance, Otar lagged behind and waited until Aaoran had crossed. Every time he entered a new semi-active ruin, he held his breath, his heart filled with a hard to grasp reluctance and anticipation—and then, one foot in, it was gone. Now that the ruin had woken, the old tingly feeling was back spreading through all his nerves, down his fingertips and toes.

He stepped through.

The ghost didn't appear when they set foot into the main dome, nor when they walked down the staircase. For once hope flared inside him, that this time the brief vision he had was a product of his imagination.

The stairs down were flanked by a pale blue light that gave everyone a ghastly complexion so alien as if they had never been part of this world—like the Ancients?

Aaoran stepped over to the smaller stone door, never stopping their stride. Beyond the now wide-open hinges, crept scholars along, their eyes sweeping every inch.

The smaller dome was cold, almost freezing. The floor was tiled in a strange spiral-like pattern in black, blue, and white—another thing never recorded before. Spread out through the room, as if a giant had taken a handful of wooden toy blocks and thrown them, stood black stone blocks of various sizes.

Otar stepped up to the closest one and stretched his fingertips out, but the ruin was alive, and touching live ruins always came with consequences for him. He swallowed the impulse down and crouched to check where the stones connected with the floor.

"Fascinating," Aaoran breathed, a few paces away—and it was. Despite there not being much, it was the most incredible find in the last big-turns. Otar rose, and was mid-motion to pat the sand and dirt from his clothing, when he found that the floor was pristine. The domes had not been merely closed but sealed—nothing coming in or out.

Out.

The one word sent a shiver down his spine, and he shook the thought away.

Humming came from somewhere, echoing around him. Not the humming of a song. The noise was slightly metallic, like thunder rolling in the distance.

Otar looked up, his eyes and ears searching for the source.

His gaze stopped at a black block in the middle of the room, towering above the rest of them, and on top, with dark soulless eyes watching Otar, sat Maugi.

186

Chapter 16

"What shall I tell you about the ghost? There is too much to understand about it, too much for me yet to discover. Not all the things make sense to me yet, and its behavior is so much different here in Adabel, than it had been in all the previous ruins, as if this place has a strange power to transform everything around it, as if something is lurking in the depths that has just waited for me to come and set it free. I wonder so many things while Andres sleeps beside me and I'm unable to calm my restless mind. Something is waiting and every turn I wonder if I'm really ready for it."

(From: Scholar Otar's last notebook, unpublished)

MAUGI HADN'T CHANGED. It never varied—blotchy, washed out, not quite there, a silhouette. It didn't matter, the appearance always remained the same. Otar theorized it was the same ghost, following him from ruin to ruin for whatever reasons. Or was Otar carrying it around, and in the ruins, energy was used to project it? Otar wanted to scrub his face, but he felt Aaoran's eyes on him. Showing weakness now might mean that they still thought he was too ill and would bundle him up and put him on bed rest.

No, he needed to find out what was happening.

Maugi was silent. Waiting. Watching. It did that from time to time until Otar asked it a question, about the ruin, about what he saw. Not always were the answers clear, some filled with strange words and phrases that made little sense to Otar. Sometimes they were barely audible, distorted and high-pitched. The clearest answer he had ever received was the one from the other turn—as if being here, the ghost had found a better way to communicate—if it had been Maugi speaking.

And yet it must all be in Otar's mind because no one ever pointed to it or asked what the strange thing was doing here.

But why? Why would his mind conjure up something like this, and here? What was the connection?

It made little sense.

There was a smug tilt to Maugi's head even if the ghost showed no emotions. But now it seemed to say it knew that one turn Otar would come. A headache formed at the base of his skull, tingling down his spine, and rising over the crown of his head.

"What do you see?" Aaoran's voice was close.

Startled, Otar stepped back, meeting Aaoran's eyes. Their gaze was unreadable. For a heartbeat, Otar panicked. Did his mentor suspect something?

No, neither Jasner nor Turas would have shared what happened all those summers ago, keeping it under wraps, and Otar was now living on borrowed time to find a cure—even if he came to believe that there never would be one.

Slowly, he got his pounding heart back under control and then walked closer to the middle, to the stone Maugi was sitting on, trailed by Aaoran.

Otar looked up again. The ghost was swinging its legs—did it smirk?

There was something different with Maugi here. But Otar couldn't figure out what. He squinted at it. What was it hiding? What did it want from him?

All those puzzle pieces weighed on his mind, and he knew, felt it inside him, that he was missing so many more, but he had no clue where to even look.

And yet, somehow, it all tied to him. His search for a cure, for the secrets of the Ancients, for any information about the monster, about a past.

Or had he collected all the pieces, and he was just not ready to take in the full picture? Everything was dark and nebulous, legends half-pieced together that formed a rather strange pattern, with many holes and contradictions.

"Otar? What do you see?"

"A block." Otar snorted.

Aaoran sighed.

Before Otar could explain himself, a scholar, measuring things at Otar's feet, jostled him, and to not fall down, Otar braced himself against the stone.

For a long heartbeat, nothing happened. Then the floor rumbled. The tiles moved, turning around, changing place, forming strange patterns and swirls until settling in two rectangles. A black one as an outer perimeter, and an inner one in blue. When everything stopped and the scholars, who had backed away confused, were returning to inspect, then the stone blocks glided around, settling neatly on the tile lines, as if a ghost was rearranging them.

The voice returned, the one he might or might not believe to be Maugi.

Hm. There is something not alright with you. I can't let you contaminate me, so I'll shut down and revoke everything.

Maugi disappeared, and the lights went out. The doors, secured, stayed open. Murmurs rose, witch lights flared on, and more were brought in to fight the sudden darkness.

Otar, inch by inch, moved his hand away, his heart pounding. Aaoran's eyes tracked the movement, their gaze almost setting Otar's hand on fire.

"I wonder what happened," they said, their gaze never leaving Otar.

"No idea." Sweat trickled down Otar's back, his fingers tingling. Otar was sure Aaoran heard the lie in his tone. But Aaoran only hummed.

Hunger slammed into Otar. Bad hunger. His vision doubled, then snapped back to normal. He itched to put his palm on the stone again, but fear stopped him. Then his knees wobbled.

"Otar?" Aaoran's voice came from far away.

"Just exhausted, long hours, not enough rest. You know how it is, and with the injury…" This time, he was glad he could use it.

"I do." Aaoran forced a chuckle. Their gaze stayed on Otar until they shook their head. They turned and called out to two scholars to tell them what they had found out.

Otar stared at the spot where Maugi had sat and then tracked back to the underground chamber. He stopped in the middle—the well was dull. Carefully, as if he was inspecting it once more, he kneeled down, and after making sure that no one was paying attention, he put his hand down. It had worked the last turn, so it should again, right?

He waited a moment with his hand on the stone, but nothing happened. Had he been wrong? Had it just been a coincidence?

A zip passed through his fingers, sparking along his nerves and up his arm, down his body. The monster came fast, pouncing at the intruder, opening up what was stored inside him. He had always known that the energy he took was put somewhere separate inside him, and now for the first time he glimpsed the vast ocean inside him while nothing more than a bucket full was taken out.

But for what purpose? It didn't heal him, didn't curb the hunger, and never left him.

Ah, there you are. Hm, I see what is wrong with you.

Another zip down his back.

I isolated the problem and took what is needed to begin all the repairs to work on a normal level. Let me check for more of you.

More?

No, only you remain.

The lights flickered on again, the scholars, humming in surprise, looked around and waited for a heartbeat, then two, but when the ruin remained alive, they returned to work. Otar stared at the well. It glowed now in a faint off-blue. A soft golden glow, which also circled around the black rings on the walls accompanied the black lines in the floor.

Questions. So many questions. He had wanted to ask more, but the moment the lights flickered on, the presence in his mind receded.

His eyes followed the lines to the circles, and he wondered what would happen if he touched those. He rose and looked down at his hands.

They had taken. Never given.

The first time he had taken the life force of a living being, he had been ten summers. An accident. Hunger had plagued him for turns. A deep-seated hunger, never going away, gnawing at him, a dark black hole inside of him, that nothing could soothe.

One turn, he had found a bird in the middle of the road with an injured wing, hopping around frantically. He had been so careful in scooping it up; he wanted to bring it to their doctor, who also took care of the animals. But as soon as his hands closed around it, his icy fingers touching the soft feathers, the thing, the hunger, had taken over.

Just one heartbeat and the bird's body stilled, dying instantly.

Then Otar didn't understand. He'd been sad, and a bit confused, but he thought he was too late, and buried the little bird on the side of the road.

In the evening he had found himself less hungry, the aching hole inside him not as tormenting, but he never connected the dots.

More turns went past, and the hunger returned growing and growing until Otar couldn't ignore it anymore; this time it was a rabbit.

From then on, he learned what he needed to survive, taming it enough to snatch bits and pieces but never giving it full control. One wrong step, one letting go, and it didn't stop. By accident, he realized that sleeping with other people allowed a constant flow of energy without harming the other.

But he had never found another person like him. Only in legends about the Ancients.

Otar took the way back to the main dome and stopped in the middle of it. The scholars and workers moved around him, their voices melting together to a muted background noise. The strange things on the murals shifted, danced before his eyes, flowers swaying in the breeze, fish swimming, and the strange things above them flying through the sky.

What was he? Who had been his parents?

He turned on his feet, the blue stone on his skin shifting with him. In the morning air, it was cool. Now it was skin warm, resting over his heart.

More questions.

Why did Andres give it to him?

What did anything mean anymore? The ruins, the Ancients, his ancestry, Maugi, Andres, the stone? The more he searched for answers, tried to grasp for things to make sense, the more questions emerged, without answering any of those before.

The headache pounded behind his eyes, and Otar closed them for a moment. Exhaustion gripped him. Well, he was still recovering. Maybe rest was what he needed. The last turns had been intense, and with his thoughts muddled like this, he wouldn't be of any help. Otar opened his eyes again and sighed. It was time to return to the camp.

THE FIRST THING he did was stopping at the kitchen tent to get a fresh cup of brew. He stared at it for a long moment before shyly asking for wild honey and spices to be added. The kitchen matron beamed. She rolled up her tunic sleeve revealing tribe tattoos, while her braids hid under the headscarf she wore. Either way, she prepared him an entire pot of brew.

When Otar bent forward to take it, the blue stone slipped out. The matron's eyes zeroed in on it, and she looked elated. She rummaged around in one of her various baskets and then stuffed some grain cookies, the same type Andres' tribe would eat at a fire in the late afternoon, into his other hand. Otar ducked his head into a resemblance of a bow, and the kitchen matron shooed him away with kind laughter.

He hurried through the tents and then settled cross-legged in front of his own, enjoying the soft breeze, while the sounds of the camp ebbed and flowed around him. He took out his notebook. Note sorting helped him sort his thoughts as well. He got lost in making connections and annotations, sketching what he had seen in the small dome and the underground chamber, speculating about meanings, noting down the words Maugi had spoken, trying to understand them.

The sun shifted, the shadows growing longer, when someone walked towards him. Otar slowly raised his head when the figure blocked the light, his mind occupied with racing thoughts. He blinked a few times, to focus, to find the present, and a voice. Bit by bit was the waiting shadow revealed.

His eyes went wide when he recognized him.

"Andres?"

The steppe rider smiled at Otar and then shifted on his feet, as if he was waiting for something. Onder, who had arrived shortly after his brother, didn't even look at Otar and went off to search for Aaoran.

That didn't bode well, so Otar suppressed the spark of hope that thundered through him like a lightning bolt. The sun sunk lower, twilight stretching through the valley, shadows grasping for each other.

Otar asked what he was doing here, but Andres only shook his head. Silence reigned, while his former lover turned his face to the sky, with, as always, one hand in his sash and the other on the pommel of his sword.

Trying not to make the situation any more awkward than it already was, Otar gathered up his notes into a neat pile and held up the brew pot. Andres unclipped his cup and, after taking a first sip, raised his eyebrows in surprise, before his gaze softened.

Otar's cheeks turned red, and he looked away.

"I found them!"

They both startled at the shout. Onder strode up to them, closely followed by Aaoran.

When they huddled into a small circle, Onder stole Andres' cup, took a sip, and as his brother had done, raised an eyebrow at the taste. Otar concentrated his gaze on his mentor.

"What's going on?"

Aaoran's eyes danced, amused. "The Heir apparent will grace us with his presence, and the Kruson tribe is asked to provide safety as a sign of good will between the regions."

Otar blinked, not trying to reveal that he knew Jasner would be coming. And yet he thought he had more time to—what, exactly? In all the summers traveling he had found precisely nothing.

"When is he to be expected?" he asked instead.

Aaoran rolled his shoulders back. "The Heir is known for not sticking to a timetable. He arrives when no one expects him to."

Story of Otar's life. His gaze flicked to Onder and Andres, taking in the guilty slope of their postures.

"You knew."

Andres didn't flinch, but his fingers on the sword pommel twitched. "There have been talks for many big-turns now. We considered accepting the offer when you were there, but we had other matters to address first, before the council allowed it. The message arrived two turns ago." His eyes flicked to Onder.

Otar frowned, calculating in his head. How could Andres be here already?

Before he could voice his objections, Aaoran was talking.

"When will your warriors arrive?"

"In three turns, maybe four. They'll bring support from other tribes." Andres huffed. "The other leaders butted in and wanted a piece of the brew cake."

Aaoran grinned and asked after something else, but Otar tuned them out.

Things weren't adding up. Arriving before the main party wasn't unheard of, but coming alone all this way?

Another puzzle piece Otar didn't know where to fit. Nothing made sense anymore.

He was tired, tired of this conversation and tired of these people.

"Please excuse me," he mumbled.

Otar crammed his notes under his arm, took the cup and the pot from the ground, turned and slipped into the tent. The flap fell close behind him. He put everything on the table and then braced his hands against the wood.

His vision blurred—his thoughts swirled and danced, shifting between his mind's fingers, slipping through his grasp.

Why did he feel no one was ever talking to him?

Because he did the same? Kept everything close, bottled up? No, he had opened up to Andres, and where had that gotten him?

But had he been honest?

Should he open up more?

Otar hoped there would be more time before he had to face Andres again. Time to lick his wounds in peace and find his equilibrium again—yet the lords seemed to have other plans.

Did it matter now?

Turas would arrive soon, and he had made it very clear the last time they had met, that if he didn't present a cure for Jasner, he'd face imprisonment or death.

Otar exhaled. His turns were numbered because there was nothing to be found.

The air behind him shifted, and even without turning around, Otar knew who was standing there.

Andres' presence tingled down his spine—as if the other was the center of everything, a consistent pull on what made up Otar. Worse, the monster inside him took notice, reaching its ghostly fingers out. Otar clamped down on it, but of course, it ignored him. It touched the life force of the other, and in some kind of twisted greeting, didn't pursue more. Almost curling around the other man like a cat demanding to be petted.

The outside sounds spun over them. Shouting and laughter, singing and music, the night descending.

The soft shuffle of boots coming closer.

"Otar, won't you face me?"

He was closer than Otar expected, closer than he wanted and not close enough. He balled his hands into fists, swallowed, and turned. His heart thundered in his chest; the pain of his fingernails digging into the soft flesh of his palms gave only a temporary reprieve.

It had only been a few turns since they had parted and Andres hadn't changed—the scar, the dark armor, the colorful sash, the golden beads in his hair, the endless braids—and yet there was something in the tilt of his shoulders, in the lines around his eyes, it all appeared softer, as if he had found inner peace.

Otar wanted to hate him for it.

Andres' gaze flicked over Otar's face to his throat. Stopping at the stone that had fallen out from the tunic, Otar suppressed the urge to put it back.

"You're wearing it." Andres' voice took on the deep growl of his tribe's tongue. A tone that shot right through to different regions in Otar.

He forced himself to shrug and loosen the fists to a more relaxed hand.

Andres blinked. "Did my brother not explain?"

There was no sense in lying. He shook his head.

Andres muttered something unflattering under his breath. "And yet you are wearing it. Why?"

Embarrassment prickled down Otar's neck, spilling over his cheeks. He cleared his throat and stared at a point near Andres' collarbone. "Because it was a gift from you." The only one Andres had ever given him that hadn't been a necessity. He bit his lips, still not daring to look the other in the eyes. "Should I give it back?" He didn't want to, but if he had overstepped in accepting it…

"No!" In two steps Andres was so close, their noses almost touching, his gaze blazing, yet the gesture to take Otar's face into his hands was gentle. "Please don't."

"Then tell me." Otar said hoarsely. "By the lords, tell me what is going on."

"Akamar daro." You reside in my heart.

Otar froze, his mind coming to a screeching stop, and he stared at Andres. He blinked, and then again. But

Andres didn't vanish, the words vibrating between them didn't dissipate. His knees buckled, and he sank down to the floor, guided by Andres.

Otar tried to get his thoughts in order to return to a passable state of functionality, rationality—

"You bastard, you utter bastard." It burst out of him, and he cried. Warm arms wrapped around him, the smell of spice and smoke, sweat and leather encapsulating him, enveloping him like a long-lost lover.

Andres rocked him in slow motions, while tears flowed freely, uttering sweet words and pressing butterfly kisses into his hair.

And Otar let himself go.

Chapter 17

"The northern lands are similar and different to the steppe. Both regions are governed by tribes. But while the steppe people wander through the plains in search of pastures for their yardar and other livestock, the northern tribes are sedentary. They supplement their food with hunting and trade. The settlements are self-governed, with some forming alliances and even bigger settlements. The harsh winters don't leave much room for petty squabbles."

(From: "The North", in: "The Seven Lands in its Entirety", Vol. 8)

THE SHADOWS HAD overwhelmed the turn when Otar finally got a grip on himself. His eyes were gritty, his nose stuffy, and his limbs heavy. He was tired, and yet he fought against the embrace, there was too much still unexplained, he shouldn't let himself sink into the other until he understood what was going on. Andres only let him go far enough that Otar could lean back but remained in his arms. Andres' gaze was soft and open.

"What does the stone mean?" Otar's voice broke, hoarse from crying, but he didn't care.

"It is a promise of intent."

Otar stared, and Andres blushed. He swallowed, his throat bobbing nervously. "When we believe we have found the one we want to spend the rest of our life with, we search for the blue stone in the big river that cuts through the steppe further to the east. When we find a piece that is suitable, then we carve it. We give it shape and intention and adorn it with signs and symbols that have meaning to us, the intended, and the tribe. They offer protection, fortune, good wishes, and speak of intent and the feelings we hold. And then…" He swallowed again.

"You give it to the intended."

Andres nodded.

Otar fingered it, his fingertips seeking the lines and markings like an old friend. It was delicate work.

"Why now?"

Andres looked at a point over Otar's shoulder, the red spots on his cheeks darkening. "I started carving the stone after I left you that first time in the southern jungles."

Otar furrowed his brows. "But we never said anything of our feelings."

"I wanted to. And yet, whenever I tried to bring up the matter, you avoided it and changed the subject."

Otar found he couldn't deny it. While he didn't remember Andres broaching the topic, he had always spoken about them being friends, being casual, being companions.

While their parting five summers ago had been friendly, it had also been awkward.

He hesitated, while he thought about it, and then opened his mouth, but Andres put a finger on his lips. "I could have been more forceful, maybe got a letter out to you, done anything. I didn't, and yet I couldn't forget you. In the end it was rather cowardly. I didn't confront you and what we had, but I carved the stone."

"Is that why you wanted to be close to me, after you saved me?"

"Until you told me your feelings, I swore to not see more in you, because there was also the topic of me being promised to someone else. I had never been so confused in my life, unsure what my path should be." He cradled Otar's jaw again. "When you declared your love for me, everything changed."

Otar licked his lips, a nervous gesture, and raised his own hand, laying one on Andres' cheeks, going all soft when Andres nuzzled against it, pressing the other hand against Andres' chest, feeling the steady thump of his heartbeat.

"Tell me about it."

Andres smiled, but instead of answering, he helped Otar up. Confused, he followed.

"The ground in these tents is quite hard, and I'm not young anymore," Andres grinned. "We should get something to eat."

Andres let Otar go and stepped to the tent flap. Sudden panic gripped Otar, that as soon as they walked out, the dream would shatter, and Otar would be alone while Andres was swallowed by the night. He clutched Andres' wrist.

His lover looked back, watching him.

And Otar kissed him. It was meant to be short, to feel the other against him, to make it true, anchoring Andres into this reality. An answer almost to Andres' words, a reassurance for them both.

But as soon as their lips touched, the dam broke. Andres turned, one arm circling Otar's waist, tugging him close, the other sliding into Otar's hair, angling their heads just so. Then he answered Otar's kiss with his own, ruthlessly plundering what was denied him so long.

Otar didn't hesitate, raising his arms around Andres' shoulders, pressing them even closer together.

The monster circled them, and Otar let it.

Mid-kiss, Andres hoisted Otar up, and Otar encircled Andres' waist with his legs. It was only a few steps to the small bed, but it could have been continents. It didn't matter. Andres laid him down so gently, with such a soft expression, that Otar wanted to weep.

They parted, catching their breaths.

"Are you sure?"

Otar raised his arms and pulled Andres close.

IT WAS DARK in the tent when they watched each other with sleepy eyes while drawing lazy circles on their cooling skins. Otar hadn't felt this sated and loved in a long time. Andres smiled, touching Otar everywhere he could reach.

"Will you still marry?" Otar asked the questions that had been on his mind the last few small-turns.

"One turn." Andres' voice wasn't more than an exhale.

Otar swallowed. It shouldn't hurt so much as it did, and yet—

Andres tapped him on the nose, and then against the stone resting on the bedding between them. "When you permit it." Otar blinked, and Andres chuckled. He pulled Otar close, whispering in his ear. "One turn, when you allow me, I will wed you."

Was this what happiness felt like?

"What will your tribe say?" He said it at the same time as his stomach growled.

Andres kissed Otar's temple. "Food first."

They cleaned up as best as possible. And right before they stepped out, Andres hugged Otar around the waist and kissed him gently.

A reassurance. And everything in Otar broke free once more.

They walked side by side. Otar resisted grabbing Andres' hand—not that his lover would have done it, anyway. Andres clad himself in his usual armor. When Otar had pointed that out, Andres had shrugged and said, "This is who I am." And so he had one hand on the pommel and one hand in his sash.

It didn't matter.

He was walking beside Otar, cutting an imposing figure. His dark eyes sweeping left and right, taking it all in. From time to time he would turn his head to ask Otar a question about the dig, its process and the layout of the camp, always with a smile.

It warmed Otar to his very toes.

The kitchen had already closed down the big pots, and the matron was only able to offer them hot brew and cold leftovers. She winked at Otar after she had studied Andres, and Otar fought hard to keep the blush down.

They settled at a smaller fire off to the side occupied by Onder. He was watching their approach with glittering eyes but didn't comment when they settled opposite him.

Silence stretched between the three of them, while they ate; around them songs and laughter rose. Occasionally, someone would stumble past, greet the warriors with a nod, and then drift away.

When they were done and settled with the brew, Onder leaned forward, the fire throwing dancing shadows over his face, painting harsh lines and an even harsher gaze.

"What is your decision, brother?" His eyes were the same color as Andres', but colder now.

Andres laid his left hand on Otar's knee. Onder studied it for a moment and then nodded with reluctance.

"So be it," he said.

"So be it," Andres echoed.

Otar looked from one to the other, raising an eyebrow. Andres chuckled.

"I promised to marry you, ana."

Otar turned to Onder, who watched them with an unreadable face. "What am I missing?"

Onder sighed, his shoulders dropped. "The tribes marry, not the people alone. Long ago, many winters in the past, the elders agreed that Andres would marry into a small tribe in the east. It needed the added protection we offered in exchange for resources we desired." He took a sip from his cup. "But when my brother returned from his travels to the south and west, he wasn't making up his mind. And then he carved the stone. One doesn't do that when the marriage is arranged." Onder stared into the fire. "So I asked him, but he never gave me a straightforward answer." He punctuated every word and flicked his eyes up at Andres, who smiled ruefully. "Instead, he let the proceedings go on, but wouldn't involve himself. He brooded, of all things, taking long trips to the outer regions." Onder huffed. "I let it slide, because he didn't say no to the marriage and promise given—and then you came." Onder's gaze snapped to Otar, who resisted the urge to hide behind Andres.

"The moment he saw you, I read it in every line of his body. It all made sense then and there. He had traveled with you way longer than he had said he would, and when he returned, he was changed. But even with you there, he dithered. Oh yes, he made sure that you were taken care of, but once more he let you go. And then, the colossal idiot, sent the stone along." The fire crackled. The songs and laughter around them slowly fell away as the night went on.

"So, I waited. I delivered you to Aaoran and when I returned, I gave him a choice."

Andres sighed, picking up the story. "I was in contact with the other tribe to settle the matter. But it wasn't easy to ensure protection and still get the resources in exchange. I didn't want to give you false hope even after you made your feelings clear, because if everything I had planned fell through, I would have to marry into the tribe indeed."

Onder shook his head with fond exaggeration. Andres shrugged his shoulders, and Otar's heart swelled.

"So that was good. But I made the promise to marry."

"Aye," Onder threw in before taking another sip.

Otar turned to Onder. "You didn't tell me the stone's meaning on purpose."

"Andres had already burned that bridge twice, so I wisely said nothing to you about its significance. You and him, you needed distance from each other, to think about what either of you really wanted, and if it was time to let the other go."

Andres leaned against Otar. Their bodies flush together from knee to shoulder. Otar basked in the warmth.

"What would happen if somewhere in the future I didn't marry him?"

Andres growled, and Onder cackled.

"He must marry. That is the pledge he made, and our way demands that a promise is honored, however possible. If you don't wed him, I'm sure we can find someone willing to put up with him."

Andres stared at Otar, his gaze pleading.

Otar smiled and touched his cheek. "We'll talk about it later," but his eyes crinkled in the smile that took over with a life of its own, and Andres relaxed against him once more.

"To end this tale," Onder spoke. "After you and him spoke to each other like adults, he was to tell me if he still wanted to marry you or if there had been a change of understanding between you two. And now you will have to figure out the rest. The tribe gives you its blessing."

Andres inclined his head.

Onder sighed. "And with this, I'll retire for the night." He stood, and without a glance back, vanished into the darkness.

Otar watched him until the shadows swallowed him up completely.

"What are you thinking about?" Andres' words were a whisper in his ear, his breath puffing against the delicate skin. Otar shivered and caught Andres' satisfied grin out of the corner of his periphery.

He rolled his eyes and then, more somber, said, "Does he hate me?"

Onder had always been friendly to him, but since he had given Otar the stone, a distance had opened up between them. The closer he got to Andres, the more seemed to stand between him and Onder.

Andres sneaked an arm around Otar's waist and pulled him snug to him, almost into his lap. He pressed a kiss against Otar's temple. "He fears that I'll leave him and the tribe behind."

Otar's heart did a double beat. "Will you?"

Andres shrugged. It was a careless gesture for such a significant topic. He was a steppe rider and warrior, born and raised on the great plains. Otar wasn't. Maybe he'd even live with the tribe and study and document its traditions, but that wasn't the path he had chosen, the path he wanted to take. He needed to find answers, and those weren't found in the steppe.

And there was still the question of what Andres would do if he knew about Otar's secret.

Andres untangled himself and turned to face Otar. "Do you think we are there yet? That right now we can make that decision?"

Otar shook his head. Five summers ago, they might have been, but at the moment they needed to rediscover if they fit together, or didn't.

Andres smiled and kissed him. "Then let's see where the next turns lead us to first, okay?"

"So be it," Otar whispered against his lips.

Andres laughed, free and satisfied, and pulled Otar closer again. They stayed in front of the fire until it died down, the ambers glowing in the night.

OTAR WOKE THAT morning with a lighter heart than ever. When he opened his eyes, Andres' soft smile greeted him. A hand reached out to stroke his cheek, and then Andres leaned forward and kissed him. A greeting.

The gong for breakfast startled them and broke them apart. Chuckling, they climbed out, dressed, and then joined the stream of people walking to the kitchen. They nodded at Onder and Aaoran, who were sitting with different groups, and settled down further away, to keep to themselves for the moment.

When they finished, Andres accompanied him to the ruins, saying he wanted to take a look for himself and check how the security could be enhanced.

Otar kissed him goodbye at the entry of the main dome and went back to his research.

Night had fallen when Andres came and dragged him out, herding him to the kitchen before it closed down. After grabbing their food, they joined Onder and a group of warriors around one of the bigger fires as they were discussing something in Tribe. Otar let their voices wash over him, enjoying the warmth of Andres' body at his side.

Back in what now seemed to be their tent, they rediscovered with kisses and touches how they still fit together.

The next turn, they repeated it again.

And again.

And again.

The turns drifting into each other.

It was the most peaceful Otar had felt in a very long time. Closer to what they both had experienced when they traveled—but it was also more grounded, clearer in where they stood with each other.

It made Otar forget about everything else while he crawled over every inch in the domes and surrounding buildings. He measured the endless passages and walkways, sketched spires and symbols and strange things on the murals with wings and wheels—he pressed everything else down and away, letting himself get lost in his research and Andres.

And then one morning the drums sounded.

Chapter 18

"When I look into the stars, there are many feelings inside me. I wonder what lies beyond them, if there is even a beyond, another world, another something to discover. I spoke with scholars about it, and while they do wonder and try to see what might be out there—we do have some pretty pictures of the moon—it feels as if no one is really driven. Or am I just, as always, imagining things? Out here under the vast night sky of the steppe, I feel utterly alone and at home at the same time."

(From: Scholar Otar's last notebook, unpublished)

IN THE MORNING, Andres promised him he would return earlier and that they could have a quiet afternoon and ride out a bit, just them and the steppe. Otar was looking forward to it. The notes he was sorting blurred before his eyes and his head was overstuffed with information. Maugi hadn't reappeared, and since he had pressed his hand to the well and had felt the energy drain from him, the ruin hadn't talked to him. He was unsure if he should see this as a bad or good sign. Probably both. That his mind was now silent should soothe him, but it was also frightening as it made chasing answers more difficult.

He scrubbed a hand over his face and wondered if talking to Aaoran could help him find some clarity when a drum sounded.

A beat that moved closer, rising over everything else. He froze in the motion of stacking his notes and swallowed. Drums only ever meant one thing, the rhythmic thundering and vibrating bass heralding that the Heir apparent Jasner ne Rasanell and his close adviser Turas ad Temar had arrived.

Otar sunk down in his chair, staring at the sunbeams falling in through the open tent flap, tracking the dancing dust particles in them.

Wondering if this was how it all ended.

HE FOLLOWED THE masses streaming to greet the Heir, but stayed far back, closer to the overhang than to the road that came through the crevasse. The parade that thundered through was smaller than he'd expected.

One flag bearer rode in front, holding up the sun banner of Rasanell high, the blue and green banner fluttering in the wind. He was followed by a handful of soldiers, which flanked Jasner and Turas on both sides. The two drummers made up the rear.

From the distance, he couldn't quite make out Jasner's or Turas' expression. But he assumed Jasner was smiling and waving, while Turas looked grim and pained, hating to be on the back of a yardar for an extended period.

After their friendship broke, the fallout had been intense, leaving a lasting impact. Turas had wanted to brand Otar as a traitor, and only Jasner's interference had saved him from that fate and the proposed execution.

It had been an accident, and Jasner had never blamed him, even if Otar had almost killed him, the monster sucking all the life force out of him.

But Turas never forgave him.

Otar couldn't fault him for it. If the same thing would have happened to Andres, he was sure he would take his revenge as well.

So to buy him some time, he swore to find a cure, to restore what had been taken and to make Jasner whole again. A pipe dream.

The procession stopped and Aaoran, already waiting, stepped forward and greeted them with a deep bow.

Turas dismounted and walked around to help Jasner. The heir looked at the offered hand and then got down on his own. Turas frowned, but let it go. Then he turned from left to right, as if he was searching for something or someone in the crowd. Otar sunk deeper into the shadows and focused on Andres instead.

The steppe rider stood straight with his head held high, the beads glinting in the sun. As always, when he was amid friends and trusted allies, he had one hand on the pommel of his sword and the other in the sash. Otar's heart swelled. Even when he bowed to the heir, he didn't give an inch about his own position.

Otar contemplated slipping away. Not just to his tent, but further beyond the ruins, wandering the Seven Lands indefinitely. He turned his body; the foot hovering over the stony ground—leaving Andres was the most unbearable thought he had ever had.

He huffed. Not losing out on the ruins had come first to his mind, but Andres stole himself into them as well. He planted his feet and thought it through for once. Giving up this place would be hard. These ruins held secrets he was desperate to uncover. There was an air of something he couldn't quite put his fingers on; he was still missing a puzzle piece.

The crowd in front of him shifted. Otar used the moment to slip back to his tent. Soon they would summon him. He sunk down on his chair, his arms on his thighs, his head down, his thoughts running in circles.

It was Aaoran who found him first.

"Hiding?"

Otar raised his gaze and tried for a smile. It felt stretchy and fake. "You have no idea."

Aaoran stepped further in, let the flap fall close, and stopped. "I have more of an idea than you may think."

Otar realized they really might. He hadn't been subtle in his letters after the incident, including his sudden departure from the university. Before he wrote at length about the two and later three of them, and then they were just forgotten. His mentor must have been curious, but they had never pressed for more.

"You never asked what happened."

Aaoran crossed their arms, studying Otar, choosing their words with care. Their eyes flickered through the tent before they snapped back to Otar. "Would you have told me?"

"I wouldn't have lied." He never did.

"Ah," Aaoran stated and then, "you would have said it's complicated and left it at that." Their eyes twinkled, and then the amusement dimmed.

Otar looked away, fiddling with his tunic. Aaoran was right. That is exactly what he would have done. Every question about himself, his past, his family and especially his research, he deflected.

And he was tired of it. Tired of keeping those thoughts and weird truths inside him, all these fears and questions without answers. There was no help, no one to sort it through with, to make sense of it all. He inhaled. The weight of what he was about to do crushed him.

Aaoran wasn't prone to hysterics or fast verdicts. He weighed facts, considered options, and thought about possibilities.

Otar licked his lips. The words were on the tip of his tongue, knocking against his teeth. The silence dragged on too long already, but when Otar dared to look at them again, Aaoran was watching him with an open gaze.

"I think we need to talk." Otar's voice almost broke, fear choking him.

"As you wish." They accentuated the words with a formal bow, folding their hands in front of their chest, and then bowing down, bending in half. Otar was embarrassed at the level of reverence Aaoran showed but didn't dare to dissuade them from it.

The tent flap moved, and Andres stepped through, stopping when he noticed them both. His eyes darted from one to the other while taking in the somber air.

"Anything I should know about?" His hand tightened around the sword pommel. The fingers in his sash twitched—Otar flustered at the protectiveness.

Aaoran rose from the bow and smiled at Andres before speaking to Otar. "We'll talk later."

Otar nodded, and then he was alone with his lover.

Andres rolled his shoulders back, letting go of something, then looked at Otar. With one step, he was close, knelt down, wound his arms around Otar and tugged him close.

Otar came with little resistance, pressing his face against Andres' stomach as if it was the most natural thing to do. The smell of leather and sweat and dust surrounded him, calming him. They didn't quite fit together yet, but here, like this, it gave Otar hope. Perhaps they'd never get back the easy rapport from five summers ago, but as long as they were being honest…

Honesty. Had Otar ever been honest?

"Not eager to see the heir?" Andres rumbled.

Otar collected his thoughts, disregarding all the words that wanted to spill out of him. "There will be enough time to meet him properly."

With the little patience Turas had, it would probably be sooner rather than later.

Andres hummed. The vibrations tickled Otar's face, fingers curled into his hair, scratching at the nape.

"You know whatever happens, I'll be by your side."

"I know," Otar mumbled into the clothing—because that was the logical answer.

Leaning back Andres cradled Otar's face in his hands. His callouses scraped over the soft skin of the cheeks, those dark eyes wild.

"No, whatever comes, I'll stand with you."

The emphasis wasn't lost on Otar. He searched Andres' face for a sign of what he meant, but they remained unreadable—another piece missing.

"Andres?"

"Andres!" someone shouted at the same time, and the moment broke.

Andres studied his face again and then, after a demanding kiss, he was gone, demanding in a gruff voice what was going on.

Otar sunk back, blinking into the dancing sunbeams, wondering what had happened.

WAITING FOR SOMETHING to happen could fray even the greatest of patiences. After three turns of neither Turas approaching him nor a messenger coming for him, Otar, overcome by the jittery feeling inside him, got tetchy and started snapping at everyone. With Andres receiving the brunt of it, yet taking it in stride.

But after yet another minor incident morphed into a full-blown shouting match, Andres took his unused bedroll from his pack and left their tent in the middle of the night.

Otar curled into himself, staring at the tent wall, not finding any sleep.

AAORAN HANDED HIM a fresh cup of brew in the morning—just the way he liked it—before Otar was even close to the kitchen line.

He raised an eyebrow but took the gift.

"News travels fast," they said cryptically and then nodded at a tent, where Onder emerged, followed by Andres.

Heat spilled over his cheeks, and Otar sighed before taking a sip. He needed to apologize, but for that, for it to make sense to Andres, he needed to explain what was eating at him. But was he ready for that?

"Shall we talk?" Aaoran said from his side, sipping his own brew.

Otar exhaled and blinked into the rising morning light. "We shall."

A man, wearing the colors of Rasanell's royal family, materialized beside him, startling Otar enough that the brew sloshed out of his cup.

"Yes?" Otar asked while mourning his drink.

"His Imperial Highness Jasner ne Rasanell, Heir apparent to the throne of the Jewel of the Wooden Lands, requests your presence."

Otar stared at the sad remaining dregs. "Now?"

The messenger stared at him as if he didn't understand the question.

Otar sighed and looked at Aaoran, who smiled serenely. "I'll find you later."

Aaoran nodded, turned, and strode away.

Otar made a wavy hand at the messenger. "Lead the way, then."

THE HEIRS' ACCOMMODATION, the royal tent, had been erected at the furthest end under the mountain cliff. There was a small indentation there, almost like a cave, but not as deep. The royal tent stuck out from all the surrounding tents by its size and elaborate designs painted on the outer walls. Four grim-looking soldiers guarded it. In the distance, close enough to come running when needed, steppe riders made their rounds. Otar was sure that atop the stone walls other lookouts kept watch. No harm would befall the heir to the throne.

Otar snorted.

The messenger threw him a gaze that stated Otar wasn't displaying sufficient humiliation for being summoned, but was too well-trained to comment on it.

The guards checked the courier first before they scrutinized Otar. Then they nodded and stepped away to let them through.

The messenger held open the left side of the double flap and announced Otar before scurrying away. Otar wished dearly that he could do the same.

He looked over his shoulder and wondered how far he would come before the rustling of clothes drew his attention back.

The tent was sectioned off. There was a front room with seat cushions and colorful rugs, and a low table held confections and fruits. Through a thin gauze fabric, Otar glimpsed a small desk covered in papers and scrolls. Jasner had always been diligent in his duties. Somewhere to the left, heavy fabric obscured the sleeping area.

Turas was seated at the desk measuring him through the delicate curtain. Movement behind the sturdier one indicated Jasner's whereabouts.

Otar kept his gaze steady and his feet planted at the entrance, not moving an inch—he knew the protocol. Otar hated it, but Turas wholeheartedly embraced it, wearing it like a shield around him. Because the only thing Turas ever wanted was standing beside Jasner, but many envied his position, and protocol kept the balance in his favor. That was probably why he had been so hard in letting the accident go and shut him out. Jasner remained friendly after everything.

Turas didn't rise or motion him forward. They were locked in a stalemate until Jasner emerged. He paused, looked between Turas and him, and sighed.

Otar furrowed his brows. That was a weakness Jasner had never allowed himself to show before. At first glance, the heir appeared as always, dark skin, even darker eyes and black hair, kept in a low bun at the nape of his neck. Maybe it was the dim light in the tent, but there were lines now around his eyes and mouth that hadn't been there seven summers ago.

Jasner looked tired, a tiredness that was Otar's fault.

To distract himself from the uncomfortable feeling in his stomach, he bowed deep. "My prince."

There was another sigh, but Otar waited, keeping his gaze firmly on the floor. They knew that this display of submission wasn't for Jasner alone, but also for Turas.

The murmured command for him to rise sounded loud in the quiet between them. When Otar was looking at them again, Jasner waved him to the cushions, and he and Turas settled opposite him.

As there were no servants present, it was on Turas to serve them brew. First Jasner, then Otar, and lastly himself.

The silence stretched as they all took a sip. The brew had a more earthy flavor, imported from the northern regions. Otar let the taste roll over his tongue, chasing the bitterness embedded in it.

They had summoned him, so it was on them to start the conversation. As he had previously found with Aaoran, he was tired. He had done what they had asked of him, written endless letters of his findings, or the lack thereof, talked at length about everything he tried, and it wasn't enough?

"So, nothing new to report?" Turas' tone dripped with contempt.

And Otar was done. "By the lords, you know I'd tell you first!" he hissed, too angry to keep his voice level, tired of the games and charades.

Seven summers he had wandered now through the Seven Lands. Seeing all its wonders and endless beauty, researching the Ancients, crawling over every inch of stone he could find, but finding nothing. Leaving behind a despair in him he couldn't quite place, and that had had nothing to do with the accident.

Many scholars before him had been in the same situation, and yet they had carried on—had none felt the abyss inside them?

"Are you sure?" Turas put his cup down with more force than necessary. Apparently, he wasn't the only one with a temper. Otar looked at his once friend—the rumbled robe, the blond locks in disarray, the brows drawn together—he appeared as exhausted as Jasner, even more so.

Guilt gnawed at Otar's stomach.

"Turas," Jasner said, and with that one word, they fell silent.

Otar stared into his brew. They had had endless cups of this blend back in Rasanell, talking endlessly, discussing all things of interest. His heart made a double beat, and he ignored it, not dwelling on the painful feeling.

"I found nothing because the Ancients left nothing behind besides crumbling stone and strange symbols on the walls." When he had asked Maugi, the ghost had fallen silent and not returned for three ruins.

"You said that you would find answers, that you would find a solution to restore what was taken from Jasner, to make him whole again. Have you failed?" Turas leaned forward. "If so, you know the punishment."

"I never agreed to anything! I stated I'll try, but I didn't make any promises," Otar hissed, mindful of the guards outside.

"You willingly hurt him!"

"Enough." Jasner's voice wasn't loud, but it cut through their shouting. One flick of Jasner's eyes and Turas closed his mouth with a click, brows drawn together in confusion. Besides his own turmoil, Otar felt pity for him.

Jasner then turned his attention to Otar. "I apologize. This wasn't why I told Turas to send for you. I should have read the letter before he sent it out. But as previously, he cannot let the matter go."

Otar blinked at him.

Jasner smiled. A true one, not the ones reserved for court. "Yes, I wanted to ask if you had found something new, and while I didn't expect it, because, as you said, you would have informed us, there is always the slight bit of hope. Also, it would be fascinating from an academic viewpoint to know more. That has been the reason for the continued support of the excavations."

Otar stared at him, at the soft smile and the gentle expression. The feelings he once had for him, for them both, had established a strong friendship—the ending had been devastating.

"Then why am I here?"

"I miss you, my friend."

"Oh," Otar said stupidly. Was it as simple as that? His eyes went to Turas, whose face was a thundercloud. The lips pressed into a thin line, the whole body coiled inward, ready to jump forward.

Otar's gaze drifted around to collect his thoughts. This was a development he hadn't seen coming—not since he had almost drained Jasner of all his life force.

"This wasn't what we talked about," Turas said into the silence, his stare glued to Otar.

Jasner took a sip from his brew, putting it down in a delicate movement. "No, you told me what I should do and never listened to my objections in this matter."

Turas sputtered, his cheeks turning red in anger.

"It was an accident, Turas, because I thought I knew better. I was arrogant, and for that, I paid the price." He sighed, exhaustion spreading over his face as if he had been holding it together until this moment. "But you? You never accepted my view, thinking I couldn't understand what had happened." He shook his head. "I had always hoped that you'd come to your senses on your own. But this ends now. For the last time, I'll repeat myself: This was never Otar's fault, and I wish it would be handled accordingly. If you disagree, I will release you from your vows, but don't expect me to ever take you back."

Turas' eyes bulged, his mouth open, but no sound came out. His fingers trembled, from anger or fear, Otar couldn't tell.

Jasner interlaced his hands and rested his arms on his legs, sitting upright, his head high, unwilling to give in even an inch. There he was, the ruler he would one turn become. The eyes polished stone, unwavering, unforgiving. Turas' entire posture turned to stricken, as if everything he had ever cared for was now slipping through his fingers.

Then, as if the strings were cut from a wooden puppet the entertainer on Rasanell's streets used to tell stories with, his body collapsed into itself.

"I understand."

Chapter 19

"You never asked what happened at the university. Why I stopped mentioning Jasner and Turas and what we had. I know you said it so that I wouldn't lie to you, but I'm nonetheless grateful. The horrors of that day followed me for a long time into my dreams and waking moments. Touching someone filled me with dread for a long time. When Andres sought me out in the jungle and saved me, it was the first skin-to-skin contact in many turns, and I was so surprised by it, that I forgot about it all for a moment. Accepting Andres' closeness after that was almost embarrassingly easy."

(From: Otar's letters to Aaoran, unsend)

OTAR'S MIND WAS still reeling when he walked back. Once Turas had bowed his head in submission, they had turned to more inconspicuous topics. It was surreal after all of Turas' accusations and hurtful words. When Otar had left, he could feel eyes burning into his back.

Was it really over? Jasner had saved Turas' life when he had been very young, and he paid the life debt with absolute devotion to Jasner—maybe it was even love. Would Turas ever accept a truce?

Otar strode down the stone road to the gate. The sun was now low on the horizon. When he had arrived at the royal tent, the guards had him classified as not a threat. Which was ironic, because he was.

Long ago, he had found a small leather-bound book, wedged between two old encyclopedia volumes in a corner of the Rasanell library that saw little traffic, if the amount of dust and cobwebs was any sign.

The text was a transcript of a transcript from an even older document that held a witness account told by the second cousin of an archivist and so forth, speaking of old legends and myths that were transformed beyond recognition. A half-page near the end, talked about soul eaters. The soul eaters lived in big white buildings, with round roofs and twisted spires. They could travel vast distances in the blink of an eye, wore peculiar clothing—long flowing robes—and ate the souls of people, sucking them dry and leaving only a husk behind.

At that point in his translation, he had stopped and stared. The descriptions of the buildings made it clear that this must mean the Ancients. His hands had trembled and after giving himself some small-turns to only breathe, he double checked the words, and yet retranslating brought the same conclusion. The Ancients had somehow sucked the life force out of living things, the same as Otar.

Even now, he wasn't ready to face the implications.

This was why he was also wandering the Seven Lands for the last seven summers—not only to find an answer and a cure, but to look for *them*.

Because if he was alive, then…

And yet, he had found nothing besides crumbling stone and a ghost haunting them.

Otar stopped at the dome entrance and looked around. He was alone. Most scholars had left when the night crawled in, either because they were hungry and tired, or because at night, the shadows in the ruins moved, and ghosts whispered.

For Otar, it had always been soothing. Dwelling on that, he walked through. It was as if the ruins were never empty, as if the Ancients still lived here, and at any moment one would emerge from the darkness and stride past him. Their long white hair and flowing tunic trailing behind them, the fair complexion a stark contrast in the gloom, glowing in the faint wall lights.

Specters. Ghosts. Soul eaters.

He stepped up to the mural, his eyes tracing the pictures. Words dropping into his head. A fishlike creature with too many fins and all the wrong colors whispered, "*Ementis*", and then swam away, scales glittering in the sun; a small tree with little round leaves and black twigs was named "*Eka*", bowing in strong winds almost to the ground; a tiny flower with white blossoms like twinkling stars was called "*Asamara*", blooming under rust-colored skies; on and on it went. Maybe they had once been part of the Seven Lands, or they had come from beyond the ocean. And yet, their pictures on this mural were off.

Otar didn't flinch when the ghost appeared beside him.

"Did I summon you?"

Yes. Maugi's voice was flat and neutral—emotionless. Distinct from the voice of the ruin itself, and different from the one in his dreams and visions. Was it all the same? Did they all have the same origin?

Maugi itself was a phantom of many ruins. Otar never figured out how that worked. The most logical conclusion was, because no one could see it, that it was Otar who brought the ghost with him.

What can I do for you?

"Tell me about this place."

For a long moment, Maugi was silent. In the far distance, a steppe wolf cried. The faint tendrils of songs and music carried by a slight breeze drifted over from the kitchen area, like ghost fingers touching him.

After a lengthy journey, we arrived here. Maugi's voice had changed once more, closer to the one in his dreams. Otar felt a headache forming. *We wanted to build an outpost and then communicate with home. We brought everything with us we might need, and we built the sender. This world didn't like us and interfered. We couldn't make contact. We were left alone. We searched and found another source of energy—*

"Otar?"

He turned, his gaze meeting Andres'. In the pale ruin light, his face was all harsh lines and deep shadows, but his eyes were kind.

His mind was still on Maugi's words. They had come from the other side of the ocean and had been unable to go home, and for that, they had needed power? He blinked and pressed all the thoughts away, concentrating on the moment, making space for Andres.

"Hey."

"Speak to me."

Otar inhaled, already constructing deflections. Then he sighed. He turned to the mural, stretching his hand out, pointing at the fishlike creature. The warmth at his side grew when Andres stepped closer.

"Esmentis." Otar's tongue struggled with the unfamiliar word. He relied on his mind to guide him. "Eka." And then "Asamara." He let his arm drop.

Andres didn't move. "I thought no one knew the language."

"Yes." Otar waited for the questions, the accusations, the scorn. The mural blurred before him, everything running together.

"Tell me." Andres' voice was gentle. Otar used the other's calm to steady himself.

"They're in me. When I look at them, any of them, I know their names."

"Do you really know them, or do you think you do?"

Otar shook his head. He spread his fingers, close to touching, but never quite putting them on the stone. "When I look at a tree, or a yardar, or a person, I know what they are called. It is the same for those names on the wall."

"But how?"

Otar dared to peer at him. Andres was studying the pictures. He didn't seem angry, but confused.

Otar licked his lips, his heart beating a fast staccato. "There is one possibility…"

"You aren't saying…"

Otar shrugged. "Honestly, I don't know who or what I am. Nothing makes sense. How can I know when no one ever taught me? When nothing is documented? When no book is written about it?" Otar looked down at his hands; they trembled, his whole body shuddered.

Arms enveloped him. Not pressing him closer, but holding him steady, grounding him. For a moment, Otar let it be. Then he gently extracted himself, taking a step back.

More confusion flashed over Andres' face, then everything smoothed out, his gaze open.

"There is more." Otar's voice broke.

Andres stepped forward, taking one of Otar's restless hands and entwining their fingers. "Tell me."

"I have killed. More than once. There is a monster inside me. One that is always hungry."

"We all have," Andres said in a low tone.

"Not like this. It takes until the other person is all but an empty husk. I try to control it, but it slips through my grasp more often than not. And twice now I have let it reign free, not fighting it."

Andres drew Otar into his arms again and hummed. It wasn't the reaction Otar had expected.

Seeing the unasked question, Andres said, "The slavers' leader, before I killed him, he asked if we killed the demon." He chuckled. "And when we traveled, you know, there had been those odd little things over the winters. Touches that held too much intensity. Your drawn expression when we didn't sleep together for a few turns." Otar coughed, embarrassed, and Andres laughed. "It all connects. You fed on me."

"And you're just alright with that?"

Andres drew back in order to look at him. He took Otar's face in his hands, stroking the thumbs over Otar's cheeks. "I almost lost you twice. I'll only let you go when you tell me." His gaze turned intense. "Are you telling me to go?"

"No!" The word broke out of Otar before he could even think about it.

Andres hugged him tighter, and this time Otar melted against him.

"There is more," he whispered into Andres' nape.

"There always is." Andres sounded amused. "Later than."

Otar pressed his face deeper into Andres' neck. "Later."

SHOUTING SURGED FROM the direction of the ruins as Otar sipped his morning brew and wondered if every morning would now start like this. People turned their heads to the ruins. More yelling and cries of excitement carried through the forests of tents, and more and more people drifted over to check what the racket was about this time.

Had the second smaller dome opened its gates?

Otar finished his brew in measured sips and then followed the commotion.

He saw Turas in the stream of people. Their gazes met. He looked as puzzled as Otar.

They walked through the stone gate, down the buildings, and came to a stop in a semi-circle around the dome entrance.

A group of steppe riders stood nearby, watchful and alert. Off to the side, Aaoran was listening to three scholars as they explained something with flailing arms and fast hand movements.

Aaoran nodded their head a few times before they looked over. Their eyes met Otar's. Once more, he wanted to turn and run, but he kept his feet planted. Then his mentor waved him over.

It wasn't until he fought through the ring of people to reach Aaoran that he found Turas had followed him.

"And then they just moved," one scholar, an older woman with close-cropped hair, was saying as he came closer, while the others nodded. Her tone made it clear that whatever had shifted should not have been able to move. Aaoran looked thoughtful while the scientists almost vibrated out of their skins.

"What is going on?" Otar said when he was near enough. The mass of people in his back swayed forward to listen. They reminded Otar of the women in the tribe when they had asked to be drawn by him and were waiting eagerly in anticipation of his answer.

But before Aaoran could reply, the scholar who had been talking cut in. "The stone blocks changed position again, and now they are emitting a soft glow."

Murmurs broke out, but the scholar's voice was loud enough to be heard. "We wanted to investigate further, but the guards moved us out." She threw a dirty gaze at the unmoving warriors. Aaoran held up their hands in a placative manner.

"You know the rules. It was for everyone's safety." Their eyes twinkled, but the tone was resolute. The scholar rolled her shoulders back but didn't contradict them. "We'll check the situation with volunteers to make sure it is safe. If there are no concerns, then we will open it up to the rest," Aaoran said loud enough so that their voice would carry to the waiting scholars.

Hands shot up. And after some consideration, they formed two teams of four people, plus Aaoran, Otar, and two guards.

They stepped into the main dome.

The repairs are now done.

The words slithered down Otar's spine. He licked his lips and kept walking. The dome was empty. All had been driven out as the protocol demanded. In truth, the ruins had presented no real danger besides crumbling passages and walls. No one had ever been damaged by a ruin itself.

Damaging with the ruin. I don't understand.

Otar was about to answer Maugi when he found he was the last of the group trailing behind. Maugi was the only one at his side. Otar opened his mouth but flicked his eyes to the others. He couldn't just start talking to the air.

Maugi flickered, disappeared and then reappeared as before.

This might be easier to work with. The words flared to life in his mind. Otar stiffened his shoulders at the strangeness but then forced them to relax. It was bizarre. The words were his thoughts and not—they had no inflection, no intention. They just were.

So now, he should answer in his mind as well?

The monster stretched its ghostly fingers out, but before Otar could try to reign it in, it was rebuffed by an invisible barrier.

The ruins have always been strange, and people have feared them. They reacted unpredictably, so people wondered if the ruins are set to hurt them.

The palaces were built to ease the energy collection. They aren't designed to act on their own.

Otar wasn't sure if that made more sense, but he let it go for a moment. It was hard to concentrate on the questions, to not let the thoughts drift as he always did when he thought about something.

Who built the palaces?

We did. The voice was harsh, different from Maugi. Otar wondered what was going on.

Who is 'we'?

We are we, it said, and then there was silence in his mind.

Before he could inquire more, they arrived at the smaller dome. He hesitated before crossing, but there would be nothing gained if he stayed outside.

Where the stone blocks had stood before in a fence around the middle, they now formed six neat rows with three blocks in each. They emitted the same bluish glow as the ruins' lights did when they were active. An eerie atmosphere had settled over the room, as if at any moment more ghosts would break forth and descend upon them.

The scholars mingled among the stones while Otar checked the dark tile line they had previously stood on.

Was the floor still solid?

I will only act on your words. It was Maugi's voice again.

He walked over to one block, once more trying to find out where they fit together, struggling to discover the seams. Or were they cut from one big stone piece? Had they been harvested from the Black Mountains? If he remembered correctly, the rock there was more grayish, not as deep black as this here. He also couldn't find any mineral deposits or sediment lines.

It must be a resource they had brought over. It was clear they couldn't be found here.

Otar tried to do the calculations of their weight and what kind of ship would be needed to carry these all over. A nautical expert could shed some light on it.

His eyes fell to the ruin walls.

Did you also bring the stones to build the palaces?

The city growth was done as soon as the first landing was finished.

"Otar."

Otar looked to the side. Aaoran was watching him.

"What do you make of this?"

Otar studied the space Aaoran indicated. The blocks weren't smooth anymore. There were little knobs and rectangles of slightly different colors on the blocks, with lighter and deeper black depressions interspersed. It looked like a puzzle-like pattern fit together by an unknown hand, to form a picture no one could make sense of.

"Everything is divergent from what we have seen before," Otar mused. His mind was divided. One part of it was here taking in the reality he was in, and the other tried to process all the things Maugi was whispering.

Aaoran looked thoughtful. "You think this could be Eitin?"

This is Inchenor.

Inchenor?

The first full outpost. Eitin is to the north, protected by a mountain range as a last effort— Maugi cut out.

"No, this isn't Eitin," Otar answered Aaoran. Forcing himself to keep his thoughts together. "As per surviving documents, Eitin was the grandest. And while this is one of the bigger ruins we have found, it appears to be still contained."

Aaoran hummed in thought. "So a first settlement, as you have suspected." They stared at the blocks. "I wonder if the other ruins hide something similar."

They don't. Their cores are enough to keep everything in line.

Otar puzzled over the word "cores". If they meant the wells, it would make sense, he himself saw those as the heart.

"Otar?"

Otar turned his head to Aaoran, blinking. Their voice came from far away, as if he was slipping to a distant place. His mind drifted to all the events that had happened since he had arrived here and from there further back into the past.

"Are you okay? You kept staring at the wall and didn't react to anything I said."

Otar licked his lips, a nervous gesture he still couldn't curb. The world was split. He was two things at the same time. Would Aaoran understand if he explained it? Would they call him crazy? A liar? Would anyone be willing to protect him if push came to shove? His eyes went back to the stones.

"There is a ghost in my mind, whispering words. It has been there since the first moment I set foot into a ruin." Or had it been just the initial manifestation, and he carried the ghost always inside him like the monster? Were they the same?

Aaoran stilled, Otar felt their burning gaze.

"It gives me observations. I can ask questions, but the answers rarely make sense."

Otar's eyes traced the sleek blocks, willing them and himself far away. "It just told me that Eitin lies to the north. Somewhere deep in the mountains. It also told me that this, here," he made a sweeping hand gesture, "is called Inchenor, the first."

The scholars moved around them, shouting remarks to each other, murmuring curses, wanting more or less light, filling their notebooks with frantic words and drawings.

"Have you asked about the purpose of the blocks?"

Otar paused. He hadn't, he realized. He shook his head.

"Will you ask now?"

Already opening his mouth, he looked to Aaoran and heat crawled up his cheeks. He swallowed to hide his discomfort. "Maugi," he whispered, mindful of the other scholars. "What is the purpose of the blocks?"

Maugi answered without missing a beat.

Here everything is stored.

Otar repeated the words to Aaoran, who furrowed their brows.

"I'm not sure I understand. Are these like barrels or crates and we need to pry them open?"

Otar sighed. "Sometimes the ghost is more clear in what it tells me, but often it's speaking in riddles almost on purpose. As if it thinks that I understand it better than I do."

Let me check you.

A zip traveled down his back and Otar twitched. The monster growled, rising to the surface, chasing after the sensation. When nothing happened, it settled right under Otar's skin.

Aaoran stepped closer to him, not quite touching, but concerned. "What happened?"

"Something jolted down my back." The tickling spread throughout his body to his fingertips, his head, his toes, then it was gone.

You are broken. You could understand me better if I fixed it.

Aaoran leaned closer, curiosity written all over their face.

"It wants to fix me—"

"Otar."

The voice cut through everything else. Otar turned and met Andres' gaze. His eyes were stormy in the gloomy light. Why was Andres here?

Tell me when you are ready. I recommend it be done.

Maugi's voice never changed, as if it were all nothing to him, as if it were just a book, a provider of information. Otar blinked. There was something there—a spark, a world outside his grasp—his mind leeched onto it, reaching farther and farther. He was in two places at once: the room with the black stones *and* under a rust-colored sky with voices speaking simultaneously, as if—

"Otar." Andres' voice was close now. His fingers grazed the back of Otar's hand.

The worlds in Otar's mind snapped into one. His mind was sluggish to accept it, his vision doubled for a second, and his knees threatened to buckle under him.

An exhale. And it all stabilized.

His eyes searched the black stones again. Maugi was watching. Otar wanted to reach for it anew, but Andres' hands circled his wrist, yanking him back.

"It's time to leave."

How could he leave now?

"Come." Without waiting for a confirmation from Aaoran or Otar, Andres dragged Otar out of the room, up through the stairway, into the main dome, and out into the open air. Never stopping his stride nor letting go of Otar's hand until they rounded the outer wall of the smaller dome with no one in sight.

Here, Otar regained his senses and wrenched his hand free, dancing a few steps back out of reach, while massaging his wrist. "Care to explain?"

Andres watched him from hooded eyes and sighed. "I felt you."

"What?" Since his confession, there had been no time to talk more about it. A part of him was ready to forget it all.

Andres pressed a fist to his heart. "Right here, as if something was moving inside it, and then outside, to where you were." He rolled his shoulders back and shuddered as if he were trying to dislodge the sensation. "The closer I got to the dome, the stronger the impression became. And then I felt you move to a far away place, and I knew if you stayed there, I would never be able to reach you again." He shook his head and let his hand drop. "I fear I'm not explaining this right."

Otar swayed; he reached out to catch himself at the nearby wall. When Andres moved closer to help him, Otar raised an arm to stop him.

"Was it the ghost?" Andres asked after a small-turn of silence.

Otar nodded, and the tickle spread like a phantom sensation through his body. "It did something. Then it said that I needed to be fixed, that if it were done, I could understand the ghost better. Maybe that also means I can regain some kind of information that tells me who I am."

Andres studied him. He'd crossed his arms over his chest. "Do you think this is a good idea?"

Otar shrugged, looking down at his hands; they had killed and taken life force, dug into souls and turned fragile paper, and had touched skin and blood.

"Otar."

He was tired of hearing his name. "I always knew that I didn't belong. That I differed from everyone around me." Otar chuckled without mirth. "Don't we all think that we are special?" He let his hands sink again and looked out over the ruins. "But there was always something moving in the shadows. I wondered if Maugi was part of the ruins or a part of me. I believe now that the ruins and Maugi are the same, or at least an extension of another. There is a connection between them. More than once has the monster reached out to the ruin, to the ghost, to the memories that seem to haunt all of them." He turned to Andres. "I just separated them, or the further I'm away from the ruins, the less clear any of them becomes, the harder I can control it."

The monster had been so very docile since he had arrived here. Otar shrugged and turned his head to the sky. The blue was endless. Was there a beyond as endless as this? Otar put the thought to the side and met Andres' gaze. "Doing what the ghost wants to do could give us all the answers we are seeking."

"Answers for the scholars, from a world so long-forgotten that it doesn't touch us anymore. For something we don't need to understand. Why should we know how this was all built? Where did they come from? Why did they leave? What matters is the now, and the future, and what we make of it."

"Knowing the past helps us understand where we come from, and it helps us to move forward." Otar sighed. "It helps us to see how the world was shaped and how it defined us."

"Are you in need of that, defining your past? Can't we just puzzle over it and call it a turn? Do you have to do something potentially dangerous with an unclear outcome? To fix you? What will happen to the you you're now?"

Sudden anger bubbled under his skin, his hands trembled. How dare he…He looked at Andres, registered the concerned lines around his mouth and eyes, the desperation, and the fear.

The fear of losing Otar.

Has anyone ever feared for him?

Otar turned away. He could answer that he knew what he was doing—yet, it would be a lie. In truth, he was terrified. The implications of everything had haunted him ever since he became aware of the possibility that he could be related to the Ancients. What else would he discover? Would he lose the *now* in the process of it? And yet there was a burning curiosity, a drive he would never escape from.

"Andres." It was only a name, but it carried everything he felt for the man inside him.

"No," Andres commanded.

Otar turned to him and took his hands between his own, let his fingertips dance over the callouses and scars, the deep ridges that spoke of a hard life lived.

"Please, no," Andres pleaded, his body bowed forward, protecting himself against the next blow.

"I need to know."

"Why? Is this life not enough? Am I not enough?"

The question broke Otar's heart. Andres had always been enough, more so even, and yet this was the only way forward. He kissed Andres' knuckles.

"Akamar daro."

Andres grabbed him and hugged him close, engulfing Otar completely. "I don't want to lose you." The voice wasn't more than a whisper. The unspoken "again" hovering between them, then dissolving in the midturn breeze.

"You won't."

He hoped it wasn't a lie.

Chapter 20

"I know you must wonder about a lot of things, and I never wanted it to come to this. I admit it is a mess of my making, but then what would happen otherwise? We both know the world isn't ready really for what the Ancients hid. The only regret I have is that I might never be able to tell you or even show you the whole truth. An incredible truth that goes beyond my wildest dreams."

(From: Otar's letters to Aaoran, unsend)

OTAR WAS SITTING with his bowl in his hand, staring at the other people seated around them. After they returned, Aaoran didn't comment about Andres' interference, but Otar saw the questions dancing in their eyes.

They ate in silence. When finished, Andres was called away by Onder, and, after a last glance at Otar that clearly was a warning and a plea, he walked off with his twin. Aaoran lingered for a moment longer, but Otar wasn't ready to talk yet, so they left him alone.

His feet took him to the road, and he stared down its length until it disappeared into the crevasse. He didn't react when Turas stepped up to him.

"Show me."

Otar dropped his shoulders.

They walked down the paved path, through the gate, down the ruins, through the dome, and down to the smaller one. Witch lights threw the world into harsh lines and shifting shadows.

Scholars inched along the blocks, noting down any of the markings down to the smallest details, from the different colors on the walls down to the composition of the dirt—if there was any.

"You know what this is?" Turas asked as he stepped closer to one block, making sure not to be in the way of a crouched scholar taking a better look at the connection between the block and the floor.

"No, I don't." Otar brazed himself for the accusation, but Turas only nodded. That was new. Usually, the other would argue that Otar was lying, that he was withholding information; after the accident, he had never accepted a word from Otar without questioning everything about it.

Seven summers ago, scholars had found a small piece of a ruin crystal, taken from a well that had shattered. One of them had brought it back to the university so it could be examined. Otar had been allowed to study it, and he wondered what would happen if for once he didn't take but gave his own life force. If he could even do it. He told Turas and Jasner to stay away and that it was dangerous, without going too much into the details of what he was planning to do.

But Jasner had barged in when Otar had been trying to channel the energy. The monster, agitated by what

Otar was doing, latched onto the heir. Otar took too long to realize what was happening, and even longer until he could detach himself from the fragment.

He had been too late. Jasner had lost a lot of his life force. While he was recovering, he regained a portion of it, but not all, and now his condition was more delicate, and he was prone to illness and fatigue.

Otar shook the memories away as he walked with Turas around the perimeter and stopped at a block in the corner, currently unoccupied.

"Turas."

The other turned to him and furrowed his brows. "You want to try again," he concluded.

Otar nodded, while Turas hummed in thought.

"It won't be like then."

Turas crossed his arm, looking up and down the dome. "How can you be sure?"

"Because this time, no one else will be here."

Turas pointed to the scholars still crawling around. He raised an eyebrow, and Otar smiled. "Not in broad sunlight, obviously."

"And who will inform the guards? Don't tell me that steppe rider you are close to will."

Otar refrained from sticking out his tongue. "He knows."

"I'm surprised."

Otar rolled his shoulders back in a gesture that showed it didn't matter. "It was time."

It was late. The moon stood high, throwing pale light over the grayness of the night. All that Otar wanted to do was to lie down again in his bed and curl up to Andres and forget everything else. Andres had said little when Otar had instructed him to tell the guards to make sure that no one was in the dome that night. It wasn't a hard task; with the independent movements of the blocks, they cited security measures, and the scholars accepted it with only minor grumbling.

Otar slipped in unseen, letting the shadows welcome him. The ever-present pale light guided his way. His steps echoed unnaturally loud, even when Otar moved carefully to not attract the attention of the guards.

Maugi flickered into existence the moment he descended the stairs. Everything about the ghost was muted; its presence, its colors, its voice in Otar's mind.

"Okay Otar, you've got this," he murmured to himself. He stepped down and peered into the main underground chamber. The well inside glowed. One turn and a few more steps and he would be in the small dome. Everything was as they had left it. The blocks hadn't moved again.

Otar crept forward, his stride slowing the closer he came. Then he was within reach.

There was no escaping it now.

He exhaled and put a hand on the wall.

And then…nothing.

Otar huffed. That was anticlimactic.

Your memory is imperfect, blocking everything. Fixing it is still recommended.

Otar swallowed. Was he ready for it? Or could there be another way?

No other option detected.

Otar inhaled.

Do you want to proceed?

He exhaled. **Yes.**

As you wish. Please give me proof of who you are.

I'm Otar.

This isn't enough.

Otar looked around. An eerie blue light, deeper than the usual faint hue, drew his attention. A small rectangle indentation to his right was now alit. He poked it.

I need a drop of blood.

In front of Turas, Otar had spoken with confidence—but he was scared. It felt as if he was giving in to something of a magnitude he wasn't prepared to understand.

And yet it was the only way.

He steeled himself and fished in his pockets for anything sharp to prick his finger.

"Otar."

He closed his eyes. "Why are you here? No one is supposed to be here, or—"

"It will be Jasner all over again?"

Otar whirled around. "How?"

Andres kept a hand in his sash, the other on the pommel, alert but relaxed. "I had some concerns after our talks. Things weren't adding up. So I asked the only person who could give me some answers. I went to Aaoran, who sent me to his highness. It took the Heir apparent only a few drinks to spill it all."

Drunk-Jasner was still a blabbermouth.

"And he told me enough that I could piece it together with everything else you said to me. He also reassured me again and again that he has forgiven you. So why do you insist on going through with this?"

"Because this is my ancestry!" The shout echoed around them. The simple truth hanging between them: He was an Ancient, however impossible or improbable it may be.

Andres watched him for a moment before nodding.

"Okay," he said, his gaze as steady as the sun rising.

Otar narrowed his eyes. It seemed a weird answer. Was it that easy?

"You were right, ana." A rueful smile stole onto Andres' lips. "This is your chance to know more. Jasner, Turas, me, Onder, Aaoran. We know our history, our stories. We recognize who we are—but you? You never had that privilege. You are different. Maybe you are an Ancient, perhaps you are something else, who knows, but that is the point, isn't it? These ruins and that ghost, they can tell you. Because all else has been lost to you."

"No, not everything," Otar murmured. Fragments of memories floated in his mind—his mother's face, his father's, his sister's, the people from the village, Aaoran, Andres, Onder, Jasner, Turas—they all formed parts that made Otar who he was today.

Was that what Andres wanted to imply before? That it wasn't the distant past alone that shaped them, but even more the present and what they carved out for themselves?

"Andres…" Otar was helpless, the different truths battling inside him, but his lover shook his head.

"I don't want to discourage you. We all," he made an encompassing hand gesture, while his eyes never left

Otar's, "we have the luxury of knowing our past, and it's easy to overlook those who haven't been as fortunate." He paused, an impish grin on his lips, making him appear so much younger. "Will you forgive me?"

Otar snorted. What a ridiculous question. The man that forgave Otar all his secrets and half-truths didn't need his forgiveness.

Instead, he sighed. "I realize you were also right. So, we're even." He made a wave gesture with his hand. "But now you need to go or you will end up like Jasner."

Andres didn't budge. He widened his stance before settling in. "Neither will happen."

Otar pressed his lips into a thin line.

The other reached out and laid a hand on Otar's cheek. "Do you believe I would ever lie to you?"

He didn't, even when things were unclear between them. Andres never uttered a lie—he skirted the truth for sure, but Otar did it so many times as well.

Otar shook his head. "I can't trust myself. I don't know what will happen."

Andres grinned. "I have a feeling."

"You want to let me in on it?"

"I'll explain after."

That wasn't good enough, he wanted to say, but the curiosity mounted. His lover sounded so confident. Could he live with the consequences?

He cleared his throat. "Swear to me, you'll run."

Those dark eyes stared into his, but Andres bowed his head. "I promise."

Otar nodded and hoped that there would be enough time left to tell him, "I told you so."

His gaze found the blue rectangle. He stepped out of Andres' reach and then looked again for a needle or a sharp pencil.

"What is it?"

Otar eyed him. "It wants a drop of blood."

Andres raised an eyebrow but didn't comment. Instead, he said, "Allow me."

For a moment, Otar feared Andres would use the sword, but he drew a dagger from his boot and held out his hand. Otar put his own hand into Andres', wincing as the metal tip pierced his skin. Red welled up, and he stared at it fascinated.

"Go," Andres said.

Otar caught himself and then stepped to the rectangle, putting his hand on it.

An inhale. An exhale.

A zip through his body once more.

There you are. It was the second (or third?) voice, the one when he touched the well. Not Maugi, not the harsh one. The one from the ruins itself. *What you want to do is now possible. Shall I do it?*

"Yes."

The tingle spread from the tips of his fingers down his arm to his spine and from there to his entire body— checking every inch of him.

I have given you memories you were missing. It is a lot to take in. They will take time, unfurling bit by bit. I can't say how long until you adapt to them. It was a better way than forcing them open and endangering your state of mind.

Otar swallowed and was about to move his hand away, when another tingle stopped him.

The tone shifted. *But there is more. You are filled to the brim. Give it to us!*

There was a presence at his back, but it felt off. It wasn't outside, but inside. Otar saw in his mind's eye the connection to the ghost—which wasn't a ghost, but an intangible presence made from light.

He stood on a shore overlooking an endless ocean, similar to the one he'd seen before when the ruin took some of the energy for the first time. It stretched endlessly, further and further inside him.

Transferring live force.

The ocean rescinded, pouring out of him and into the ruin. It was more than he had ever fathomed he had taken. Was it really so much? All these summers, all this energy, never used. But why? What was the purpose?

The ocean dried out, and a steady pulse beat through him. The monster rose, a shadow stretching over the empty ocean and beyond, reaching for more energy. A line glimmered in front of him, shimmering in a slightly different hue than the world inside him, barely noticeable. It led outward again and then into…Andres?

The monster pounced on it, like it did with Jasner, and once more he was slow to react, to grasp it back—it had been so docile the last turns that Otar had almost forgotten how fast it could be, he tried to grab for it, but it slipped through his fingers.

No!

Suddenly the monster paused, like an overgrown dog who had found something unexpected, shuffled around before settling down again, evaporating in gray smoke.

"It is done," he said aloud, or in his mind? Once more, it was hard to differentiate where the outside world ended and where he began. What was inside his mind and what was real?

"What shall I do now?"

You can wake it up.

Otar blinked, his eyes focusing on Andres again and said, "Wake up."

It was as if the ruin exhaled, as if it had waited so long for him to arrive so it could finally be something again. It rumbled under their feet. A tremor moved through the ground from the middle of the room, rippling outward—the whole structure shifted. The blocks changed their glow, now the same blue light from the rectangle in his hand was on, spilled from all nooks and crannies and lines the scholars had mapped earlier so carefully. Symbols danced in abstract patterns over parts of them, showing rows and rows of ever-changing numbers.

Life force is readied to deliver to Eitin.

We can call for home.

Otar took his hand away and danced a few steps back, he was back in the real world. His fingers still tickled, and he used the other hand to massage the sensation out. The tremor subsided, and the ground returned to its steady self. Otar blinked once, twice, waiting for anything else to happen, and when nothing did, nodded.

"Let's go."

Andres touched his arm in confirmation, and they stepped out. Light spilled out from everywhere. In the underground chamber, the black lines shimmered, the crystal glowed, and at the far end, on the surrounding walls, the circles gleamed, as if they were doorways covered by thin gauze shifting in the wind.

Memories scratched at Otar's consciousness, something from the legends, words Maugi may have said.

A touch at his lower back, gone as fast as it had come.

Andres looked at him. "Are you alright?"

Otar pinched the bridge of his nose, to focus on the now. "I think so."

His lover studied him a moment longer and once more touched his arm in a silent confirmation. Together they climbed up the stairs, up into the proverbial lights. Everything was flooded. Not the eerie blue light that did nothing to dispel the shadows, but bright, as if the sun had risen in the building.

There was only one guard, the other gone to inform Aaoran as soon as the ground rumbled. After they slipped out in his back, they found that not only the main dome was alight, but the entire ruin. The outer buildings glowed. A strange sound filling the air, not a hum but as if a low fire was popping somewhere.

They chose a nearby building to hide in to not be caught, and Otar peered around the door opening to look back. The spires crackled. Tiny light bolts, like sparks when lighting a fire, arced over them. As if it was gearing up for something. An ominous feeling formed in the pit of his stomach.

Steps thundered from down the road, and Aaoran swept past, followed by guards and a handful of scholars. Andres and Otar looked at each other, nodded, and when the rear group was high enough they slipped out, mingling in. Onder saw them do it, but at his raised eyebrow, they shook their heads.

When they reached the dome entrance, Aaoran was already pointing scientists in different directions. At last, they spotted the two of them and waved them over. For a moment, their face was unreadable and then they smiled.

"Is this your doing?" They kept their voice low, but their eyes twinkled, amused.

Otar nodded.

"So this is how a ruin looks when it's really alive, hm?"

They turned around, taking it all in. The now glittering stones, the brightness, the constant noise. "You think the second dome opens now?"

Otar had all but forgotten about it.

Would it be alright to open it? What if a different monster was waiting there? The same type he had encountered in the ruins in the mountains? And why was he thinking about that one now?

Interesting.

And the voice was gone again.

"Let us check," he found himself saying.

They walked in the main dome, across, down the staircase to the lower level, and stopped in front of the closed dome door. Two scholars were already on it, trying to find a mechanism to open it.

"Any luck?" Aaoran asked them.

"We tried."

They don't have the right.

Otar almost sighed. **Can you please unlock it?**

Do you want me to give them the right?

Yes.

A hum.

They are allowed.

The light of a small block to the side shifted. No one besides him noticed it. Otar looked at it and back at Aaoran. He licked his lips. "Try again."

Aaoran narrowed their eyes at him, and Otar resisted the urge to scratch his neck or shuffle his feet.

"Okay," they said, measured, "let's try again."

One scholar huffed, clearly put out, but he did as he was told, probably to prove a point. He laid his hand on the stone and pushed. For a split second, nothing happened, and a smirk had already formed on his lips when it suddenly gave way. It had opened a fraction, but it was visible. The scholar frowned and shoved harder. When he proved to be too weak, Andres and Onder, who had followed them, stepped up.

Each chose a wing, and they pressed on three.

The doors swung inward.

They stared at each other and grinned. Otar crept a few steps forward, followed by the other scholars.

The dome was lit. Large stiff canvases hung down from the ceiling and around the walls, with dancing pictures on them. Otar had encountered nothing like this before. An army of blinking lights was everywhere. There were metal stairs leading up to a narrow gallery that ran the entire circumference of the room, barely wide enough for one person. Round, long cylinders were haphazardly clustered throughout the room, connected by ropes to the ceiling. There were tables made from the same metal as the walkway. At the far end was a bigger cylinder.

Different tools littered the surfaces. Some looked familiar, but others were too strange to even guess their function. A low-grade huffing and puffing came from somewhere and a high-pitched whine grated in Otar's ears.

It gave the impression of a workshop, still in use, the inhabitants having stepped out for a moment to return at any small-turn.

They all stood in stunned silence. This was something they had never found. Tools and materials and other strange things were all here, as if whatever had befallen the other ruins did not extend to this dome, keeping it preserved and pristine.

The scholars spread out, carefully poking at the flickering lights that danced over the same type of black stone that made up the blocks in the other dome.

Otar tried to make sense of the moving pictures. They played over sections of the blocks and over the canvases hanging throughout the room.

There were mathematical graphs, symbols, and numbers. Intersecting lines with numbers growing and growing before wiggling lines that spiraled together in a helix form replaced them. From time-to-time parts were highlighted, numbers and more symbols scrawled close to it, before moving on again.

Maugi, what is this?

Here I made you.

It shouldn't come as a blow. But it did. He staggered back and exhaled. His vision blurred, and then he had himself under control again. So it was true he was connected to the Ancients, maybe even was one of them.

"Otar?" Aaoran and Andres stepped close. They all stood now in front of the big cylinder. A glass window let them look inside. Cords and ropes in various colors and thickness hung down, some of them touching the bottom. A row of lights blinked at its base. Otar pressed a hand against the glass. It didn't feel different from the glass they used in the buildings in Rasanell and other places of the Seven Lands. It was smooth and cold.

"I was born here." And it rang true. Otar asked about the room, what the purpose of the room was, instead it told him about the cylinder.

Otar was born in there.

Why?

I was told to keep watch. And I did. I was also told to release them every hundred years. To disguise them so they wouldn't be discovered. So I made them small, released them all earlier than I would have in the past, and sent them all out into the world. But none returned. Until I found you. I wanted to call you back right there, because you were the only one, the last one I could build. I didn't have more material. But I couldn't do that. That wasn't your purpose, so I let you be.

"Otar."

He shook his head and turned to Onder, who was pointing at a smaller frame attached to the cylinder running numbers—numbers that disappeared and were replaced by a picture of Otar.

The sudden ringing sound in his ears overtook everything. Otar swallowed. He darted his eyes to the side, but none of the other scholars had noticed it yet.

"Not only was I born here, but I was the only one who survived."

No one was left. He was the last. Grief spread through him. Even if it was impossible from the beginning, meeting someone like himself was the dream he held deep inside him. But now it would never come true.

There, he had his answers. He pressed his forehead against the cold glass, feeling hot, disturbed, and lost.

Am I different? Because why else would he be the only one left?

The tone of the voice shifted. *How so? Different from what? When I looked into you, you were exactly as I built you, down to every little bit. The perfect machine.*

Otar trembled. He pushed his hands tighter against the cylinder, to find a focus point. The word machine rang in his mind. It sounded repulsive.

Am I not like you?

Like who?

You, Maugi.

Someone or something tittered. The voice shifted again.

Maugi and Otar are very different.

Otar closed his eyes. He tried to make sense of all the things swirling through his head. He felt Andres' presence on his left side, and Onder's on his right. Aaoran was close by. The people who had protected and helped him hadn't left him, even when his secrets had all spilled out. Whatever happened, whatever came, they were still with him, and he could count on them.

He exhaled and asked.

What is Maugi?

Maugi is the guide and the knowledge, but Maugi is also many. Maugi paused. A distorted sound broke out of it, and after it fell silent again.

The words didn't make sense, but they invoked an emotion, a picture of a black tapestry of a space more endless than the ocean.

But what was his role? Why was he taking life force and why could he give it to the ruin?

What am I here for?

To collect life force.

Otar shook his head as those words resonated deep within him. Forming pictures and memories not his own, and yet they existed. Screaming people, bodies with his face that moved and took and took and took.

He swayed; his stomach lurched. "I need to get outside."

And he ran.

He hurried through the gaggles of scholars without noticing where he was going. He turned to the right at the main entrance and rounded the building before he was sick in the sand.

There wasn't just a monster inside him. He was the monster. It was him. It was his only purpose, his only whatever. To collect life force out of what was living and bring it to the ruins. Was that why he was so driven to research them? Because he was made like that? The monster always perked up at the mention of the ghost, tried to reach out for it many times.

His thoughts swirled. Otar looked down at his hand, imagined them taking and taking and then touching Andres, his sisters, all the other people he knew, and he was sick again.

He sank down, rested his head between his knees, and yearned for everything to end.

He wanted answers, he had gotten them, and now he wished…for what? Not knowing them in the first place? Different answers? He inhaled and exhaled, concentrating on his breath, pressing the panic away.

The most important thing Otar had learned in his scholarly life was if he wanted to be respected and show any integrity, he needed to follow the facts and not use them to support the answers he wanted to see.

The evidence pointed him in the direction of a plausible answer, one that was monstrous and improbable in the first place, and now he found it was even worse…

Steps came from behind him, and a hand settled on his back. Andres didn't say a word and Otar was grateful. He felt rattled to the bone and didn't have the energy to even talk about what was going on inside him, and what the ghost had spoken about.

Not a ghost, but Maugi—a thing also created by the Ancients. At least it had hinted at it. Neither it nor he were natural.

Andres handed him a water flask, and Otar rinsed out his mouth before taking a few sips to settle his stomach and chase away the choking feeling inside him.

He was exhausted.

Andres hauled him up and led him back to the camp and into their tent. He swayed when Andres undressed him to his underthings and didn't protest when he put Otar down into the bed. A kiss to his forehead was the last thing he noticed before sleep claimed him.

Chapter 21

"The monster is always there. It seems eternal—it doesn't matter if I'm sick, injured, tired, happy, sad. It's a constant in my daily life. Often I wish it gone, but then would I be able to communicate with the ghost as I do, would I be able to wake ruins up to even have a chance at deciphering their secrets? Probably not. So I accept it, and the danger it holds—one slip up with the wrong person and I'll be dead. The thought is nauseating and at the same time exhilarating. As if a part of me relishes in what I would be able to do."

(From: Scholar Otar's last notebook, unpublished)

OTAR WOKE AT night. Andres' heavy arm was thrown over his stomach and his lover's deep breathing was bordering on snoring. Tenderness rose in Otar, mixed with sadness. He realized now what he needed to do, but he also knew it would hurt so many people. Unexpected people. He had always thought himself alone, that no one would ever care what happened to him, that none of them stayed close because they loved him—but they did. He was unsure how he should feel about it.

He wriggled out from under Andres' arms and then took Andres' thick robe, smoothing his hands over the embroidered pattern. It was almost too long, but it carried Andres' scent; that mixture of smoke and spice and sweat, soothing Otar's frayed nerves.

He stepped outside and turned his face to the sky. Night reigned, but the pale light shimmering over the towering stone walls told him that the ruin was still ablaze. He swallowed.

Maugi?

The air next to him glimmered and Maugi materialized. He supposed that answered the question if Maugi was a part of the ruins or of Otar. It had always been with him. Whatever the ruin had done to him, repaired inside him, Maugi was now at his side.

You have been born with a fraction of me in you.

A new wave of nausea swept through him, but he pressed it all to the side. There were more important things to take care of. It was time that he understood what lay beyond.

But Maugi is also many.

The phrase kept rattling around in his mind. Since coming here and interacting with the ruin, he could make out three distinctive voices.

A Maugi voice that was neutral and lacking inflection; another similar to it, but with faint emotions, longing, and regret creeping through; and another one that spoke of 'we'. It hadn't been there often, but Otar had felt a force behind those words, a power contained, ready to break out.

It was time to understand it all because he now knew what he was. However, his creators were still shrouded in mystery, and he had the distinct feeling that if they didn't figure out what the ruins were for, they all would be in danger.

He hurried down the stone road, trying to keep out of the sentries' view as much as possible. If he was spotted, he needed to at least be fast enough to go through with his plans before the cavalry, meaning Andres, arrived and hindered him once more.

Maugi, what is the risk of forgetting my current memories if I force the recovery?

So far his memories had only come in bits and pieces—not enough to understand what was going on.

Higher than the average.

Otar cursed. He imagined that to be the case, but the risk was more than he had expected but less than he had feared. Maybe he could rely on his connection to Andres to even out the odds. He shook his head. No, he wouldn't drag his lover into his mess any more than he'd already done.

But hadn't he also said that he wasn't alone? Didn't that mean that he also had the capacity to lean on other people?

Everything had become so onerous.

Otar slipped through the ruin buildings, hiding from the guards. He arrived just on the other side from the dome's entrance. The main entry point was in a diagonal line to his right, and two grim-looking steppe riders swept their eyes around.

The blazing lights would hide nothing.

Otar gnawed at his thumbnail, thinking fast.

Maugi, distract them.

Not sure what you mean.

Otar sighed. **They need to vacate their post for a brief turn. Don't hurt them.** He added that last part hastily, not sure what Maugi was capable of.

Thinking up scenarios.

Otar didn't find that very assuring, but let it slide.

Then one half of the ruin was plunged into darkness, emitting a high-pitched whine. The guards at the entrance looked at each other and started moving towards that direction. Otar waited long enough for them to be as far away as possible, then he hurried into the building, down the stairs and only came to a stop when he slipped into the dome with the black blocks. He dropped behind the last row and halted. But no steps had followed him down, no shouting reached his ears.

He forced his heart back under control and righted himself. The robe hung heavy around his shoulders. An embrace from a ghost. He shuddered and clamped down on the thought. Instead, he fingered the blue stone over his chest and clasped it tightly. Then he walked over to the block he had touched before.

Maugi.

Yes?

Force the memories into me.

It can be done, but the other method is the recommended one. It will be less dangerous and destructive.

Give it time, they will come to you, the process has already started. The voice with resignation and regret.

I don't care.

Oh, Otar.

Do it. The one that held pressure, a tempest contained.

As decided. Please proceed. Maugi's neutral tone.

The same square depression he had touched before lit up again, and he put his hand down without hesitation.

Maugi was inside him again, fluttering through every part of his body, down the nerve endings, filling him out; he was Maugi, and Maugi was him.

Something else rose in the back of his mind.

Andres had woken up.

Otar kept himself as calm as he could, pushed the rising panic down and away. With each new connection Maugi made, with each new memory, it became increasingly hard. Until he drowned in images and words and everything was laid out before him.

Screams threatened to break out. He pressed his lips and teeth together.

The world shifted. Buildings rose and fell before his mind's eyes, impossible spire-like creations touching clouds and stars. Ruins alike sprawled endlessly. Flying things, those he had seen on the murals, floated in the sky. Energy zipped from spire to spire, akin to fireflies dancing in the twilight.

Otar was here and there at the same time. Everything rushed into him. Rearranging what he knew, what he was.

What was his name?

Where was he?

Why had he come here?

Otar. It whispered through his mind in an oddly familiar voice. Deep and growling, rough with anger and sleep and resignation. Why? Who was he?

Another shift.

An endless steppe. The sun rising. A warm body beside him. A tent. Shadows shifting. Fingers on his skin. Lips on his. Something sweet and soft.

Andres.

Return.

We can begin.

And then the storm came.

WHEN OTAR BECAME himself again, he wasn't alone. Aaoran and Andres stood beside him. Not talking, waiting. Otar took his hand down and turned to them. He read anticipation, worry, and anger on their faces.

"Otar?" Andres hesitated where he stood, clearly wanting to touch him, but unsure if he was yet the same Otar.

Otar nodded. And Andres hugged him. Otar, too overwhelmed, sank into it. His voice was a far away thing, his mind trapped in that talking space, pictures chasing each other in his thoughts.

This is everything. All the memories are now there. They will settle down, but it will take time. Your entire conscious-ness will break down otherwise.

The words slid through him. He knew when the sun rose, all of it would be finished. He opened his mouth and closed it again. Feeling as if he hadn't slept for hundreds of summers, he swayed. Everything in his mind intertwined—the then and the now—making it hard to sort through it.

A rumble caught them by surprise.

Eitin has answered. Sending life force.

An ominous feeling settled in Otar's heart. He raced through his memories, but it was all still fragmented.

Soon, soon, we can call for them soon.

Counting down the time until establishing communication.

"Otar?"

Andres was looking at him, his eyes searching his face. He couldn't answer. He needed to let his mind settle to make sense of it all. They needed to wait.

…call for them…

He licked his lips. He was sure that it meant only one thing.

"They will be coming."

OTAR STARED INTO his cup of brew. He didn't remember arriving in his bed a second time that night. He had slept through the sun rising and when he woke, the world was still standing. The side next to him was empty.

The thoughts rearranged themselves in his mind, and it was now easier to separate the different pieces of himself and the past, when the Ancients had arrived here. There wasn't a lot he could recall about them. Either it had never been part of his memories, or they were still closed to him. It didn't matter.

He rubbed his temples and decided he needed more than one cup of brew to sort through this mess. The kitchen matron was as kind as always. She took one glance at him and gave him an entire jug and a platter of cold, grilled vegetables, porridge, and fresh fluffy bread. The same food they made in Andres' tribe.

He was so grateful he almost cried. After walking over to the furthest corner of the tables and sitting down, he inhaled the food. He had been ravenous. For the moment sated—yet the monster burned under his skin since the ocean was drained out of him—he filled his cup with brew and contemplated what to do next.

"Call for them." The word kept echoing in his head. Meant "them" more Ancients?

Was it his fault? Because he'd woken the ruin?

No. They prepared it many summers ago and concealed it. They played a long game, biding their time. They knew how long they needed to wait until it all came together. Your life force helped to do it earlier.

So, a coincidence and half his doing. It didn't make him feel better. Otar took a swig from his brew and thought about the whole situation. He still wasn't sure what to do next, and he had lingering questions about how he had been born here but found by his father in the north.

I transported you to Eitin before Inchenor went dormant.
"They could travel in the blink of an eye."

The lines on the ground with names on it pointing to ruins, the shimmering circles on the walls, together with the hidden purpose of the underground chambers—they were the means to move from one ruin to another, a network of travel posts. Not unlike those they had for the yardar. Maybe different colors meant specific places or regions.

Could they access it now? Or would the other end just be closed off, and they would perish if they attempted to use it?

Questions and speculations.

Something was coming. Every time his mind circled back to that, he shuddered. More of the Ancients? What would happen then? Were they friendly or not? It was unclear. He was to collect life force to be used as some kind of fuel, like fire logs that burned, providing warmth and helping to cook—he powered the ruins.

We only wanted to survive. The plea whispered through his mind. Another voice snorted and then his mind was silent again.

There was one thing he could do: He needed to go to Eitin.

As soon as he realized that, a shadow fell over him. Andres' face was unreadable. He'd said nothing since last night.

Now, he was watching. Waiting for him to say something, to explain, to guide him. He was right. It was time to tell them why he was created, and what they had made friends with.

OTAR CHOSE THE underground chamber as a place to talk. Most scholars had moved to the two smaller domes or were still trying to figure out how the murals now fit into the new discoveries. No one said anything about his picture in the workroom, and he wondered what Aaoran had told them about it.

They clustered around the well, the energy humming under their feet. Andres was there as well as Onder, Aaoran, and to his surprise, Turas and Jasner. All the people who knew parts of his secrets—but no one who understood it all.

Among them, as if the others had subconsciously made space for it, hovered Maugi. Ethereal as always, a construct like him bound by their purpose. They all had a specific role to fill until the very end. Or had they? Maugi had come with the Ancients, that much he knew. There were bits and pieces about it in his mind, but once more it seemed not to be his memory alone.

Otar entwined his fingers behind his back and sighed. "I'm not sure where I should start."

"The beginning helps." Aaoran's eyes twinkled, but their brows were furrowed, showing deep ridges and worry lines.

Otar huffed. "The beginning, you say?" Where was that? When the Ancients arrived? When he was born? When he understood what he was?

"As we have gathered, the Ancients came from a different place and landed at the shore of the Seven Lands, many, many summers ago. They built this ruin as their first outpost and wanted to establish communication with their home. They brought everything for it, but they failed. They were left stranded, with no way back and no way forward. So they built more places."

"Couldn't they have used the resources to return instead?" Turas asked.

Otar shrugged. That part was blurry for him—there was something strange about it. All he knew was that it hadn't been possible. "I think they had hoped to find the resources here they would need to return, and when they didn't, I think they decided to just expand to gather what they needed that way." He shuddered.

Maugi kept its vigil.

"Why did they come?" It was Aaoran.

"Probably the same reason why we travel anywhere—to explore, to understand, to find something beyond our own purview." He stared at Maugi, but the ghost was still. "I don't know for sure. Just that they came and built, and they created me."

At that, Otar looked at each of them. Aaoran watched, fascination on his face; Jasner had the same excited gleam in his eyes; Onder blinked rapidly, as if he was unsure what he was listening to; Turas was thoughtful, his arms crossed; and Andres had his eyes fixed on Otar.

"I never thought something like this could be possible, creating a living person," Aaoran said.

"To what purpose?" Onder asked, brows furrowed.

Otar peered into the well, avoiding their gazes. "To collect life force and transfer it to the ruins to power them." He raised his hands, as he had often done in the last turns, and looked down at his palms, trying to understand how they could do what he did. "They created me to be a monster."

No one moved. Otar let the silence settle, imagining that he was alone and not confessing his deepest sins.

"That explains the accident," Jasner mused.

He nodded.

"You know, before it happened, I could power witch lights and read the politicians around me like an open book. After, nothing of that remained."

"Are you saying that life force and magic are the same?" Aaoran asked.

"Interesting thought. Maybe you're not here to take the life force but the magic inside us, however marginal it is, and use it as fuel. But for us it is the same, and therefore it can be deadly," Jasner murmured, his tone hesitant.

Did it even matter anymore?

He took, and he killed, and he gave it to power stones.

"So you woke the ruin?"

Otar nodded and glanced up again. They all appeared puzzled, trying to fit it all together.

"Most ruins are dead or kind of waiting for energy to come to them, so they can wake up." He pointed to the well. "This is the heart that holds the power of a living ruin."

His knees felt weak, and a headache was forming at the base of his skull. There was more information inside him. A lot of it didn't quite fit, fragments he didn't know where to put.

"You said they will be coming?"

Otar spread his fingers. "I did. And I'm not sure if this is a good or bad thing. The energy I poured into the ruin was sent to Eitin, the main city of the Ancients, and is there to be used to call the others. But for what purpose?"

Run little Otar, run.

His head snapped to Maugi, but it didn't move, or waver, a statue made of air.

"What happened?" Turas eyed him.

"I think Maugi just warned me."

"The ghost?" Aaoran flicked their eyes from him to the open spot between them.

"Yes. It said: Run."

But where to and from what?

He swallowed. "There is one way we can find out more." He met the gaze of each of them before he looked back at Maugi.

"I need to go to Eitin."

Chapter 22

"Eitin is truly the grandest. One day you'll find it, hidden in the icy valleys of the north. It's a sight to behold. There won't be any more dangers lurking there when you finally arrive, Aaoran-peras. When you come, this will be my gift to you."

(From: Otar's letters to Aaoran, unsend)

IT WAS TURAS who found him sitting on higher ground looking down at the ruins. Upon hearing his steps approaching, Otar didn't look up but deflated.

"Come to finally pass your judgement?"

Turas didn't say anything but settled down next to him, and for a moment, they sat in silence. A light breeze flowed in and ruffled Otar's hair. There were sounds from the camp below mingling together; it was peaceful. Otar closed his eyes and let the sun warm his face, burning all those doubts and thoughts coursing through his mind away.

"I was jealous."

Otar turned his head to face Turas but didn't probe further. Turas looked straight ahead, squinting a little when he looked up high into the sun rays.

"You came into our lives so effortlessly, and you took Jasner's attention. I liked you, but Jasner was fascinated by you for some reason, and I feared…"

"That I would take him away."

Turas rolled his shoulders back, not outright admitting to it, but his words were clear enough.

"It's hard to believe what you are telling us now."

Otar hugged his knees. "Would it be easier for you when I say I can hardly wrap my mind around it?"

"Not really. It's hard to believe that you were created, not born, that there had been someone with so much magic to be able to create another living and breathing person. I won't diffuse your claim but, in my mind, it's still just an elaborate con to get out of your responsibilities."

Otar sighed. It would be a long time, if ever, that Turas fully changed his mind on what happened, but it was to be expected. "I wish it was the case."

"When you go, I'll come with you."

"To keep an eye on me?"

"Forgive me for that. I try as Jasner demands, but it is hard for me. He is everything to me, he was so much and still seeing him reduced like that…it is hard."

There was nothing Otar could say to that besides, "As you wish."

OTAR PACKED HIS pack and wondered if he really needed any of the things he'd put inside it. Notebooks and pens seemed kind of silly to him. When they had emerged from the underground chamber back up to the main dome, he stepped up to the murals—the pictures invoked a familiarity, but he still didn't understand them fully. Some of them he'd seen in the sky of his memories, high above, hovering just like Maugi did, but they made little sense to him.

Andres was watching him from the bed, while Otar packed and repacked and gave up.

"Talk to me," Andres said when Otar stopped moving around, staring at his belongings.

"What is there to talk about?"

"Otar—"

"Don't!" He put his head in his hands. "Please don't." This wasn't a name—Otar meant something bad, a monster, something created. He wasn't anything anymore, he had no history, no nothing. His shoulders shook.

"Look at me, Otar."

He flinched, but he raised his gaze. Andres wasn't touching him, but his expression was tender.

"You know why I like your name? Why it stuck the first time Aaoran introduced us?"

Otar shook his head. A long-lost memory broke loose. The widening of Andres' eyes when Aaoran had said Otar's name, quickly replaced by a twinkle.

"*Otar*, in our language, means 'Gifted by the lords', something precious."

He wondered if he should laugh hysterically or cry.

Andres rose from the bed, circled it, and sank down before Otar, taking his hands into his own.

"However you came to be, you are a gift to me. Akamar daro. Whatever may happen."

He reached into his hair and tugged a braid loose. It held two golden beads, so finely engraved it would take turns to make out all the lines and symbols.

Andres took a strand of Otar's hair behind his ear and twisted it into a small braid before securing it with one bead.

"You are now family. My family."

"But, you…we said…I…"

"I know," Andres smiled. "And this isn't the complete vow, but a reminder for you. I won't let you go. Whatever you may think, whatever you may believe, whatever may happen," Andres pressed one hand over the stone resting against Otar's skin, and with the other he cupped his cheek, "I won't leave you alone."

"Akamar daro," Otar whispered, too overwhelmed to voice anything else.

Andres smiled, the soft and small one reserved just for Otar, and then kissed him.

THEY GATHERED ONCE more in the underground chamber. The others, Onder, Aaoran, Turas and Jasner, looked unsure as to why they would start the journey right here. After some heated discussions, they decided that Turas and Andres would accompany him, and Onder would remain to oversee the guards. Jasner was too important as the heir to travel with Otar, and he complained about being left behind. Aaoran was needed to monitor the ruin and the scholars. Initially, Otar wanted to go alone, but that had been strongly vetoed. It crossed his mind to run away and leave the others behind, but the thought alone exhausted him.

He was tired of being alone.

"Shouldn't we set out?" Turas was impatient. "As I understand, time might be of the essence."

Otar shook his head. "Even if we left last turn, or the turn before, it would take too long to travel up north and find the correct place."

"Then how—"

"Maugi, open the way to Eitin."

The well glowed, the light spreading to the black line on the ground marked with Eitin. From there, it traveled across the floor to the opposite wall. The circle attached to the line there wavered, rippled, and turned a solid color of gold.

"They traveled in the blink of an eye," Aaoran quoted the legends.

"I think this is how they moved from one place to the next. My assumption is we will arrive in one of the colored rooms designed for arrivals. We step through, and we will be in Eitin."

"You think this is safe?" Turas asked, eyebrows furrowed.

No disruptions detected, the line is stable.

Otar shrugged. "Maugi says it's safe enough, and our only option. If you would rather remain here…"

But Turas didn't rise to the bait and only rolled his eyes.

Otar stepped closer to the waiting ring, when a hand caught his arm. "Return safely, Otar," Aaoran said, their gaze intense.

Otar swallowed around the lump in his throat and nodded. Out of the corner of his eyes, he saw Andres and Onder whispering to each other. No one had commented on the braid and the golden bead in his hair. But Onder had eyed him, his face, as often these turns, unreadable.

It didn't matter. Otar stepped further to the gate and turned back again. Turas and Jasner had their hands clasped, and Onder and Andres were hugging. Once more, the urge to go was overwhelming. He was sure as soon as he emerged on the other side, the portal would close. He would leave the others behind, with no way of finding him—but would that help?

Andres looked at him, but didn't move, his gaze steady for a moment. He turned back to Onder. They also clasped hands. Then he walked up to Turas and together they made their way over to him. They stepped up to the shimmering ring.

"Ready?" Otar croaked.

When they nodded, he took hold of both their wrists, just to be sure, and all three stepped through the portal.

As he'd expected, they emerged in a colored room. Otar took note that it was yellow, almost golden. He wondered if the colors said anything about the departure point or if they were assigned at random. The whole mechanism was fascinating to think about. How did they know which rooms were free? How were they connected? What happened if someone was in the room when another arrived? How did it look like? He rolled his shoulders back. It was hard to wrench his thoughts away from the puzzle. Instead, he checked on his companions. They looked dazed but alright.

Otar crept forward and peered into the hallway, half-expecting an Ancient stepping past. Had any of them survived over the summers? Keeping out of sight?

Maugi?

Yes, Otar?

Are there more of the Ancients?

Yes.

Okay, there should be some. They needed to be careful. It was still not clear if they were friends or foe. Yes, Otar sucked the life force out of living things, but not always, especially with Andres. Something held him back. When he was close to him, the monster heeled.

The hallway was dark. As soon as they stepped into it, ghostly blueish lights flickered on. So Eitin was maintained but not alive. And yet, Maugi had said that there were more Ancients. Another puzzle.

Maugi, can you guide the way?

I can give you a map.

A map? Maugi wasn't solid. How could it—

And then he had a plan in his head, the complete layout of Eitin, with everything that they had built. Otar stumbled, and Andres caught his arm.

"I'm alright, but somehow Maugi forced a map on me. It surprised me."

Andres nodded, but his hand lingered. He had the other hand on the pommel of his sword, his gaze alert.

"Which way?" Turas asked, and Otar closed his eyes for a moment to understand where they were and where they needed to go. First thing was to find a path out and then figure out what they were looking for.

"Left and then up. Then we should be in one of the five domes."

"Five?" Turas breathed, and Otar chuckled. In his mind, Eitin was a grand city of spires and domes and endless rows of buildings, all interconnected by bridges and pathways. They walked down the narrow path, Andres taking point, and then up a staircase and emerged into the central dome.

It was breathtaking, stretching over them, bigger than anything that had ever been documented. The floor was tiled in gold and silver, the murals painted in saturated colors, as vibrant as if they had been drawn that turn, reaching high over them.

This was the main city of the Ancients.

Turas turned around a few times, muttering words to himself.

They stepped out.

Eitin sprawled before them, hugging close to the mountain it was built in, going down in a terrace-like structure. There was a massive dome on every level surrounded by buildings. It looked chaotic, but with the map Otar could discern the system. Otar imagined it bustling with life and noise and shuddered at the emptiness.

What had happened? Where were they?

He wanted to ask Maugi, but something held him back.

"And now? Where to?" Turas asked.

Why had they come? To find out what was happening at Eitin. The life force had been sent here, calling for others, so they needed to locate whatever the Ancients used as communication and then…well, no clue.

Run Otar, as far away as you can.

There it was, the other voice again.

Let him come, show him, make him understand. He can't do anything. Followed by laughter.

The other, or was it more? It sounded like many voices, laced with anger and glee.

"Maugi?"

Yes, Otar. Neutral again.

"From where did they call the others?"

A red dot appeared on his map, marking a smaller dome. Otar raised his hand and pointed in the direction. "Over there."

"Will we meet with resistance?" Andres' hand wandered from the pommel to the scabbard, the other he kept out of his sash. His whole body was relaxed but alert, his gaze sweeping over the ruin.

Otar thought back to the black shadow in the mountains, the red glowing lights, its rage. "I'm not sure," he said, his eyes scanning the narrow pathways and stairs down the terraces. Nothing moved in the shadows, and the ominous feeling of something waiting was missing. Perhaps there was nothing there, and the guardian was a one-time thing.

They stepped forward.

Silence enveloped them, their steps echoing around the empty houses and the high stone walls.

On the first flight down, they stopped. The dome was two stories further down, emitting a faint bluish hue. All the smaller domes had a distinct tinge. Otar's fingers itched to note it all down, to dig deeper into this city that could give them more clues about the creators. But there was no time. He hoped he would keep some of this information. Maybe after they returned, they would allow him to study these ruins and not outright execute him.

What had Aaoran told the other scholars? About how they activated the transport? About what happened with the ruin, not once, not twice, but thrice? About what was going on?

A tremor rippled through the ground; they looked at each other.

"Let's hurry," Andres said and quickened his steps.

They rushed down the numerous pathways and stairs, weaving their way through a maze of right and left turns. It felt chaotic and organized at the same time. Otar navigated them sure-footed, the map in his head overlapping with reality, while he tried to catch a myriad of new information with his eyes and engrave them in his mind.

Another tremor traveled down the terrace. Andres made them stop and looked around. Otar squinted down the ruin. Did that shadow just move?

He licked his lips and felt dumb.

"Maugi, is someone guarding this place?" he asked aloud.

Yes. The guardians.

He cursed and relayed the information.

"What can we expect?" Andres drew his sword and fell into a defensive stance, his body taut.

Otar was about to ask when an image of red glowing eyes flashed through his mind.

We built five. One died early. One turned mad. We took three to Eitin.

Shadows detached themselves from the surrounding darkness. Growing bigger and bigger, nine red glowing lights zeroing in on them.

Turas cursed.

"Otar, can you tell Maugi to stop them?"

"Maugi?"

You don't have the rights.

You aren't us. More and more voices chimed in. *Not one of us. Not one of us. Not one of us.* It echoed all around him.

"No, it can't."

Solidified shadows, deep black that swallowed all the light and fuzzy at the outer edges, glided closer and closer, enveloping houses as if they weren't solid.

"I don't think a sword will help," Turas commented.

"Any better ideas?"

Turas shook his head.

"Then run," Andres called, and they all turned and pounded down the streets.

When Otar looked back over his shoulder, it was as if the guardians hadn't moved but were suddenly closer. He ran faster, stealing a glance over his shoulder. And yet nothing changed. The guardians came closer and closer, as if they were an image moved by a hand.

The third time he checked, they were close enough to breathe down their necks.

This wasn't working.

Struggling to catch his breath and unable to use his voice, he used his mind.

Maugi, where are we safe?

Let me check.

A new dot, in blue, appeared on the map. A line was leading them right to the domes.

"Follow me," he shouted and hoped the others would hear him. Shadows snipped at his feet, and he stumbled, a hand under his arm holding him upright. Turas shoved him forward, while Andres tried to deflect the tendrils with his sword. They dissolved and reformed, like smoke over a fire.

Otar pointed to the dome the blue dot on the map showed. "In there."

Maugi, open the door.

Checking rights.

It was the longest moment of Otar's life.

Door open.

Close it tight and lock it as soon as we are through.

They crashed through the opening. Tendrils trailed after them. The first guardian was almost inside when the door snapped shut, cutting it off, at the same time as a static humming went up. The shadowy left behinds dissipated.

Otar fell down on his knees, trying to get his thundering heart back under control. His lungs hurt, and his stomach heaved.

Hands checked him over, but Otar waved Andres away. "I'm alright, just out of breath."

"What was that?" Turas asked between his own lungful's of breath.

"Maugi called them guardians. I think I met one in a ruin in the mountains. That one seemed to have gone mad, set to destroy anything that had to do with the Ancients. It hunted me through the ruins."

Andres raised his eyebrows but said nothing else.

"What now?" Turas asked when he could keep upright and breathe again.

Otar looked around. The dome was dark.

"Maugi, can you make light?"

Maugi hummed and the light grew. The dome was smaller than it had appeared from the outside and it wasn't ornamented, like the smaller domes in Inchenor.

"Will we be able to access the place of communication from here?"

This dome isn't connected to the underground.

Otar sighed.

"I'm guessing not," Andres said dryly.

Otar checked the map but didn't quite understand what the measurements meant. "How far is it?"

The projected picture wasn't promising. They still needed to continue down a full terrace and then make it to the end to access the bigger dome, and from there, a passageway would lead them deeper into the mountains.

Turas, who had been inspecting the building, called them over. "There is another door. We could slip out, but the moment we do, they will be upon us."

"Maugi, can you distract them?"

Like the guards?

"Yes, like you did to let me creep into the ruin."

Andres rolled his eyes, and Otar smiled ruefully.

A rumble went through the entire dome.

I erected a barrier to keep them here. They will take it down soon.

That made Otar pause for a small-turn, but he shoved it away for the more pressing concerns.

"Maugi bought us time, but we need to hurry."

Andres and Turas nodded, and they ran for the other door, which opened for them. Outside, Otar took the risk of looking back and found the three gigantic shadows hovering in front of something shimmery. Their red eyes didn't turn to them, but Otar was sure they knew where their little group was.

They hurried through the streets as fast as they could.

They broke it down. They are coming.

Otar repeated the last sentence aloud.

They were close now, running parallel down the terrace as the stairs they needed were located at the other end.

Sudden air movement made Otar look back, and he almost faltered. The guardians' red eyes filled his field of vision.

They reached the stairs; Turas took a wrong step and tumbled down the second half, Otar helped him up with Andres dragging them both along.

"I'll shield you." Andres' breath came in harsh puffs. Otar shook his head.

"No, you can't fight them. They are shadows."

"I'm here to protect you."

"If you try, you'll die." Or worse. Otar suppressed that thought as well and kept on running. His knees threatened to buckle under them. Everything hurt, but stopping wasn't an option.

Maugi let us in the dome.

No!

There they were again, the multitude of voices. The second non-Maugi.

I'll ignore you, because Otar has precedence.

Otar felt himself smirk.

Dome is open.

Thank you.

There was no reply, not that Otar had expected one.

The door slid open, and they stumbled into the darkness. The opening closed with a thud, cutting off the shadow tendrils that had followed them. Once more, they sank to their knees to catch their breath. Otar contemplated never getting up again.

"Let's not do this again," Turas gasped, and Otar laughed, bordering on hysterical. It triggered a coughing fit. Andres put a hand on his back, stroking gently. Otar smiled up at him. And maybe, just maybe, everything would be alright in the end.

Chapter 23

THE DOME WAS different from the one they had been in first. It looked more like the workroom they had found in Inchenor. Low slaps that must have functioned as tables, dark blocks with flickering lights, and the same low hanging canvases with moving pictures they had seen there. The arrangement looked as if a kid had taken a handful of toys and threw them around. But there was a method behind it.

His memories were still coming together, and he knew he had massive gaps where more knowledge should be, but he recognized some patterns in how things were arranged. The layout of the workroom was close to Inchenor, but slightly off, as if someone else had worked here and rearranged the place to their liking, similar to how a blacksmith worked—smithies looked the same, with fire, workbench, anvil, and tools, but every blacksmith used a different setup.

He pondered that while he led the others throughout the dome, down the connected hallways deeper into the rock. It was a maze of rooms he had never seen in a ruin before. They were filled with rows upon rows of black blocks. Some of them had dancing lights flickering over them, others showed graphs and numbers.

It was eerily silent besides a faint static hum.

They subconsciously quickened their steps until they were nearly running down the hallway, until they were blocked by another stone door.

It was harder now to get anything from Maugi. The multiple voices that seemed to live in or alongside Maugi interjected like petulant children, throwing tantrums. In the end Maugi got the upper hand again, but Otar was exhausted. He swayed on his feet, wondering how much time had elapsed. When he toppled to the side, Andres caught him by the shoulder.

Opening the doors will take a while. The call home is still proceeding. I can't stop that.

"It will be a few small-turns until the door opens," Otar mumbled.

Turas looked around and then nodded at Andres. "Let's rest here."

Andres agreed, and then manhandled Otar into a corner, took off his cape and enveloped him in it. The cape was made from thick wool and soft to Otar's touch. He put up a token protest for Andres now being cold, but the other hushed him. Snuggling under the cape, he watched with half-lidded eyes as the others moved around. They checked the various rooms carefully and talked in low tones. It was friendly noise in the silence, and secured by that, he let it lull him to sleep.

The third Maugi voice, not the one that used 'we', came to him in his dreams. A ghost touching his mind and slipping in. It was quite a distinct presence, more alive than Maugi had ever been, distinctive by nature and yet familiar.

"Who are you?"

The voice smiled. There was no body or face to it, but Otar knew it grinned. "I'm your creator."

"Maugi created me."

"Yes. It created the current you."

Otar paused at that. His mind stretched and stretched, trying to comprehend the words.

"I don't think I understand."

"Let me show you then."

THE WORLD TURNED fuzzy, muffled sounds all around him, as if someone was speaking through thick stone or water.

Adjusting hearing.

"…the first—"

"Was a failure. This one seems more promising."

"I wonder—"

"Speak. You have been in a strange mood for weeks now."

An inaudible murmur… "—correct use of resources."

"You know perfectly well that we didn't have another choice." Agitation and desperation.

"Did we, really?" Wondering.

"They have a natural barrier. They won't come to harm, and we will have enough to call home. We are dying here." Pleading.

"I know, but I have a bad feeling." Resignation.

Laughter. "You and your feelings…"

"THIS WAS THE beginning of you. I made you, so that you and all the others could collect the energy of this world and give it to us, so that we could live and even return home," the third Maugi voice said.

"Why were you dying?"

The voice dissolved for a moment and then returned. "We come from another place. There, the world feeds us. When we arrived here, this world didn't want us, and we couldn't access the energy, the aether, to keep us alive."

"So you created me, created a monster."

"No, I didn't." A sound like a sigh. "We found by accident that when we touched the inhabitants, a bit of the life force could transfer to us. Enough for us to survive and make a living here. But we were home sick, cut off. We needed more energy to make the passage. For that I created Otar to collect, wandering around in groups and swarms to take and store and bring back."

Otar kept silent.

"It wasn't enough. We needed more to live, to maintain our homes and to return. So much power. But the barrier the inhabitants of this world had, the magic, prevented us from taking more, allowing only for floating bits but not full access. So we developed a virus to change you, and it worked. Not for all—some proved to be resistant to the changes, but most lost their magic and we could take what we wanted."

He wondered if he could be sick in his own dream. His stomach roiled, and bile rose in his throat.

"What happened then?" Because the Ancients never went home. They were still here. Where have they been hiding?

"The people revolted. They drove us out. We locked down the more central cities and turned to Eitin as our last stand. We gave everything to go home. But it wasn't enough. Some of us just wanted to give up, to end it, but the elders devised a plan. Keep building Otars, keep collecting energy, take whatever scraps the world is giving us, put our cities to sleep, and save it all up. So that one day, when there is sufficient power, we can send for help."

"Help?" Otar swallowed. Not only calling home, but getting more Ancients here?

"Yes." The chorus of voices chimed in. "To take revenge and rain fire on this world." Hollow laughter.

"Otar?" Someone was shaking his shoulder. Andres crouched before him, his eyes intense.

"What happened?" Otar scrubbed his eyes, struggling to get his bearings back, trying to understand what had been in his dreams. Had it even been dreams?

"You slept so soundly that we thought you slipped away," Turas said from above him. He looked worried. A look Otar hadn't seen for a long time on his face.

Otar fought himself out of the cape and shook it out, before offering it back to his lover. He took it with gentle amusement.

"Has the door opened?"

"There was a strange clicking sound, but we haven't checked yet."

Otar nodded and walked over. He pressed his hands against the stone, but they didn't budge. "Maugi."

Say please.

He rolled his eyes. "Please."

A loud click and the doors swung inward, as if pushed open by a ghostly hand.

Light flickered on, illuminating the room beyond, and Otar froze. His mind was taking an endless time to catch up with what he was seeing.

It was a dome-like structure but made of metal. The upper dome showed filigree metal arms interwoven with each other, interspersed with unusual glass. It reflected the light in a strange twinkly way. Beyond that, everything else was gray stone. The wall around was covered in the same type of gates they had used to reach Eitin, but smaller, barely wide enough for one person to step through. The Ancients' symbols were written over each portal. But no line led to them, and in the middle there was no well.

Only after Otar took in all those details, storing them away safely, did he turn to the thing that was also there, and what he had never seen before in any ruin: Bones.

Bones covered the entire floor. Some were close to each other, some haphazardly thrown around.

"By the lords!" Turas exclaimed, stepping to Otar's right.

Andres stood frozen to his left. "Are those…"

Otar nodded. "These must be the Ancients."

They came from all the other places. There was a plan I wasn't privy to, they—

The multi-presence again, stopping whatever Maugi wanted to say.

In his dream, the third voice had spoken that they gave everything to go home, but he hadn't realized it meant death.

Otar itched to take a better look at the skeletons. And yet he recoiled at the mere thought.

"What happened here?"

"More guardians?" Andres was already drawing his sword, but Otar shook his head and put a hand on Andres', pressing it down. He resisted for a moment, but he sheathed his sword and turned to Otar.

"What is it?"

Otar licked his lips. "They took their own life."

"Why?" Turas asked while he strode into the room, crouching down by the first heap of the strange silvery bones—thinner than a human one—but formed similarly. Otar could name all their parts and place them in a skeleton while the empty eye sockets of the skulls watched him.

Turas stretched his fingers out to touch the bones, and Otar resisted the urge to run over and slap the hand away.

He looked at Andres instead. "They did it to call the others."

"But that still doesn't explain this." Turas made a wavy hand gesture.

Otar sighed. "To put the plan in motion, they needed more energy than they had thought. To gain that, they created…well, me. But not just me, more than one of me. A lot more things went down, but in the end they overstepped, and you, the people, revolted against them and drove them out. They barricaded themselves here, and most gave up their life force to call home. But it wasn't enough. So they waited, sending out Otar after Otar, collecting energy, until I brought them the last bit."

"How many winters ago was that?" Turas rose again and squinted into the light.

"Too many to count."

"But if you want to call home, why give up your life?"

"To call the others here and exact revenge."

The words hung in the air and both stared at him.

"That doesn't sound good," Turas commented, crossing his arms.

Otar huffed.

"And now?"

They searched around, but there were only portals and death.

There is a door behind you.

Otar blinked and turned around, searching every inch of the walls, then he saw it; hidden between two circles, was an outline the size of a door.

"There." He pointed, and they hurried over.

"Will you let us in?"

I can't, Maugi answered. *I have done my part. I brought you here as she has told me to do.*

There was a pause.

I can.

It was the third voice.

Open sesame. Try now.

He stepped closer and pushed against it. It opened with no resistance.

Inside was a small room, not much bigger than Otar's living area in Rasanell. In the middle, stood a tower, made of metal. Lights blinked on the lower third, while a blue light ringed the rest. Protruding from the ceiling was a spire pointing down, with arcs of crackling energy dancing over it. The highest point of the tower and the spire met, sparks jumping between them.

Next to the strange construct stood a massive arrow on legs. It was long, almost touching the opposite wall, and thicker than Andres' body. Light from the tower flowed into the arrow. At its pointy end, something had formed that looked like a star in the night sky, a crack that was widening, the longer Otar looked at it.

Canvases hung from the ceiling and the constructions, showing graphs and numbers.

Otar stepped closer to get a better look. He couldn't make much sense of them, but the third voice whispered they were close. Andres followed him and then recoiled with a hiss of pain.

Otar whirled around, and there was a shimmery barrier between them. It had let Otar through but rejected Andres. They watched each other for a few small-turns and then Andres nodded; he would wait outside without complaining.

Whatever was happening, it needed to stop, and neither Andres nor Turas could help him.

He turned back to the arrow and then to the tower. As if guided by a ghost hand, he raised his own and tapped against one canvas. It was smooth and cold to his touch. With every tap of his fingers, the layout changed, showing graphs, words, pictures, numbers.

Download triggered.

"What?"

Something hissed. A multitude of voices all at once, all hissing, screaming.

Static ran through Otar's bones. His mind broke open. He clenched his hands and hunched his shoulders forward to brace against the storm, biting down his own screams that threatened to rip out of his throat.

"Otar!" Andres must have felt something. He had almost forgotten about the bond. "Lower the barrier."

"No." This was his to take, the last part of an agenda hidden in the ultimate plan, drafted a very long time ago.

"What is happening?" Andres looked so confused and desperate that Otar's heart clenched.

Andres stepped forward and stretched his hands out, not touching the shimmery veil. Turas hovered at his side, watching them with furrowed brows.

"You know, Maugi isn't only Maugi."

"More secrets?" Andres asked exaggerated with a touch of fondness.

Otar smiled. "It did take me a while to figure it out, but now I'm sure." He turned his gaze to the door that led to the dead. "Maugi speaks sometimes in different voices, while its appearance never changes. One was a single voice, more emotional than Maugi. My creator. And then there was a multiple voice, speaking not as one, but thousands at the same time, they speak as 'we'."

Otar looked at the tower. It had shifted its color from a steady blue to a pulsing gold. "After Maugi triggered my first memories, I didn't know yet that what there was to know wasn't for me but for the Ancients. But I wasn't an Ancient. They built me just as they had made the guardians, and I was not the only one. So they kept me out. But then…"

"…you touched the well." Turas said and nodded.

"It allowed my creator to circumspect the plans of the elders and slip in." He groaned as pain pulsed in his head.

Andres stepped even closer to the barrier.

"But what does all of this mean?"

"The Ancients believed themselves to be above all. And this world defied them. As I mentioned before, they wanted revenge. Your ancestors drove them from their cities to Eitin and imprisoned them there. The Ancients couldn't leave on foot, as secure as Eitin was, it is in the middle of the mountain cliffs, the only way out was through their travel system, but with no one to maintain it at the various points, it crumbled away. They also had closed down almost all smaller ruins; they were trapped.

"So they devised a plan. They waited. They tasked Maugi with building me repeatedly and sending me out. No one suspected a small child. It could live undetected and fill up to the brim and bring it all back. I don't know how many came back."

None.

"I was the last chance. The resources were nearly spent. On the other side their energy collection was close to being finished. A couple hundred summers more and they would have enough. The moment I uploaded the life force back in Adabel and basically told the ruin to send it over, the call started. But how to tell the folks on the other side what happened and what was to be done? Easy. They transferred their minds into Maugi so they could move it over with me, maybe even be given new bodies."

"New bodies?" Turas was aghast.

Otar shrugged. "It's what they have been whispering about. It makes little sense to me." Maybe one turn he would understand. "I was meant to take them over, but my creator hatched a different plan."

He turned back to the console, his fingers flying over the smooth canvas, while his creator poked picture after picture.

Traitor. The voices hissed. *And still too late.*

A shudder rolled through the room. At the end of the arrow, the fissure spread out, growing faster.

"You know, they created the Otars as a one-time use."

"No!" Andres shouted, and Otar didn't dare to turn around, his fingers dancing over the numbers and graphs on their own.

"We were meant to collect as much energy as possible, until we brimmed with it under the skin, and then release it—submerged into a liquid that would dissolve our bodies and absorb the life force storing it away. And then form a new Otar." Fragments of memories remained. He was many.

"Don't, please don't."

Otar let his hands sink. "They locked Maugi out of this."

The creator in his mind cursed.

"And they also locked out the only Ancient that would help me. But I still have energy left. I collect it, it makes me *me*. And I know when I release it here…"

The fissure at the tip of the arrow grew broader. With it came sounds, strange noises, explosions, screams. Something bad was happening on the other side.

The pulsing golden light changed to silver strands, overlaying each other, as if the arrow had only warmed up and was now preparing for the full impact.

It fired. A blinding ring formed around the tower, traveling down to the arrow and crashing into the fissure, and again, and again.

More sounds drowned them. A thundering echo that hurt in their ears, more explosions, and strange words.

Otar climbed atop the arrow, hissing when the rings of light hit him. He crouched down and pried a metal sheet away. Heat burned his fingers, but he gritted his teeth and pulled. Strands of lights were now laid bare.

"Otar!"

"I'm sorry."

His hands closed around the naked energy. He exhaled and let go.

Chapter 24

"I grasped for the sky, and it grasped for me. Riding under the blueness of the steppe was all I wanted to do, until I met Otar. For him, I diverged from my path, which disqualifies me as a leader, but you know what, Onder? I don't regret it. I made my decision, and I made my peace with it. I know what will come when I follow him. I knew it the moment he said he would travel to the other city. He is the sun and the sky and the moon. He is *otar*, and I'd be a fool to not hold onto him."

(Letter left behind from tribe leader Andres to his twin, tribe leader Onder)

FOR A LONG moment, there was nothing. No pain, no energy, no feeling, just him and nothingness.

Then the power surged through, and Otar's mind traveled with it. To where the arrow touched the fissure and beyond.

He saw the world on the other side, white buildings broken to dust, skeletal-like structures stretching into a red sky filled with strange things and explosions. Distinct people, in forms and shapes he had never seen before, crouched around the crack, watching him.

One, with almost yellow eyes, his body big and broad unlike anything he had ever seen, said something to him he didn't understand.

He shook his head and pointed to the fissure. He smiled. "I'm here to close what should never have been opened."

And for a small-turn, they understood each other. The other nodded.

Hundred, thousands of voices thundered through him, clawing at his mind. As he had entered the stream of energy, they had invaded him. They fought him, pressed into every minuscule space he was, into his cells and thoughts, his dreams and hopes, his fears and weaknesses, his love. Clawed at the fabric, he was made of, demanded to be let out, to be set free.

And he took them, let them come, embraced them as close as he could.

Then he stepped back, tearing the ghosts with him, and he plunged.

There was something neither of them had thought about, not Otar, not Maugi, not his creator, not the Ancients.

The energy they had taken wasn't only the life force of the inhabitants; it was the aether of this world, merely loaned to those who lived in her. It was a primal force, without thought, without conscious will.

The fissure splintered, and he and the ghosts of the Ancients were thrust into a vortex of stolen energy. It leaked out, into the nooks and crannies around them— into Andres and Turas, into the ground and beyond, to Jasner, to Aaoran, to Borroi, Onder, the old man and

Marit, his mother, his sisters, to all the beings in the Seven Lands.

And the world roared, clamoring for what was stolen, thundering through rock and water, through dirt and stone, rumbling across to take it all back.

The ghosts screamed and pushed. They tried to hold on, clawing into Otar by pure will. But they had given up their bodies, trusting only their minds, with nothing to hold on to, unlike Otar.

He held onto his body, held onto the bodily sensation rushing through him, held onto his memories of what was real.

Still held on, until the screams fell silent, and only he and the world remained.

Otar hadn't lied to Andres—he wanted to live; he wanted a future; he wanted to make an impossible dream true.

And yet, he was prepared to die since he believed himself to be an Ancient, because he wasn't of this world. He was an anomaly—created, not born.

Had he any right to live?

The world reached for him. He was in its domain, and everything that came was hers to claim. Pain and endlessness stretched before him as she hollowed him out from the inside, claiming all the energy, taking the ocean with it.

Should he let go?

Should he accept?

He touched the people and beings of this world. They all knew what he was, what he'd caused.

Death was waiting.

A tug.

A second tug.

Something strung tight in him, a thin glittering twine. Reaching to somewhere far away.

To Andres.

He reached for it, but the world stopped him. She had claimed it all, and she was claiming him. But as he said, he wasn't of this world.

There was no place for him.

The fissure cracked even more—a world beyond, a world that was tied to him, a place he had come from.

But Andres.

He grabbed for the bond and pulled. The world crashed after him, faster than Otar could escape. Otar stretched himself further and further, the world curling around his insides, ready to yank him out.

Wanting to end him here.

Otar yanked hard. The bond broke in a shower of glittering rain. Otar stared at the fraying ends, dissolving between his fingers. Despair spread through him at the sight.

The world enclosed him.

Anger beyond anything he had ever known thundered through him, and he reached for it himself. The life force the world took flowed back into him, faster and faster. The bond was broken, the control gone, the power was his for the taking. It settled under his skin, brimming and crackling.

The world, giving one last effort, tried to fight, but Otar held on, gaining what was lost.

In a last measure to save herself from being devoured by the monster, the world bowed and cast him out.

OTAR STUMBLED TO the ground, batting hands away that wanted to help him up; with the bond to Andres gone, the monster would reach out uncontrolled. He got to his feet and eyed Andres and Turas, who were watching him with wild eyes.

The fissure to his left crackled, slowly closing on its own. The Ancients ghosts were gone.

"What happened?" Turas asked.

Otar shook his head and turned to the tower. Energy was still arching over it, but it had gone back to the blue light while the arrow smoked.

"Maugi?" Would the ghost even answer him?

Yes, Otar.

Otar nearly sacked with relief.

"End this, when I'm gone."

As you wish.

There was a stunned silence, and then the other two spoke at the same time.

"Otar—"

"But—"

He held up a hand and tried to sort through his mind. He only had one chance to do this right, otherwise…

"Turas, I will tell Maugi to open a portal to Eitin to send you and Andres through. It is your only chance to return home. I don't know if the guardians are still alive, or if there is a way down from the mountains. The map Maugi had given me doesn't show any—so when I say run, you run."

"And what about you?"

"I will follow you, but I need to make sure that whatever happened will never happen again."

"Promise," Turas demanded.

And Otar nodded.

The other two looked at each other.

"Maugi, open the portal to Eitin."

Portal opened, closing down soon. I can't hold the energy stable for much longer.

The tower shuddered, and sparks flew from the spire on the ceiling.

"Run!"

The two of them obeyed. Otar turned back to the construct.

"Maugi, what can I do to help?"

Nothing, Otar. I'll destroy it and myself.

"You will die." Otar felt queasy at the thought. They had known each other for a long time now. Even if it was constructed, it had been a companion, making his explorations less lonely.

What is death to a ghost?

Otar laughed and exhaled at the steps in his back.

"You are making it easy for you again, sending me away," Andres said, coming to a stop next to him. "You have no intention of coming through. What is on the other side?"

"A world to explore."

Andres hummed. "You want to slip through. You are running away again."

"Am I?" Otar countered, but even before he spoke, he knew Andres was right. Didn't he swear not to do it again?

"Why aren't you asking me?"

"How can I?" They both watched the light flicker over the tower, shifting now from blue to green to red. He was calm. "Asking you to leave the steppe is one thing, but going beyond this world, never to return, how can I?"

"Am I not an adult? Am I not a leader of my people?"

Otar turned to him, confused.

"Am I not a person who can weigh his options and opinions and make decisions I am comfortable doing?" Andres looked at him, his eyes intense in the flickering lights. He stretched his hand out and touched the braid with the golden bead that hung behind Otar's ear. "Ask me, ana."

The red flickered faster and faster, throwing harsh, strobing shadows over them. A high-pitched whine echoed around them.

"Will you come with me?"

"Always."

When the ground shook, they turned to the crack.

Goodbye, Otar.

"Goodbye Maugi." Then he advised Andres. "Don't touch my skin, but hold on to me."

He nodded, and slung his arms around Otar's waist, careful to not touch bare flesh. Otar exhaled and thrust his hand into the fissure.

Nothingness flowed around him once more, and they stumbled out on the other side.

He sprawled on the floor, his mind dazed. Red and white danced before him. His eyes went to the fissure that snapped close right in the moment.

And then, "Let's not do this again."

Otar rolled to his side and stared at Andres, who was sitting up next to him, massaging his temples. But he smiled.

"Are you alright—"

A massive shadow fell over him. The same person he met when he slipped through for that first time, the one with the yellow eyes, scrutinized him, then held up what looked like a weapon, pointing it straight at him.

"I'm Lord Commander Baresh, and this is Aluriana. Who are you?"

Otar smiled sheepishly and raised his hands. "I am a scholar."

Epilogue

"Aaoran-peras,

I don't date this letter as I don't know what time it is. They tried to explain it to me, but I can't get a grasp on things like years, hours, and months, and time moving differently in different places. I'm well, and you can tell Onder that Andres is also well. Still very confused, as I am, but you won't believe what is out here.

Did I make the right decision? Who knows and only time (ha!) will tell, but I think you might understand why I didn't return and why I left when I could. Dragging Andres along was a choice, I know, and Onder is surely cross with me, and yet, I'm grateful for his presence. I could have made it without him, but knowing he is at my side leaves me more anchored in this new, strange reality.

Whatever the Ancients did to me allowed me to at least understand their languages—well, most of them—which is a boon and a disappointment at the same time. Learning languages to understand a culture is half the fun as you have always taught me.

What happened after we crossed over? We arrived in a world they call Aluriana, which is somehow tied to the Ancients, based on the descriptions we gave. They are not entirely sure that those we encountered in Eitin are actually the Alurians that live in that world, or have lived. Because the Alurians were conquered that very turn—or more, if I understood correctly—they were eradicated for crimes they had committed. It is a rather complex story that spans too many summers to count. I'm sure you remember the Western War, where an Alliance between neighboring states went against the Usara Kingdom, so that the Kingdom's raids into their territories would end. I think it's something along those lines. But the scale is so much bigger that it is hard to grasp for me.

A world is a planet, a round shape floating in a sky beyond the sky and which they call the universe. The planet is often not the only one. There are others close by, and they form a solar system. Not all of them are inhabited, and some are strange. Then there are other such solar systems nearby, and they form a galaxy, and so on and on. An infinite number of worlds.

They tell me it's not infinite, but the number is so big it feels like that.

We travel in ships made for this universe-sky. It's dark and cold, and those ships that are entirely made of metal just fly through it. As if we were in the stomach of a bird—a bird as large as Rasanell's university.

I'm learning so many things each turn. New, strange, and fascinating facts. It's wonderful and overwhelming.

I wish this letter and all the others I'm writing, with all my notes and observations, would reach you, but they told me it is impossible. As they explained the time concept to me, they also told me not all places are in sync, that the Ancients have traveled differently to arrive at a different time, and that you are not born yet or are long dead. A sobering thought and hard to keep. But it also means that you should be safe now; at least they say there is a high probability—I'll make sure that it's true.

One turn, I will return and bring all the letters and all of my findings to you.

Until then, I'll remain your faithful student,

Otar"

"Finished?" Andres asked from the side of the desk. He was sitting on the bed in the small space they had given them. There wasn't much: a bed, a desk with a chair, a low table with seating cushions, and something they called a bathroom. Meals were delivered to them. Andres and him weren't trusted, which was understandable. He wouldn't trust a person just appearing out of thin air either, telling wild stories about Ancients and soul-sucking monsters.

The commander with the yellow eyes, Baresh, had brought them to a doctor, to be "scanned", which seemed to be a word to look them over more deeply than any other doctor back home could have ever done. They also gave Andres an injection that allowed him to understand the people around them. Odd people in all kinds of forms and sizes and colors.

The doctor had said that Andres and Otar were healthy and carried no danger. When Otar had tried to warn them about the monster inside him and what he was able to do, the doctor had shrugged and said he would run more tests but told Otar there wasn't any sign of it.

Otar had later risked touching Andres. Nothing happened.

Had his last encounter with the world itself burned it all out of him? Was that good? He suddenly felt lonely without the second presence inside him.

"Otar?" Andres prompted again.

"Sorry, yes, finished." He smiled at his lover, who smiled back.

Andres was surprisingly calm about everything. He was, however, many miles away from home, stranded in a world that made absolutely no sense to him, and he hadn't once complained or commented that he regretted his decision to come through not knowing what would happen. Otar had tried to broach the subject a few times, but Andres always shook his head and told him he was fine.

"Andres." Perhaps this was another chance.

Andres blinked at him. The steppe rider had foregone his cloth armor and changed into something more local. Baresh had explained it was also an armor, but it was thinner than anything Otar had ever seen before.

The armor was all black with silver threads and came with sturdier boots. Andres still wore his sash, but they took his sword and locked it away.

"Are you sure that this is okay for you? That we may never return?" Otar started again, when the silence stretched too long between them.

Andres sighed, but it was more exaggerated than annoyed.

Otar turned his head to the letter he was writing—on a device they called a pad, which didn't need any ink—and further to the window that showed the place the ship was docked at. A space station they called it, a travel point in this whole big something where people resupplied and mingled. The station was another metal structure with bridges and pathways, not unlike the ruin structures.

Andres raised a hand and with gentle pressure at his chin made Otar look at him. "If there was an easy way to travel back, I would take it to visit," he rumbled. "I would make sure that Onder was okay and the tribe properly taken care of. I would also get the wedding mantle for us."

Otar blushed and swallowed.

"Would I stay when faced with the choice?" He shrugged. "I don't think so, because you wouldn't stick around. You would visit and then leave again for the stars, with or without me." Andres looked over at him, amusement in his eyes.

And Otar couldn't deny it. Andres was right—after learning what was out there beyond the sky and the sun and the moon, how could he stay in one place?

How could anyone expect him to remain? There were endless things to discover: possible answers to where his creators had come from, uncovering answers to so many other questions, and all those yet to discover puzzles. He needed to know: What was out there?

Perhaps there was also a way of allowing them to visit home, or maybe just Andres. Otar was unsure about his own welcome.

"Here with you, Otar, this is the right path to walk. I will learn, and I will adapt. I don't think this will be a smooth ride. It will be terrifying trying to understand everything that is going on and what all these magical things are."

"Technical," Otar corrected. He blushed at the raised eyebrow.

Andres tried the word out and repeated it a few times to himself. "Technical then. They seem more like magic to me, but that only shows how little I have learned so far. I'm glad I can at least understand them." He reached out to Otar, who took his hand with hesitation, always waiting for the monster to come back and pounce and do something terrible. But so far, the doctor had been right. There was nothing anymore. Even when he tried to look into himself, he was met with silence.

He needed to find out more about it.

"We are in this together, and I promise I won't abandon you, and stay by your side, whether you want me or not."

Otar huffed. "Getting full of yourself."

Andres grinned and tugged him close, holding him in a slightly awkward position, but Otar didn't care.

"Akamar daro," he mumbled into Andres' neck.

He hugged Otar tighter, and they stayed like that until the ship set out again.

The End
(for now)

Afterwords

AND THERE IT is, my first novel. Writing this afterword is an incredible feeling. How often have a I stood under the shower, brushing my teeth or waiting in a line and thought about what would I write if it ever came to this. Most of those thoughts I have long forgotten, but some still remain in my heart.

This book took me three years to write, you hold the sixth version in your hands. While a lot of Otar and his journey was set in stone from the beginning, the people around him changed a lot, as well where his path started. Even his ending was meant to be different, but my lovely development editor asked the right question about where the book and ultimately Otar should go, sparking in me an idea about something beyond. So, if you want to grumble about not reading a stand-alone, it's their fault (in a good way).

Writing is a very solitary endeavor. Paper and pen, or document and keyboard are the only witnesses for the struggles and hours of thought and hard work and often despair. And yet an author isn't a solitary creature. Writing communities, friends online and offline, partners, acquaintances, circle around me, and they have all supported me and continue support me in their own way.

My grandfather always wanted to read a book or a story I have written. Sadly, he never had the chance. But he firmly believed that one day I would make it.

All the discord writing communities I'm part off helped me to put my own struggles and insecurities and questions as a writer in a broader perspective. They told me that I'm not alone, and that I don't need to solve my problems alone, I can always ask, and people will answer.

Social media is a bane and boon. On some days I can't look at it but being able to connect to other indie and trad authors once more allowed me to be less alone.

I thank especially my beta readers who beside my lovely editors were the first people to ever read the work in its entirety, and that they liked it was such a massive relief.

My editors, who probably had to deal with a lot of confusion on my side, with being a total novice to the entire process of getting a book off the ground. My artist and my typesetter got also a lot of messages and needed to clarify a ton of things. I really thank you for your patience.

My husband. My partner. My best friend. I wrote it in the dedication, but I'm sure while one day this book might have seen the light of day if would have been far in the future without your continued support. Creatives are riddled with self-doubt but you always believed in me and my skills, and that allowed me to give it my all.

But what would be an author without their readers? You, who is holding this book in their hands having read it and hopefully liked it, you as well I thank from the bottom of my heart for giving this story a chance. And I thank you for your time, which is the most precious thing a reader can give to a writer.

With that the only thing that remains to be said is: Otar will return and this time there will be dragons.

All my love,

JD Rivers
October 2024

Credits

Development Editor
K.B. Spangler

Line Editor
Nikita Kannekanti

Cover Artist
Planetsandmagic

Type Setter
Hermit

About the author

JD writes queer speculative fiction where they fall deeply and madly in love while figuring out the world around them. She collects hobbies as others collect books and has an unhealthy addiction to watching competitive cooking shows. JD lives close to the woods with her husband and the cutest dog in the world.

For more information: https://jd-rivers.com